No Pleasure In Death

Pauline Bell

MACMILLAN
LONDON

First published 1992 by
MACMILLAN LONDON LIMITED
Cavaye Place London SW10 9PG
and Basingstoke

Associated companies in Auckland, Delhi, Dublin, Gaborone,
Hamburg, Harare, Hong Kong, Johannesburg, Kuala Lumpur,
Lagos, Manzini, Melbourne, Mexico City, Nairobi, New York,
Singapore and Tokyo

ISBN 0-333-58037-0

A CIP catalogue record for this book is available from the British
Library

Phototypeset by Intype, London

Printed and bound in Great Britain by Billing and Sons Limited,
Worcester

Prologue

The letter, painstakingly written in a schoolboy hand, lay on Chief Inspector Browne's desk. Answering his summons, Sergeant Hunter closed Browne's door, crossed the office and bent to examine the single white sheet. Its texture was coarse, cheap drawing paper, perhaps, and the lines drooped downwards as they traversed the page, suggesting a dispirited mood in the writer.

Hunter's thin lips formed the words, though he read soundlessly. 'Dear Sir, I'm very sorry about the girl. I didn't mean to do it. Yours sincerely, John.' He continued his silent study of it for several seconds whilst Browne, with growing concern, studied his sergeant. The narrow face, with its sharp features, was always pallid, and the brilliant winter daylight reflected from the clean snow covering the landscape outside his window was kind to no one's lines of fatigue, but, taking all this into account, he still looked ill. Hunter, aware of his superior's scrutiny, tried not to wince as he swallowed.

'You want to get yourself to a doctor, Jerry.'

Hunter grimaced. 'I've been. Had no choice. Annette made the appointment for me. Fat lot of good it did. A week of antibiotics has made no difference. It's only a sore throat anyway, hardly life-threatening. Question is, is that?' He turned his attention back to the letter.

Browne sighed but desisted from offering more advice or sympathy. Hunter was embarrassed by them and would quietly expire at his feet rather than complain. Still, his wife was obviously aware of the problem. He waved Hunter to a chair and answered him. 'It's very likely some joker but we'd better not file it in the bin. Anything useful from the Smithson youth?'

5

Hunter cleared his throat before answering, a proceeding that was manifestly painful. Browne's patience ran out. 'Get yourself home, Jerry, now, and that's an order.'

Thus chidden, his pride intact, Hunter departed thankfully.

Browne refolded the letter, using tweezers, and sealed it carefully in a plastic bag. For now, it could join the odd assortment of objects that belonged as yet to no particular case that he kept in the bottom one of his four desk drawers. Later, he would bawl out whichever of his underlings was responsible for his not seeing it until today when the postmark on the envelope showed it had been sent on November 21st, almost a week earlier.

Preliminary inquiries had drawn a blank. Missing Persons had added no young girls to their list in the last two weeks or so, nor were there any reports of young females who had suffered physical harm on his patch, except for a couple of traffic accidents. He could safely let his thoughts travel towards lunch.

The overhead heaters at the main door did little to prepare him for the enervating chill, and after only a few steps the wind in his face had his forehead numbed and aching with the cold. No wonder Hunter had gone down with some bug. Getting his workload redistributed would have to be the first job after lunch.

The carpark sloped upwards. At the far end, the thin snow covering was fresh and unmarked, but in the entrance brown tarmac was revealed where tyre marks had met and crossed till the snow was all dispersed. A humming in the air came from the factory across the road with its grey slates topping huge blocks of millstone grit. A powerless but cheerful sun glinted on its rows of windows and its garish metal signs, yellow with bright blue letters, screwed to the wall.

Spindly apologies for trees fought for survival in the gale that whistled between its two buildings. On the immediate horizon, scarlet and white banners flew from the new DIY store further up the hill.

Browne turned as he stood beside his car, fishing for his keys, and faced the building he had just left. It was too new for its yellow sandstone to be much discoloured in this relatively smoke-free zone. Beyond it the land dropped steeply, so that the buildings in the valley appeared as merely a huddle of roofs and a regiment of chimneys, and behind them the great hump of moorland that usually lowered over the town today, with its sparkling thin crust of snow, seemed to smile on it.

He found his key, inserted it and thankfully escaped from the wind into his car. Pausing in the gateway, he looked down on to the main road, white edged this morning, with a broad dun-coloured central stripe, over which vehicles hissed through the slush to Leeds and Bradford or dived under the flyover towards the town centre.

The station's local was one of the hundred or so pubs in the area called the Fleece. Standing below its sign, which featured an animated woolly ball with a surprised expression, Browne reflected, not for the first time, that he could paint a better sheep himself. Then he dived into the welcome warmth of the interior.

He wondered whether to celebrate the confirmation he'd received that morning, that he was now an actual, rather than an acting, CI by ordering steak, but decided it was a heartless way to mark the retirement through ill health of his predecessor. In any case, he marginally preferred the crisp perfection of the pastry that topped the Fleece's meat pie.

As he waited for it he scanned the notices and advertisements on the board beside the bar. It was dominated by a poster publicising the local choral society's Christmas concert and Browne pulled out his diary to note the date and time. He was looking foward to having his daughter home from her first term at Oxford and his son from his final year at Durham. Alex had been abroad to work during the summer vac, but, with finals on the horizon, he would be at home studying during this one. Still, he would suggest they went to the concert as a family. A few carols and a chunk of the *Messiah* was part of the Christmas tradition in this part of the world.

Chapter 1

Howard Mellor was attending his first rehearsal with the Cloughton Choral Society. He was proud of his mellifluous bass and had sung at his audition less than an hour ago without a qualm. He would have been exceedingly surprised if they had turned him down and he sat now, on the back row of tiered seats, watching the other members arrive and fiddling with his copy of the *Messiah*, from which he had just rendered 'Why do the Nations' to Mr Cully's satisfaction.

He wondered why the three officials who had listened to him had seemed so amused by his choice of demonstration piece. His copy fell open at the flyleaf and he looked at his father's name, John Howard Mellor, the same as his own, in the careful writing of a man younger than he himself was now and of a generation that placed high value on a neat and attractive script. The copy had done his family good service.

He was less than impressed with his surroundings. His choir in Surrey, for whom he had sung all the bass solos, had practised in a new and lavishly equipped leisure centre. This was some sort of lecture room, the dais in a well at the front. The white-painted Victorian panelled doors were attractive and the other surfaces were a pleasant apple green, except where the paint on the ceiling was falling in fragile, brittle sheets from the plaster. The windows were at elbow level at the back of the room but high up in the wall for those who were seated at the front. The floor and stepped aisles had sensible green and black mottled lino, the padded sort that muffled your footsteps and felt warm.

The place had obviously been built before it became the custom to sink the mechanics of heating and lighting into the wall, so the conduits were in metal pipes, painted to match the plaster behind, that criss-crossed themselves and each other round the radiators and light switches. A grand piano on the dais was swathed in a velvet covering in a nasty chocolate brown lined in a dull green. It looked like a discarded curtain from a huge window.

He had been told that the room doubled during the day as a slimming club and a Well Woman clinic. It explained the reason for a hospital-type scale with a vertical measuring rod and sliding gauge which stood beside the piano. Music-stands stood guard round both. The heaters were huge metal cuboids with grilles at the top that were throwing out gusts of warm dust-laden air. It would dry their throats and their voices would have to be forced over its chugging mechanism.

Cully was now seated on a tall stool, his legs comfortably hooked into its rails, a laden music-stand before him. His voluminous sweater made his spare form seem emaciated. His fingers were long and beringed, his feet enormous. The blind at the window above him was pulled slightly away and Mellor could see the snow building up on the sill outside. The rows of seats in front of him were filling up.

The Choral seemed to contain a fair cross-section of towns-people. Luxurious fur jostled against a padded anorak patterned with polar bears and worn by a female old enough to know better. Lower down, a teenager prepared to settle herself. Her leather skirt barely covered her knickers and her legs seemed to be bare. Mellor supposed he had been equally tough in his youth. The men weren't so easy to categorise. He watched a voluptuous black girl in a full and flowing black coat dance on the spot as she spoke and laughed, her great dangling gold earrings dancing and laughing too.

A blond man in his thirties appeared in the doorway. Cully caught his attention to indicate their new bass and the blond man bounded up the steps and pumped Mellor's hand. 'Jack Chance. Secretary. Glad to have you aboard. I'm a tenor so I have to sit across the aisle but I'll see you afterwards and get someone to show you the pub we use.'

Mellor returned his grin. 'Good of you but it will depend on the time. My wife's had an operation. She's a bit touchy at the moment if I'm away too long.'

Cully rapped sharply on the music stand with his baton. The chatter hushed immediately and all eyes were on him. With no more instruction than an opening note of the piano and a pointing from the baton, the assembly embarked upon a series of warming-up scales that was obviously an established routine. It was organised, Mellor noted, so that the two sections of the choir reached their top notes alternately. Tenors and sopranos were invited to sing a descant to the scales at intervals of a third, fourth and finally a fifth. Mellor was impressed. Cloughton might be only a small textile town but these people knew what they were doing and did it competently.

The accompanist played rapturous trills and arpeggios along with them to liven things up until after a few minutes Cully was satisfied and brought things to a halt by repeating his tapping. He held up a pink booklet. ' "Adam Lay y-Bounden".' There were groans but he continued unabashed. 'You're going to get fond of this one.' The groans became disbelieving. 'It's rather like a mock-serious setting for a nonsense song. You didn't do too badly with it last week, except in verse four. Basses, you were dragging there. It sounded like community hymn singing!'

To a man, the basses took pencils and marked up their copies. Mellor peered at the squiggles his neighbour was making and the neighbour moved closer to share his copy.

'It's high for the sopranos at the bottom of page six,' Cully continued. 'Don't reach for it. Get beyond it and come back. Chins in for the Gs and As. Pretend you're in the bath! Let's go straight through it to start with. Don't make your first note sound exploratory; go at it confidently. If you aren't sure, make it up in the right style.' There were grins from those who knew how he would react if they actually followed that instruction. 'Watch the time carefully. If your note values are the least bit ragged the rests are completely ineffective.'

They began on a creditable performance of the piece. Mellor followed his neighbour's music with his eyes, deciding that his bass solos were in jeopardy and that there was much he could learn from this lively group. Towards the end, Cully had more instructions and he raised his hand to stop the overwhelming waves of sound. Those who were watching him stopped first, then the order gradually percolated to those whose noses were glued to their copies until the final embarrassed few stuttered to a halt. 'That will teach you to watch.' He began to demonstrate to the various parts what he wanted from them, singing to them in an amazing three octaves.

John Simmons listened carefully. It was his second rehearsal and he was feeling slightly less at sea than he had a fortnight ago. He couldn't describe the effect the sound had on him as he sat in the middle of it. He could hardly believe it was made by people. If anyone stopped, the effect would be slightly different. He didn't want to break into it with his own voice, concentrating on his own line. He'd sung in the school choir from going there when he was eleven until he left in the summer but it had been nothing like this. He'd had no understanding of the work involved. He'd been to the Choral's concerts and thought that they might sometimes have to sing a piece through several times to get it right but he'd had no concept of spending half an hour on three bars so that you lost the general effect but eventually got it how Mr Cully wanted it.

He thought the audience had even less idea. They imagined the music floated out of the copies when they were opened. He quite enjoyed this detailed work now and he was even beginning to get it right himself. Mr Cully put new singers sandwiched between experienced ones and Mr Chance helped him very patiently, but to be sitting next to someone who got everything right was very off-putting.

Mr Cully often stopped and asked if anyone was having any difficulties. He sounded quite friendly and approachable, but then someone would put up a hand and ask a technical and complicated question that discouraged him from admitting that his own chief problem was that he was no longer sure what page they were on.

The choir was a big compensation for having to stay in Cloughton. He'd have missed it if he'd taken up his scholarship in the autumn. He looked up. They'd moved on to the final section of the work now and Mr Cully was beginning a diatribe about their expression. He was getting used to that too. He'd been very surprised at first by how much time was given to how to put over the words.

'If you say something, you have to sound as though you mean it. It's exactly the same in singing.' They tried again but he still wasn't satisfied. 'You're singing that last alleluia like a reveille. I want it like a grief-stricken last post, as though Gabriel has just disappeared and you can hear him in the distance on his way back to heaven – or the echo of what's been said in Mary's mind. Use any image you like but give me an intangible, ethereal alleluia. Write in anything that reminds you about it. Copies won't be examined afterwards.'

A smile went round the room whilst Simmons scrabbled for his dropped pencil.

As Cully made his points, the accompanist underlined them, finding unerringly the phrases under discussion and playing them through. No instructions were given him; he seemed to read vibrations from Cully. His hands seemed to work of their own accord. He never looked down, keeping his eyes for the most part on Cully, with an occasional glance at the music. His amazing virtuosity was matched only by his infallible good humour. He wasn't at all jolly but smiled quietly to himself as he followed the proceedings. He kept a notebook on the piano and from time to time jotted down any quirk of interpretation to be incorporated into his playing.

Cully heard the final section going wrong again. He beamed round at them. 'All right, that was my fault.' He was careful to say it at least once each practice. They loved forgiving him. He was pleased with them. They had come a long way since that first run-through, with the melody blurred at the edges as those whose sight-reading left room for improvement fell off the sides of the notes.

Where had he read about the 'discipline of music where all concur to one end'? The end was about all they had in common, this collection of students, insurance brokers, supermarket cashiers, housewives, lawyers and so on. Some had toes and heels tapping, keeping their owners' voices in rhythm. Some of them felt they would be wanting in enthusiasm if every part of their anatomy were not involved in producing their notes. Others sang with dead-pan faces, hardly moving their lips, as though to betray from which orifice the sound was coming would be in execrable taste. Some looked exhausted, others seemed to find it effortless.

There was a growing preponderance of grey heads in front of him but this was not yet reflected in the sound. And there was some new young blood. Downy-haired John Simmons caught his eye, only the top of his head visible as he glued his own eyes to the copy and tried to keep his place. The voice was remarkable and tenors were always thin on the ground. He hoped the lad had staying power, that his enthusiasm would last until his difficulties with sight-singing were overcome. He was a good keyboard player so it should come more easily before long.

In front of John, he noticed the bossy local headmistress among the altos, obsequiously following his directions to demonstrate her wisdom in recognising that, in this one field, she had a superior. Her eyes were fixed unwaveringly on the baton and she kept in strict time with the other altos to stress the novelty for her of taking directions. Further back on the other side was Stella Smith, singing her heart out and ruining the purity of the soprano sound with her uncontrolled vibrato. He hadn't the heart to tell her to tone it down, when he knew, as she did, that she wouldn't pass her next audition and this therefore would be her last concert with them.

Next to her should have been Alison. Where on earth was she tonight? He could hardly go another week before putting the solos together with the choral sections. The concert was less than three weeks away. Perhaps Denise would do it tonight. She'd auditioned to be a soloist so she should know the notes. He felt worried rather than angry. Alison had her faults but he wouldn't have expected her to cut a rehearsal without letting him know. He'd ring her as soon as he got home.

Denise obliged without demur and the second section with solo went well. He'd give her a solo verse of her own in one of the carols. He owed her at least that. He looked round again and saw that people were flagging. He'd had enough himself. Quickly he brought the rehearsal to a close and smiled as the weary voices,

14

when allowed to talk instead of sing, immediately renewed their strength.

Mellor had enjoyed himself on the whole. His interest had waned a little towards the end of two hours of listening, but with his own copies to sing from and as a prospective performer it would be different. The choir must be about eighty or ninety strong but its leader's outgoing personality as he addressed them gave the gathering quite an intimate atmosphere. He watched him now, slumped against the piano as the singers dispersed, drained and almost grey faced with fatigue, and realised that the man had given a performance as much as any Shakespearean actor.

The girl who'd substituted for the absent soloist was very attractive and her voice was pure and strong. He gave her an appraising glance before looking round for Chance. When after five minutes he had failed to find him, he spoke briefly to Cully, then left without making his apologies. As he passed Denise, he caught the edge of the folder tucked under her arm and her music cascaded to the floor. They introduced themselves as they gathered it up.

Jack Chance emerged from the group that surrounded him to view the commotion and grinned. 'An accident,' he asked his companions, 'or have we acquired another fast worker to keep Jake up to the mark?'

Chapter 2

John's mind had not been on the music for the last part of the rehearsal, but he'd managed to go through the motions despite the excitement he could feel taking him over. By the time he'd stuffed his possessions into his case he'd known that tonight was going to be like that other time. It wasn't going to be acted out just in his own mind. For the second time it was going to be for real.

Denise had asked for it using that hated expression. 'Some folk have all the luck.' 'Some folk have all the luck.' 'Some folk have all the luck.' All his life it had rung in his ears. But he wasn't powerless to express his anger at it now. Denise was going to get what she deserved.

Denise was delighted to accept a lift. It made her feel grateful to her husband again. It was good of Stuart always to leave her the car when his firm sent him away. Now that the problem of getting home on a filthy night had been solved she felt she'd been unreasonable to blame him because the exhaust had fallen off. They'd both known for some days that it needed attention and it had been her responsibility as much as his. Still, all was well now and she'd get it fixed first thing tomorrow. It was a good thing it was Sheila's turn to drive them both to work.

She luxuriated in the comfort and warmth of the big car and smiled as she recognised the music on the cassette tape her companion had slipped into his machine. 'Do we have to start our homework on the way home? Or are you showing me how "Lully, lullay" should have been sung?'

16

He turned to her, his expression serious. 'I'm not familiar with this soloist. There's not much she can teach you though.'

Not certain how to deal with this, she changed the subject. 'I'm not sure exactly where you live. I hope I'm not taking you too far out of your way.'

He shook his head. 'You aren't tonight. I have to return some books to a friend who lives on the same side of the park as you so I shall have to pass your house.'

She was puzzled. It didn't seem a particularly urgent mission. When he had offered the lift, he had seemed in a great hurry, hustling her out into the snow and shooting out of the carpark in rather a foolhardy manner. Now he seemed to be in no hurry at all, humming along with the recorded choir, his speed dropping to under thirty. The weather was bad but this was a well-gritted road. Several times he gave her a sidelong glance. Surely he wasn't going to make a pass at her.

After a while the car's speed picked up but she still felt uneasy. Her companion didn't seem quite himself. He was crouched over the wheel, his grip on it whitening his knuckles. They took a left fork and Denise jerked forward. 'The park's up the other way!'

He answered, tersely, 'Better grip on this road.'

'But there's that terrible junction at—'

'Shut up!'

Denise's alarm increased at his abrupt change of manner and the breakneck speed at which he was now driving over an untreated frozen surface.

He enjoyed her screaming at first. This was the moment he'd savoured last time. He'd trapped her. He could take all the time he wanted. When he'd had enough, he hit her.

He knew just what to do. He'd done it all before with Alison, the fast driving, then refusing to answer her when she spoke to him until she was frantic, then the tap on the head with his smallest spanner. Not too hard, just enough to stun her whilst he got her out of the car. The pressure on her neck next and, finally, the finger. He was pleased with how clearly he could think. He was in a bubble of excitement but he was completely aware of what was happening outside it. He felt a bit like this when he'd

17

written some music but there was no revenge in that. Relief of a kind, maybe, but no revenge.

Later, he drove back to the park and carried Denise carefully into the bushes, leaving her music-folder beside her. Perhaps he could enjoy some music himself now. He could remember vividly the first piece of serious music he had ever listened to. It was the Morning Song from Grieg's *Peer Gynt* suite. He had been six years old, privileged to be taught by a blue-overalled lady who had discovered its magic for herself and had been able to share it. The magic had not happened for him for a long time and so the memory was now a painful one. Perhaps tonight, after Denise, he could hear it like that again.

He set off home, this time driving steadily over the treacherous surfaces. At first he couldn't tell whether the sparking necklaces decorating the windscreen were rows of lamps in the distance or their reflections in the trickles of water drops down the glass. He forbore to use his wipers, mesmerised by the patterns and unafraid of driving into a distance he couldn't see. His life was charmed tonight.

Presently, when he knew the built-up area was near, he switched them on. The streetlamps hadn't started yet and he enjoyed watching his headlights pick out snow-laden branches and bushes that seemed to rush towards him. Then, as the turbulence inside him abated a little, he steadied to his customary impeccable driving till he reached his home and parked quietly and neatly outside.

He got out his record of the Grieg straight away but waited until he had made himself a cup of tea, before, hands trembling, he set it playing, putting off the moment when he discovered that the magic was not going to work.

It didn't. He listened and felt nothing. He knew that he himself was nothing. If he looked in the mirror he would be surprised to see a reflection there. In the excitement with Alison and Denise, he thought he'd changed something, become powerful while they were helpless, but nothing was changed; he was the same paralysed individual, tied down by circumstances so long that now he'd be incapable of reaching out to life even if he were free. Two girls were dead but his mother still had the same hold on

18

him. It wasn't any more what she was able to do to him, but what she'd irrevocably turned him into, prevented him from becoming.

He felt now as she had always seemed to, unutterably depressed. She'd blamed their poverty but poverty didn't have to be depressing. It could have been intimate; it could have been about shared hardship and pulling together. Revealing their circumstances had always been the worst sin. His top clothes had always been newer and better quality than his underclothes!

He'd escaped into books. The kerb in front of the kitchen range ran into a metal box at each end, padded on the top to make seats. They were covered in the imitation leather she called 'rexine', which had been cold to the backs of his bare legs whilst the fire scorched the fronts as he sat reading. The plastic surface could be peeled off with his fingernails when she wasn't watching. He'd found this satisfying, although sometimes the plastic had resisted and bent back his fingernail. It had been a major tragedy to injure his hands in any way.

She hadn't liked the reading, so sometimes, to curry favour, he had scrubbed the cellar steps for her, always beginning with an enthusiasm that waned about halfway down. She had praised him with mixed feelings. He'd saved her a degrading chore but she hadn't wanted him to have to do it and certainly no one had to know. It had been kept 'a secret between John and Mummy'. Keeping the cellar clean had been important. With no pantry or fridge, food had been kept on the 'cellar-head' and the weekend jelly had set in its covered glass bowl on the stone-slab table in the cellar proper.

The ground floor had had carpets, threadbare and thin but much vacuumed. His friend from the other end of the yard, with whom he was not allowed to play, had an intriguing rag carpet, 'nasty dirty thing', made with bits from all the family's outworn clothes. Their own furniture had been strategically placed over patches where threads hung loose, except for the bit in front of the kitchen sink where she'd washed him so painfully. Bathing had been pleasanter. His mother had gone upstairs, once he was past babyhood, so as not to see him undressed in the long zinc bath across the hearth. His father had supervised, pouring in saucepanfuls of boiling water, heated on the gas ring, then cooled it and left his son to wallow while replacing the water container with a huge pan in which to fry up the family tea. He'd enjoyed the rough friendliness of it all until he'd learned to share his mother's humiliation.

Baths had been on Fridays and afterwards he'd taken his book to his lino-patched bedroom with its iron mantelpiece, the chamberpot placed ceremonially underneath. He hadn't minded crossing the yard to empty it in the morning, 'nice and early, before anyone's about'.

Quite a lot of his early memories centred round that outdoor lavatory. He'd soon learned the safe way to make trips to it in the dark, across the flagstones outside the back door, being careful not to trip over the one that jutted. You knew you'd reached the asphalt stretch when your feet crunched. There was light from the kitchen window but it shone mostly on the yard wall. There was newspaper, torn into half sheets for afterwards. You could read it in the dim light during the day. The shack had had a musty damp-paper smell. It was whitewashed inside but the surface had flaked off in the damp places and the bricks became covered in a furry growth like a kind of warm frost that you could poke off with your finger.

Proper toilet rolls were bought when visitors came, the hard, shiny kind with green writing along the perforations. He'd used it sometimes as tracing paper for his geography homework.

The door was in the longest wall, so that his swing, hung in the doorway on fine days, could only move across the width of the narrow building. He faced inwards on it, pushing his feet against the wall to gain momentum, but this was disapproved of, not because of the marks it left on the wall but because it was 'dirty' to face the lavatory bowl.

The asphalt surrounded a few square feet of earth where the air-raid shelter had been. He'd planted seeds in it sometimes, but the clay had either baked hard and cracked, or if the weather was wet become the consistency of plasticine, and nothing ever grew in it for long. The excitement he'd felt if they'd showed green was less for the tiny plants themselves than for the fantasy they represented of a house with a garden from which they could feel superior to their neighbours.

20

He felt guilty and ashamed for liking the ramshackle house when he was small. It was lazy and stupid of him not to want 'a proper carry-on'. On and off, he'd been dimly aware of the camaraderie between the people in the other houses and the waves of resentment towards his own family. It had taken him years to realise it was caused by the holier, cleaner and more-respectable-than-thou attitude with which he had learned to treat the neighbours' children. He'd felt half contemptuous and half afraid of them. He was not allowed to pick up their 'nasty, rough way' of speaking. Usually they didn't speak to him anyway. He hung around sometimes and watched them, not realising that he was envying them, but more often he escaped to his books and his music.

He had once tried to tell his mother about his music. He remembered her reply. 'Oh, John, if only you were more like normal boys!' Surely that was the last thing she had wanted. 'If only . . . ' had dogged his childhood. Even on days he'd spent trying to please her from rising to falling into bed, he'd been rewarded with, 'If only you were always like this!' His music was acceptable if she directed it. He had composed a piece when he was ten and had been required to play it for a while, whenever his uncomprehending relations had been around to be impressed. They invariably talked through his performance. He trembled with rage afresh as he remembered the great-aunt who, intending to compliment him, had told him that, if he practised hard, he'd play as well as his older cousin. Incensed at this unfavourable comparison with a despised inferior, he had at last rebelled and refused to finish his piece. He felt again the agony in his fingers as his mother brought down the ruler on them. After that, he'd been unable to finish it. He'd still been sobbing when his mother had followed him up to bed to explain that the punishment was for his own good. 'What a way to behave after all we've done for you!' Tomorrow he must write a letter, apologising to Aunt Eleanor and explaining that he hadn't meant to be so rude.

Where had his father been? It was immaterial. The total submission that his mother demanded from them both had become habitual and had rendered him powerless. He remembered his father's wage rising to something just less than twenty pounds a

21

week and his quiet, beaming satisfaction that he was now a 'thousand a year man'. It wasn't enough to satisfy her though, once the novelty had worn off.

She had rejected his person too. Everything physical was dirty. He wondered how he himself had come to exist. He would never have dreamed of asking her about the facts of life. He found them out by accident, rather than because he wanted to know. She had sent him once to the chemist with a note that she refused to explain. It had made him afraid in a vague, unspecific way. The shop was along a dreary street. It had an unfriendly feel, its shelves and counter high. A man with a pinched face and an anonymous white coat had read his note, wrapped a mysterious package and sealed it with sellotape, all without speaking, and wrapped his change in the crumpled paper. He had read it on the way out but had had no idea what STs were. He went home feeling like the pawn of an international spy ring, and yet as if the parcel's bulky, squashy contents were somehow unclean and shameful. He could have accepted the not knowing, as children always accept, through necessity, the half-mysterious, the partly understood, but his mother had sent him on the errand because she found it embarrassing herself and had tacitly transferred her distaste to him.

Later he had filled in the missing facts from a magazine circulating in the school playground and was horrified when he understood. Thank God he was a man. He'd made his own arrangements about that sort of thing. Nobody else knew about it and it suited them both very well. What had that booklet been called? 'The Joys of Sex'?

He couldn't understand joy. It seemed to mean abandonment. He didn't trust anything enough to abandon himself to it, wasn't prepared to take the risk – except with the girls. Doing Alison in particular had aroused him to a sort of pleasurable terror but, afterwards, he'd felt hopeless and miserable as he did now. He'd hoped a doctor could help him but he'd been unable to explain anything to him. He'd just sat in the surgery, wishing Dr Burton could read some of his thoughts, and come away with a prescription for sleeping pills. And now he'd done Denise.

He was looking forward to the papers. He would cut the reports out and lock them into his five-year diary. Having them there to look at would make him feel a bit like he did when he'd taken the clothes from that department store when he was a sixth-former. He'd been amazed how easy it had been, bringing out another garment each time he went in. It had evened things up a bit and he'd kept all the stuff hidden in the back of his wardrobe for ages, without wearing it, gloating over it.

It wasn't as exciting as doing the girls, though. Yet, strangely, his memories of the actual killings were vague now. He just remembered the thrill, the buzz of it. He got up and put his record on again and sat staring into space as it played, not listening to it. Then he pulled a pad out of a drawer, fished for the pen in the jumble of oddments beneath and began to write. 'Dear Sir, I'm very sorry about the girl. I didn't mean to . . . '

Chapter 3

Browne woke at the telephone's first ring and answered it at the second but it had woken Hannah. He listened, spoke briefly, then replaced the receiver and began to dress. 'Young girl, Greystones Park, strangled,' he told his wife softly. 'Do you want coffee?'

She nodded and refrained from offering to make it, knowing that he'd prefer to be alone downstairs, preparing himself for a new investigation.

He padded to the kitchen, his mind fixed on the letter in his office drawer. It had been posted thirteen days ago. Had it been an apology for an intention? Since it employed the past tense, he didn't think so, but he reread it mentally as he carried up Hannah's coffee and then departed cautiously over six inches of snow. He negotiated the drifts in his own road successfully and found to his relief, as he turned at the end, that his approach to the main road was sheltered from the wind. The flakes that were still falling interrupted and reflected the beams from the streetlamps and his headlamps, reducing the world to a myriad pinpricks of light.

He reached the main road, the wintry conditions giving him a heightened awareness of the details of civilisation, the fug of the car heater and the bitter coffee he could still taste in the back of his throat. A couple of cars passed in the opposite direction, little capsules of humanity hissing through the gloom. Along the motorway, on the skyline he couldn't yet see, miniature beams slid from one end of his range of vision to the other.

He signalled and turned on to a side road. Freedom from conditions like these was supposed to be one of the few advantages of global warming. Not that he disliked snow. On the contrary, he greeted its arrival with boyish glee, but it wasn't helping matters just now. The wall on his left bounded the park and he slowed for the entrance, only to find it blocked by a huge drift. He would have to walk from here as he could see his colleagues had done.

The snow was already beginning to pile up on the roofs of a couple of parked police cars, though not on their still-warm bonnets, and the footsteps leading from them were fast becoming obliterated. He slid his woollen-socked feet into his Wellington boots and followed them. On the other side of the entrance, a young constable had gone over to speak to a swathed figure who was toiling hopefully over the luminous mound which hid his own vehicle.

Following the just discernible tracks, Browne sighted a cluster of officiating police, unrecognisable from this distance as they huddled in universal duffles. One of them came to meet him, revealing himself as DC Nigel Bellamy. 'She's just a lass, sir, behind the big bush there. Dr Stocks has been and gone, called out again, but we know officially that we've got a corpse.'

Browne took the proffered torch and regarded the body thoughtfully. He saw in the strong beam a face covered with minute Tardieu spots and recognised a death by asphyxiation before he pulled back the victim's coat to reveal the thumb-marked neck. The coat had been unfastened but pulled up round her neck and he replaced it as he had found it, then stepped back to consider. He knew that dawn was imminent, would have arrived by the time they had set up arc-lamps. They'd wait for daylight. 'Who found her, Nigel?'

Bellamy indicated with a jerk of his head. 'Chap over there with the traffic cop, sir. Robert Clarkson. He's the park keeper. Lives in the lodge just inside the gates.'

Browne nodded and went over to the man. He looked subdued but certainly not in clinical shock. 'How exactly did you come to find her, sir? Bit early for walking the dog, isn't it?' Browne had seen no signs that a dog had bounded through the snow.

Clarkson shook his head. 'I always wake early and the snow made it seem lighter. I was wide awake and looked out. It's a fairyland, isn't it? I know we get it nearly every year in these parts but the first good fall always takes you the same way. I thought I'd have a wander round whilst it was still unspoilt. The place'll be full of snowballing kids before long – not that I begrudge them, mind. There was a robin chuntering to itself on the wall and I went right up to it. They're used to me around. Then I saw her.'

'Did you touch her?'

He shook his head. 'I was sure she was dead, but, even if she hadn't been, getting her to hospital quickly would have been more use than my mucking about with her.'

The body lay in the lee of the wind and, sheltered by the bush, had only a light covering of snow, but Browne could see that it hadn't been disturbed. He picked out Clarkson's tracks from the others and saw that those nearest to the body were still a couple of yards away. He could sympathise with the man's urge to enjoy the snow.

'So, what did you do?'

'Made for the gate and the road.'

'Not to phone from your house?'

Clarkson had begun to shiver and wrapped his arms round himself. 'The wind's brought the line down somewhere. My phone's been dead since last night. When I got to the road, I had the good luck to see this constable.' He indicated Brian Jackson of Traffic Division who obviously had information to impart. Clarkson was dismissed to wait in his own house, increasing his popularity by his parting remark: 'I'll get the coffee-pot on. When any of you can be spared you can come and help yourselves.'

Browne continued as best he could with a routine that the conditions made almost impossible and, by the time Superintendent Petty arrived, he needed only to confirm and approve. The Task Force squad had each been assigned his few square yards to search. The immediate area had been taped off and detailed notes taken of the general weather conditions.

Browne turned back to Jackson. 'What were you doing up here, Constable?'

'Attending a minor bump, sir. Maestro ran into the back of a Mini van. Nobody hurt. I came because some passer-by with a carphone rang the station but, when I arrived, the stupid busybody had cleared off.' Browne sensed there was something else and

26

waited. Jackson spoke hesitantly. 'I'm not sure, sir, with her face all blotchy and swollen, but I think we've come across this girl before. PC Brenner dealt with the incident. A little girl was knocked down and killed. No blame attached to the driver. The kid came down a track between the houses on to the main road on a skateboard. Even her parents were trying to comfort the driver. I don't want to waste your time and I can't remember her name but I think it was this girl.'

Browne scribbled. 'Brenner, you said? Right, we'll follow that up.' He moved away to greet the pathologist, then moved to a distance as he and a photographer set to work on their various tasks. Behind him lay a bowling green and a children's playground, shrouded in snow as though covered in dust sheets and put away in store until they were needed again. The drifts were so deep that he had difficulty picking out which shape was the long multi-seated rocking horse and which the swings, though the climbing frame with its roofed platforms was still distinctive. Chunks of snow, dislodged by the wind, fell on his shoulders from the branches and bits of the branches themselves slapped against him. His calves ached from hauling his feet out of each deep footprint.

The sodium lights in the streets across the valley, viewed through the branches, seemed to be decorations strung along them, and although the snow was trickling down his neck and driving in his face, the blanket of it over everything, softening lines and deadening sound, created a strange cosy atmosphere. As he became aware of rose and gold streaks in the sky a sudden soft plop distracted him. He turned to see a swing, its seat tilted because one of its chains was twisted. The snow had slipped off revealing a patch of mundane red plastic, a glimpse of the ordinary everyday world hidden beneath this glimmering, transforming covering of white.

Realising his presence was no help to the experts he was watching, Browne decided it would be more profitable as well as warmer to go in search of Brenner of Traffic Division. He spoke briefly to Ledgard, the pathologist. They were old friends and he was pretty sure he could rely on a quick phone call to deliver the initial medical findings. The hovering Superintendent approved

Browne's departure and made much ado about the confidence with which he was leaving the day-to-day organisation of the investigation to him.

Browne made a tentative suggestion. 'It's been snowing solidly since yesterday teatime, sir. There must have been a fair amount of snow on the ground when the girl was either killed or dumped here and a lot more has fallen since. The evidence we're looking for is in the middle of it. What about setting canvas covers over the immediate area and getting some hot-air blowers to melt it? We daren't dig for fear of moving things from where they've been left.'

The superintendent nodded his consent and, dismissing him, called the SOCO over to him. 'I've decided it would be a good idea if we put some canvas covers . . . '

Browne ground his teeth as he returned to the station. It did not improve his temper to be told that Brenner was on leave. Politely, he requested details of the child's death to be sent to him and referred them to Jackson for more information. The rose and gold of dawn had disappeared quickly. Now the sky was leaden, promising that the precipitation would continue. Browne turned on the lights in his office and turned up the thermostat on his radiator, trying to decide what he could most usefully do whilst he waited for the arrival on his desk of a welter of reports on his colleagues' present activities. These would include the house-to-house calls which would be beginning now that the local populace could reasonably be expected to be up and about.

The most urgent business suddenly occurred to him. He'd consumed only one cup of coffee since he'd got up in the small hours. He made for the canteen.

Twenty minutes later, when in his normal agreeable humour he returned to his office, he found DC Benedict Mitchell, who happened to be his prospective son-in-law, hovering outside the door. He brought the news that Smithson, the youth he had been questioning for the last hour, had finally admitted to a series of burglaries on a housing estate on the edge of the town. He bore also the tidings that DS Hunter would not be reporting on duty today. Both facts seemed to afford him equal pleasure.

Browne sighed. Was yet another investigation to be hindered

by the mutual antipathy of his sergeant and one of the more promising of his DCs? Evidently it wouldn't be today. Browne was not surprised at Hunter's absence. He decided to face the next few hours one man light and then call in DS Clements on the next shift a couple of hours early. Clements would be glad of the overtime, and if Hunter returned within two or three days that would be enough.

Browne was annoyed with Mitchell and sent him to assist with the house-to-house inquiries to get rid of him. Mitchell, who enjoyed chatting to new people and making himself at home on their premises, strode off in high good humour. As always, Browne treated his irritation with a good dose of paperwork, from which he was glad to be distracted by a call from DC Dean.

'You don't sound happy, Richard.'

Dean wasn't. The superintendent had remained to watch over their efforts, 'teaching his grandmother to suck eggs!' He declined to go into detail, not being sure about Browne's relations with that superior. Browne sympathised. So much for 'leaving the inquiry in your capable hands'.

Dean's news was that a folder of music had turned up in the melting snow. It was now safely encased in plastic, ready to be dispatched to the lab. 'We can't read the name on the label on the front but the folder itself is covered in thick plastic so the contents are still fairly dry. There's a pink-covered booklet called "In Praise of Mary".' He described it in detail. 'Then there are three books, all called *Carols for Choirs*, but in different colours.'

'Right.' Browne looked at his watch. 'They should be under way at the central library by now. Get on to them for a list of all the music societies in the area and get the name and number of an official from each one. Then ring round until you find someone who recognises that collection.'

Knowing how Dean hated being chained to a phone, Browne chuckled, then decided to make a call himself before returning to the hated files. It would be only courteous to ask Hunter how he was feeling, though he realised that his chief motive was an inability to marshal his thoughts without a sounding board. Hunter was the sounding board he was used to and who was used to him. Besides, didn't Hunter sing in one of these fancy choirs? It would

29

be handy if it was the same one. Hunter's husky whisper assured his CI that he would be back on the job in a couple of days. Browne doubted this but accepted it for the moment.

'Is your choir giving a Christmas concert, Jerry?'

'Yes, on December 18th. We wanted Saturday 21st, but that would have clashed with the Choral's big concert in the Victoria Hall. We have enough bother selling tickets without a rival show to contend with.'

'Is your choir singing a thing by Geoffrey Bush, called "In Praise of Mary"?'

'No, it's separate carols, six for Advent, six for Christmas and six for Epiphany. It'd be a bit highbrow for you, sir, though I'll willingly get you some tickets if you want to give it a try.' Browne chuckled and declined politely. He gave Hunter a quick summary of the events of the last twenty-four hours, commiserated with him again and rang off.

An hour later, the phone shrilled again and Browne was addressed by his superintendent, his tone, as usual, half hearty, half hectoring. 'Dean has turned up a fellow called Cully. He says the music is the programme for his choir's Christmas concert. I've had him along to look at the girl and he's identified her as a Denise Kemp. He's a bit shaken up. I'm sending him over to you for tea, sympathy and the works. Making progress, aren't we?' After a click, the line went dead.

Browne snarled at the receiver and wondered why the Super couldn't leave the routine work to the team as he usually did. He noted the girl's name in his own file, then rang it through to Traffic Division. Jackson himself answered. 'That's the name, sir. I remember now that I've heard it again. We're sending the details across.'

Cully, escorted in twenty minutes later by Bellamy, seemed to have himself more in hand than Browne had expected after Petty's caveat. When invited to sit, he settled himself comfortably into Browne's armchair and crossed his right ankle over his left knee, a feat made easy by his length of leg and lack of superfluous flesh. He had removed a leather jacket to reveal cords and sweater over an open-necked shirt.

Bellamy had taken out a notebook and, without being asked, Browne's visitor supplied his personal details. 'Cavan Cully, Vicarage Court, St Michael's Lane.' He removed his steamed-up spectacles to polish them and Browne studied the face that was revealed. The forehead was very high, not because the hair was receding but because it grew like that, curling waywardly. It almost reached his shoulders but the impression was more as if a short back and sides had become overgrown than as though it was meant to flow. The nose and chin were extended so that the face seemed to be an inordinate length, yet the man still contrived to be handsome. The features were strong and masculine but the skin was like a woman's, translucent and fine-textured. He looked little more than twenty until the spectacles, steel rimmed and narrow, were replaced. Then he reminded Browne of one of Alex's university teachers, in his middle thirties but with the eager expression of a sheltered academic not wearied by the nasty ways of the big wide world.

Browne thanked him for coming. 'You're quite sure about your identification of Mrs Kemp?' He nodded. 'What can you tell me about her?' .

'Well, she was a first soprano. It wasn't the most powerful of voices but very sweet and boyish.' He read Browne's expression and changed tack. 'She's about twenty-five or -six, married but with no children. They're a pair of yuppies but very pleasant, not rich but short of nothing, well travelled. She missed a few rehearsals for the last concert because she was abroad. She's apt to pin folk down with albums of photographs when she comes back.' He frowned and shook his head. 'That's not relevant, is it? I don't know what sort of things to tell you.'

'Everything's relevant. Tell me whatever comes into your head.'

'All right. Her husband doesn't sing but he helps us by producing tickets and programmes on his computer. It's useful to have that taken care of when music costs so much. She was a bit reserved. Not shy exactly, just didn't put all the goods in the shop window. It gave her a reputation for being stand-offish with people who didn't know her.'

He stopped and stared at the wall for a few moments, then returned to the subject he felt at home with. 'When I first aud-

31

itioned her, I let her into the choir because her sight-reading was first rate. Her voice was true but weak. But, later, as she settled in and made friends, she relaxed and began to sing really well. She's very conscientious. She bought professional recordings of most of the current rehearsal material and studied the whole work as well as her own part. Lots of much less able members take far less trouble.'

A WPC came in with a tray of tea and biscuits which Browne dispensed as he prompted and listened. 'Tell me a bit about the choir. There was a practice last night?'

Cully nodded. 'Yes, we rehearse every Wednesday apart from holiday breaks. We began the material for this concert at the beginning of October, a bit earlier than usual for Christmas because we had a new work to learn.'

Browne shovelled sugar into Bellamy's tea and slid it across to him. 'I take it it's an amateur choir.'

'Oh yes. Most choral societies have to be amateurs. I'm paid but the singers aren't. They're not only unpaid, they fork out a sixty-pound subscription every year for the privilege of letting me bully them. You couldn't pay professionals in such numbers.'

'What are the numbers?'

'I try to keep it to about eighty. Much bigger than a chamber choir but a bit on the small side for a choral society. I think I have a reputation for being a musical snob for turning down some good voices that don't quite make for the right balance. They come to audition for all sorts of reasons but they're chosen for just one – because I want to use their voices.'

Browne proffered biscuits before Cully got too carried away and asked, 'Did Mrs Kemp stay till the end of the practice?' He nodded. 'And what time did it finish?'

He shrugged. 'I don't know.' Browne looked surprised and he went on, 'At some point I sense a change of atmosphere. There's a tendency to race to the end of a piece. When the choir is stopped it exchanges repartee instead of listening. If I persist much after that, I get consultation of watches, then audible groans and people creeping out. Time by the clock doesn't matter. It depends how musically tired they are and how high on a particular work. I don't know what time we broke up last night but they will. Their first job when we've finished is calculating how much drinking time is left.'

Browne nodded. 'We'd like to know whether the music we found was Mrs Kemp's or whether it belonged to the person who left her in the park.'

He blinked. 'But that would mean . . . '

'Yes, a choir member. Would they each have a folder?'

'Oh yes. Everyone has a copy even if he holds it upside-down. It's all part of the fun.'

'No one actually does?'

He shrugged again. 'Probably not, but one or two of them might as well. The voice doesn't always go with technical ability or general musicality.'

Browne desperately wished Hunter was with him. Not only would his intervention have made this interview less of a relentless catechism, but he would have made informed comments about the music which would have relaxed this man and put him off his guard. Their asides would have given Browne more of an insight into the atmosphere at last night's practice than any amount of careful explanation from Cully. Still, he could only press on. 'Did you see Mrs Kemp leave?'

Cully unhooked his right foot and sat forward. 'Can we call her Denise? I keep wondering who Mrs Kemp is.' Browne nodded. 'I haven't said how sorry I am. It isn't because I'm not, but talking about it seems to belittle it. We don't feel deep sorrow often enough to have got a vocabulary for it. That's a good thing I suppose.' He returned to the question. 'I saw several people go up to congratulate her on the solo she'd sung. Then I saw her talking to the new member, Howard Mellor, but I didn't see her leave.'

'How new is he?'

Cully shook his head impatiently as though he were tiring of the inquisition. 'I auditioned him half an hour before the practice began. I liked his voice and the timbre blended well with the bass sound that we have. I invited him to stay and see how he liked us and at the end he came to say he'd enjoyed himself and could he be taken on. He seemed in a bit of a hurry.' Cully anticipated Browne's next question. 'No one else was new last night. It's too near a concert to be having people joining who don't know the works. I took a youngster into the tenor section two weeks ago though. He's the next newest member.'

Suddenly, Bellamy asked a question. Browne and Cully both turned to him in surprise. 'Is it frustrating when your success as a conductor depends on other people's efforts that might not be made?' He tried to make his meaning clearer. 'I mean, if you play an instrument, you've only got yourself to blame if the sound is wrong. With a choir you're getting the sound from hundreds of other people and any one of them could spoil it.'

Cully became animated. 'But that makes it more exciting, more of a challenge.' Browne was delighted. Perhaps he wasn't going to miss Hunter as much as he'd thought. Cully went on, 'All music is frustrating. You can never achieve, physically, quite the sound you can hear in your imagination, whatever you're making it with. Amateurs feel it especially. They think they could have got there if they hadn't had the distraction of making money in another field. Mellor, the new bass, was telling me at his audition that he thinks he could have become a professional flautist if his mother hadn't persuaded him into a safe career. He probably forgets how much pleasure he gets out of what he does. Then I've a tenor who thinks he should have been an opera singer if the woman who should have been behind him hadn't turned him down.' He tutted derisively. 'As though it could be someone else's job in life to develop his latent genius! He's just lazy and unrealistic. Even my invaluable accompanist is convinced he'd be a successful concert pianist if he hadn't suffered a badly fractured finger as a child.' He grinned. 'I tell them how lucky it is for me that they all ended up in Cloughton Choral.'

Seeing that Bellamy seemed to have completed his contribution to the interview, Browne resumed. 'How many members of the choir, or people who were present last night, have the Christian name John?'

Cully blinked. 'I presume you don't expect me to give you a number off the top of my head. I'll have to look in the register – and it depends what your question means. Simmons, the new tenor, and Fielden, my accompanist, are addressed as John. But then there are Jake Searle and Jack Chance whose real names are

John. And what about people who have it as an additional name? I'm John Cavan for a start. I don't think even the register will help us there.'

His face revealed his speculations about the reason behind Browne's question but he refrained from asking. Browne pushed his chair back from the desk, indicating that, for the present, he had reached his last point. 'At the moment, I see no alternative to starting a tedious check on the homeward journeys of all your members. I hope you went straight home to your blameless wife.'

Cully shook his head. 'I'm not married. I couldn't be. My wife would always be jealous of all the people I fell in love with. I love everybody who makes music.'

'So your latent genius has no need of a woman?'

Seeing he was dismissed, Cully stood up to go. 'Ah, that isn't what I said.'

Having satisfied himself that his wife was as well as she had been at breakfast time, Jack Chance felt free to enjoy his lunch. Belinda carried a small casserole dish from the kitchen and transferred its contents to the two plates set out on the dining-room table.

She tried not to feel irritated by his conviction that her admittedly difficult pregnancy needed his personal supervision at least every three or four hours. Sensing her impatience he held back his catechism on how she had spent her morning. To ensure that it didn't pop out in spite of him he crossed to the music centre and slipped the nearest disc to hand into the CD player.

Belinda grinned. 'I see. Feel like a change from dreary domesticity and a lady with a bump?' She stroked her swollen stomach in mock offence.

Chance blinked, then returned the grin as he realised he was listening to Ian Partridge singing the part of Schubert's travelling millhand who fell in love with his employer's pretty daughter. They listened, companionably, as they ate.

'He didn't get anywhere with her,' Belinda observed after some minutes, watching Chance spear his last juicy piece of beef. 'You'd do better to stay with me than end up suicidal on the river bank.'

He nodded as the music continued, fresh and optimistic, not

sounding in the least like the fruit of wretched experience. Belinda rose to clear their plates.

'Didn't you do this song as your party piece at the choir social evening? John threw a wobbly about it afterwards for some reason.'

Chance nodded and reached for a banana from the bowl beside him. 'That's right. The playing has to be different in each verse even though the notes are exactly the same. It has to be the clacking of the mill first, then the water rippling and so on. He didn't think he'd got it right so he wouldn't go on with it. Actually, I think he'd had a fair amount to drink. Jackie took him home and he apologised profusely next time I saw him.'

Belinda disappeared to brew coffee and Chance abandoned himself to the rest of the song and the one that followed. There was a fragment of a psalm that he'd heard read in church that exactly described how Schubert made him feel. He'd looked it up later. 'I am poured out like water and all my bones are out of joint: my heart is like wax; it is melted in the midst of my bowels.' Chance had an idea that this was the psalmist's attempt to describe despair but it had managed to encapsulate exactly the painful pleasure that he was experiencing. It was partly the felicitous melodies and partly the consummate artistry of the performers.

Chance was no pianist but singing he understood and, momentarily, he felt a fierce envy of the effortless tenor. Then he abandoned it. A talent like that took away all personal choice. Using it, exploring it, exploiting it would be a duty. Exciting as that might be, it took away everything ordinary. Everything ordinary has great value when it has to be given up.

The phone rang and broke the spell. He became aware of the bubbling of the percolator in the kitchen and the clink of cups. Shrugging philosophically, he turned the music down low and lifted the receiver.

With the tray set ready, Belinda watched him through the kitchen door, as she waited for the coffee to finish. She listened idly to Jack's half of the conversation and tried to make her heavy body comfortable on the kitchen stool. The infant moved, protestingly and energetically. She was sure it would be born

36

safely now, though she would continue to heed all medical advice. Jack's anxiety was greater than her own.

His 'Good God!' distracted her and she returned to her appraisal of him. How different he seemed now from when she'd first married him, assured and confident, urbane, successful; but the same Jack really. It was after losing Sally that he'd submerged himself in the business and worked so incredibly hard. But driving himself, though more cheerfully of late, had become his nature now. On the whole he'd adjusted well to their adored child's death, though neither of them had forgiven the doctor who'd failed them. He'd been absolved from any negligence, but then they always were, and why else should Sally not have recovered from such a routine operation?

After the first wild accusations Jack had settled to what seemed a normal life even though the subsequent family they'd planned had taken such a long time to materialise. She'd given up hope but he never had and he hadn't been too twitchy through all the bother with this second child.

She hoped it would be a boy. She didn't mind for herself but a boy would be in less danger of constant comparisons with Sally. Jack should look forward more as she did. She picked up the large framed photograph from the dresser and studied the exquisite, solemn little features, her own but daintier, framed by the flaxen hair the child had inherited from her father. Without the aid of the picture, she found it hard now to remember what Sally had looked like, though she had vivid memories of her little ways.

She blinked as she suddenly recalled a worldly wise glance Sally had given her as she had sat at table and accepted titbits from her father's plate. 'Who's humouring whom?' the expression had asked. According to Jack, the child had had the potential to play like Menuhin, to look like Grace Kelly, and to take the academic world by storm. He'd brought her little eighth-size fiddle down from the attic this week, she'd noticed. She wished he'd buy this child a new soft toy instead. It wasn't fair to saddle it with all his frustrated dream wishes for Sally. She daren't tell him how little she herself thought about Sally now and how much her second child's imminent arrival made her look forward only.

She glanced round the kitchen and through to the dining-room, admiring the fruit of all Jack's hard work. Considering his origins, comparative riches sat easily on him. As a child he'd had nothing compared with the possessions she'd taken for granted in her upper-middle-class home. But there was no ostentation here. She watched him as he spoke in lowered tones to his caller, his left hand fingering the cover of a creamware chestnut bowl, tracing the delicate piercing of the lacy pottery. He appreciated it because it was perfect and pleasing, not because it was a symbol of what he'd become. He was fond of it too because it was local ware, characteristic of its Leeds factory of the eighteen-hundreds. As he'd grown more affluent, he'd taken to material possessions, and particularly to works of art, as if he'd been born to them.

He'd never embarrassed her, even in their earliest days, with self reproaches and apologies for taking her away from such things, though there had been the occasional extravagant present that he could ill afford at the time. And he'd had the wisdom to deny Sally frequently. There had been no nonsense about heaping on her all the things he'd had to do without.

As Belinda carried the coffee tray through to the dining-room table, Chance replaced the receiver looking shocked. She began pouring milk into cups as she asked, 'What's wrong? Who was it?'

'Just Cavan with some choir business.'

She shifted his cup out of his reach, forcing him to look up at her. 'Jack, I might be pregnant but my brain isn't addled. I still have my full complement of common sense.'

'All right, then.' He drank deeply from his recaptured cup. 'Denise Kemp has been found dead in Greystones Park. And Alison Meredith failed to turn up for last night's rehearsal. Cavan can't contact her either at home or at work.'

Chapter 4

By late afternoon the choral society register had arrived on
Browne's desk. Opening it he saw that it was a list of the singers,
divided into their various parts, beginning with first sopranos and
finishing with second basses. It was not a record of the members'
attendances at particular rehearsals. Each name had an address
and most had a telephone number too. Browne rang Denise
Kemp's but received no answer. Despite this, he decided to visit
the house. The neighbours might know where to find her husband.

As it happened, they did not, but a Mrs Freeman, who lived
opposite, knew why he was missing. 'Gone to France for his firm,'
she informed him. 'Sometimes they both go and then I feed the
cats.' Puzzled, she looked across the road. 'That's one of them,
wailing on the step. There's a cat-flap for him to get in. Hasn't
Denise fed him? I haven't seen her today.'

'When did you last see her?'

She looked alarmed. 'When she went off to her choir practice
last night. She hasn't gone missing has she?

Browne shook his head. 'No, she isn't missing.'

The woman was perplexed. She thought for a moment, then
made up her mind. 'The poor thing looks hungry. I've got a key.
I'll go across and feed them both. Even if Denise gets back before
I've finished, she won't mind.'

'No, you can't do that.'

Now, Mrs Freeman was annoyed, until Browne showed her his
warrant card. 'I'm afraid Mrs Kemp has been hurt.' He parried
her questions and extracted from her the Kemps' key and the
address of Mrs Kemp's mother in exchange for a promise to see
that the cats were attended to. He kept his promise and dropped

the key into the station, then, having picked up Jennie Smith, drove three miles due north to break the news of her daughter's death to the widowed Mrs Ryder.

She opened the door of a small terraced house to him, and he knew at once that someone had broken the news to her already. A phrase he had read came into his mind, 'consecrated by great sorrow'. She was quite unlike what he had seen of her daughter, small with delicate colouring, neatly and tidily dressed. She was not, nor had she been, weeping. Her expression was grave and composed, and Browne was amazed to hear loud and cheerful sounding classical music filling the little room which opened straight on to the pavement. 'Mrs Ryder?' He held up his card and she nodded and let him in.

She understood his surprise. 'It was Denise's favourite bit of Mozart. The choir sang it in the summer and she bought this recording for me afterwards. I've been remembering the times we listened to it together and, after all, it is a requiem.' She crossed the room and turned it off, then indicated an armchair for him and seated herself in the one opposite. Jennie settled herself on a dining chair at the table as he began to apologise for his intrusion. 'Has an officer been to see you already?'

She nodded. 'Superintendent Petty and Constable Mitchell.'

As he digested this unexpected information, Browne explained the reason for his own visit. 'You see, the more we know about the sort of girl your daughter was, the better chance we have of finding out why she was killed . . . '

She hushed him. 'Don't apologise. The one thing I want is to talk about her. What you've seen wasn't Denise. There she is.' She handed over two postcard-sized photographs that she had obviously looked out ready for him. One was a head and shoulders portrait, an unsmiling face with the hair dragged back so that its curl was only in the ends. Rebel strands in front of the ears emphasized the latent energy in the expression. The chin was raised and the dark eyes narrowed, giving an impression of arrogance, but the cause could well have been a self-conscious reaction to being photographed at close quarters. The impression was missing in the other picture where the girl was part of a group.

40

Here, the thick wavy hair fell to her shoulders, framing a square, strongly featured, but smiling face.

When he handed the pictures back, she slipped them into a pocket as though she wanted to keep them on her person. 'Have you managed to find Stuart yet?' she asked, settling back in her chair.

Browne shook his head. 'I haven't heard. We'll let you know when we do. Has he another name besides Stuart?'

She nodded, faintly puzzled. 'Yes, he's Stuart Raymond. The second name's after his father.'

'Not John?'

'No, as far as I know there are no Johns in the family.'

Browne nodded. 'Tell me about Denise now.'

Mrs Ryder looked at some point beyond Browne, half smiling. 'She was our eldest so she suffered most from my delusions about the sacred task of motherhood, like all first children do. She was quiet and rather reserved and I've never been able to decide whether it was because she was a bit over-disciplined. She certainly didn't have the freedom that helped to make our youngest so outgoing and spontaneous. But, maybe it was in her genes to keep her own counsel. She was always friendly but she liked one or two companions rather than belonging to a crowd like Carolyn does.

'Our big ideas about education and her intelligence were more inhibiting than encouraging – you know, music lessons on several instruments, serious books for presents when other children had cheap toys. I remember one Christmas when we'd spent a fortune on her and she'd opened all her parcels and she didn't seem particularly excited. I was about to tell her she was ungrateful when I looked at the gifts she'd put into a neat pile and realised that we hadn't given her a single thing she could play with just for the fun of it. I went away and wept.

'Then we took it for granted that she would go straight to university from school, and being a fairly biddable child she did. She met Stuart there. He's scarcely older than she is but he had the wisdom to start building up her confidence by accepting and loving her the way she was.'

41

She stopped and got to her feet. 'I'm sorry. I haven't offered you tea.'

Browne waved her back to her seat. He held his hand just under his chin. 'No thanks, I'm up to here with it. Keep talking.'

She complied. 'The best moment seemed the worst at the time. After her first year at the university, she arrived home and declared she wasn't going back. She'd done badly in her exams and she worked all summer for the retakes, so that she was choosing to leave rather than having to.'

Browne marvelled at the determination that could drive a youngster to study hard, merely to relinquish something with honour. The mother, one of those articulate beings who could find relief in the expression of her feelings, went on.

'She had a fair wait before a job turned up and then she went south to take it and she and Stuart got engaged. People said, "Aren't you very worried, disappointed, upset?" But I'd learned my lesson by then and what I felt was delight and relief. She had come through our mistakes and could still make her own decisions.'

She removed her gaze from over Browne's shoulder and looked directly at him. 'Children should be like Christmas presents. You should receive them with excitement and then unwrap them to see what you've got. They shouldn't be treated like a ball of plasticine that you mould into any shape that you want to impose on it.'

Browne's mind was now on matters closer to home than the Ryder family and his conscience was troubling him. All the previous summer he had refused to take seriously his own daughter's objections to taking up her place at Oxford. In the end she had departed, more or less willingly, persuaded not by himself but by young Mitchell.

Mrs Ryder was still talking. 'Of course they were living together. I couldn't stop them but, at first, I took the attitude that, at least in my house, they would behave decently. But, when I thought about it, I decided I wanted to be a friend of the person Denise really is, not of the idealised person she's supposed to live up to. Mind you, I didn't pretend that I approved or liked what they were doing. There had to be no deception on either side –

42

but I treated them, when they visited, as if they were married and within a year or so they were.'

Browne realised that this woman had fully realised her loss. Cully had wandered awkwardly from the past tense to the present and back again when he spoke of Denise. Her mother accepted that she would never again see the daughter that she had brought up with such care. He rose to leave. 'You've given me exactly what I wanted, Mrs Ryder. I may have to speak to you again but that's fine for the moment.'

But now she had lost her composure, and the face crumpled. 'She belonged to herself, not to me. I loved her but she wasn't mine. I didn't live through her and in that sense I haven't lost her. That sort of belonging was Stuart's right and responsibility and he took it so seriously. I don't know how he will bear it.'

She hid her face and sobbed. Browne took his leave with a slight pressure of his hand on her shoulder, but, first, he presumed to cross the room and slip back into the machine the compact disc she had politely removed on his arrival. Her smile thanked him as the room filled with sound. *Requiem aeternam dona eis, Domine.*

When Browne arrived back at the station, he found Cully waiting for him at the desk. 'I'm worried,' he told Browne when he was comfortably settled. 'I should have mentioned it this afternoon but I was so shocked at Denise's death that I forgot about Alison.'

'Alison?'

Cully pulled himself together and started at the beginning. 'Alison Meredith is a first soprano. She's singing the solo part in the main work at the concert on the 20th. We tried it for the first time a fortnight ago on November 19th. She was due to be starting on a course in London the next day, but she's a keen member and she came to the rehearsal, planning to drive down through the night and snatch a few hours' sleep before it all started. She said the first half-day of these affairs is only socialising so it wouldn't matter if she was only half awake. She left as soon as we'd finished and I think someone gave her a lift to the station. She was due to be away for nine days so we knew she wouldn't be at last week's practice – on the 26th – but we expected her back last night. She wasn't there.

'I was surprised, a bit worried even. I'm pretty short with people who let me down, and as I said she's very loyal. I tried to ring her when I got back last night and again this morning. I was going to try her firm to see if they could tell me anything when your people rang me and I found out about Denise. It drove everything else out of my head. Then when I got home I remembered and wondered if there might be a connection.'

Browne had been making notes on this orderly recital. Now he looked up at Cully. 'What sort of course was it?'

'To do with her work. She's a fashion buyer for a series of boutiques in Leeds.'

'Does she live there?'

Cully shook his head. 'No, in Cloughton, in a flat in Crossley Royd.'

Browne knew the prosperous residential area. 'And the chain she works for?'

'Cinderella. They sell evening dresses – ball gowns.' Cully seemed mesmerised by Browne's pencil which was now drawing figures of eight along the line as he counted. This girl was last seen by Cully on November 19th. The letter in his desk drawer was postmarked the 20th and had arrived at the substation in Crossley Bridge on the 22nd. He had an uneasy feeling that the postman might be calling there again in the near future.

'What does she look like?'

Cully raised his eyes from the pencil to Browne's face. 'Well, trendy and a bit painted because of her job. She's thirty-two but she doesn't look it – well, not until you're close up. She's blonde but I think her hair's bleached – she hasn't got a very fair complexion. Tall and slim.'

Browne nodded and continued writing. 'Married? Does she live with anyone?'

Cully shook his head. 'Not regularly, anyway.' He brightened. 'Do you think she might have met up with someone on this course and gone off somewhere with him?'

Browne shrugged. 'She might have done anything. Anyway, you can go home now. I know where to find you if I want any more information.'

Cully smiled and thanked him. 'I shall eat my supper with a clear conscience now the police machine's taking over.'

The second letter arrived the next morning, a day sooner than Browne had expected. Identical to the other, except that it bore a first-class stamp, it was delivered to the same substation, but this time reached him as fast as a police motor-cyclist could ride. Having examined it for a few minutes, Browne sealed it in plastic and placed both letters side by side. The cheap drawing-paper was the same, glue on the top edge showing that both sheets had been torn from a pad. The lines of careful writing sloped downwards towards the right in both.

He sat, immobile, eyes closed, letting his thoughts run free and missing Hunter. At this stage his sergeant would normally have been pacing restlessly round him, equally silent. Beginning with the same problem, their minds usually ran not parallel, but in opposite directions. After a few minutes they had reached widely differing destinations, a comparison of which produced a plan of action, sometimes original and imaginative but almost always justified by results.

If what he greatly feared turned out to be the case, the careful inquiries into the life of Denise Kemp that his team was carrying out this morning at her place of work, her local pub, her GP's surgery and so on might prove to be irrelevant. He had confided these fears to Superintendent Petty who had granted him two more constables to make similar inquiries concerning Alison Meredith. He willed one of them to discover that she had eloped with her lover, enrolled secretly at a health farm or entered a nunnery.

After a few minutes he opened his eyes, his decision made. Through his window, the snow lay, thawing slightly today and grubby looking. He was ninety-five per cent sure that there was another body somewhere out there. He would give his men the rest of the morning to follow routine inquiries and, if they produced no clue to Miss Meredith's present whereabouts, he wanted a team with dogs looking at the local parks and open spaces before it was dark.

At one o'clock, Mitchell reported that Alison Meredith had not attended her course in London. As darkness began to close in, Constable Dennison's labrador, Seeker, found the body of a white female in the large disused graveyard adjacent to the Methodist church behind the station. Three minutes after that, Browne received the news that Hunter's blood tests revealed that he was suffering from glandular fever and was on indefinite sick leave.

When he arrived at the Central Methodist graveyard, twenty minutes later still, he was not in the best of tempers. His eyes and ears registered the dripping snow even though the light was fast fading, but the raw chill made him shiver and refuse to believe in a thaw. A cobbled path ran between the grimy church and the graveyard, walled on each side and wide enough for two people on foot to pass. The cemetery itself was roughly triangular in shape.

He stood just inside it, reflecting that the killer they sought had a daring spirit if he had left a body here. There was nowhere but the surrounding main roads where a car could have been parked. A low wall skirted the land with narrow breaks in it for access on foot. To his left a row of trees grew along the boundary, leafless and widely spaced, giving a clear view of the houses beyond, monotonously ugly. Presumably, the houses were afforded an equally clear view of light and movement amongst the gravestones. Behind him a wide main road formed the hypotenuse of the triangle and on the other side of it stood the fire station, its forecourt lit and its windows blazing. Homegoing traffic swished briskly by, though Browne supposed that at least the traffic would have been lighter after the choir practice on November 19th, always supposing that it was Alison Meredith who had been found.

It was too dark now to see his surroundings clearly but the sky was luminous and the outlines against it clear and sharp. There were no neat modern rectangles. The graves dated from the end of the last century and all of them rose above his head with complicated curves, points and scallops, many surmounted by fleurs-de-lis or little stone pinnacles topped by tiny spheres or elongated crosses. There was not a well-kept grave in sight, though he admitted to himself that he could only peer a short distance through the gloom and most of the edifices were still partially covered in snow.

46

He couldn't remember the weather conditions on November 19th. That was something to check. The grass under his feet was blackened and soggy and his path blocked by rampaging shrubs. He looked across to the group of his colleagues already hard at work. Kneeling round the corpse, the arc-lamps illuminating the projections of their bodies and faces, they reminded him of a Rembrandt nativity. He had sanctioned none of their activities. The superintendent was obviously to the fore again.

He stepped carefully forward until he got a glimpse of the still form that lay tucked in beside an ostentatious chunk of pinkish stone that threw into relief the waxen pallor of its flesh. Superficially, it appeared as fresh as Mrs Kemp's body had done and he could see similar petechiae on the face and finger or thumbmarks on the neck. Raising his eyes, he tried to decipher whose grave the body shared, but even in the arc-lights lichen and weathering made it impossible.

At Browne's approach, Superintendent Petty had detached himself from the group and come to meet him. Seeing how far routine had progressed, Browne apologised briefly. 'I got here as soon as I could. Is it Alison Meredith?'

The superintendent waved his hand impatiently. 'Don't worry, I've got everything in hand. We presume it is. She's lying on the music-folder. We'll have it out when Ledgard's finished.' This was obviously not what he'd come over to discuss. 'Bad news about Hunter,' he went on, 'especially with this latest development. I think the best idea might be to have one of the better constables made up for the duration of the absence. It should give someone a bit of useful experience. What's the name of that bright young spark who sussed out your nicotine poisoning in the summer? He's a likely candidate.'

Browne was dismayed. Petty knew perfectly well that Mitchell was the constable concerned and his casual manner had not deceived Browne. He knew his objections were in vain as he made them. 'That would cost us. It would be cheaper to co-opt a uniformed sergeant with CID experience. We've at least a couple available.'

Another impatient wave of the superintendent's hand stopped him. 'Since when has penny-pinching been your way of doing things? And weren't you the one who brought young Mitchell's exploits to my attention in the first place? We can't afford to waste men like him – refuse to give them their chances. I'll see to the formalities as soon as I get back. Where was he, by the way, when we were going through all this preliminary business with Denise Kemp?'

'He'd taken over Hunter's interrogation – sorry, questioning – of Eric Smithson. You know, the Rampton Estate trouble. He got him to cough the lot.'

Superintendent Petty beamed triumphantly. 'There you are, then.' Dismissing Browne, he strode off to continue his conversation with Dr Ledgard.

Chapter 5

Waiting for his team to arrive for their briefing on Friday morning, Browne rehearsed his objections to the superintendent's plan to promote DC Mitchell. Hunter and Mitchell had never got on. His sergeant's nature was sensitive, his tastes artistic, his manners impeccable. The ebullient, outspoken DC, clever and practical but sometimes crude and coarse, had always grated on Hunter. Both men made valuable contributions to the work of his team which were sometimes almost cancelled out by their mutual antipathy and jealousy. Hearing that Mitchell was going to replace him, however temporarily, would be a bitter pill for Hunter to swallow. Browne was not looking forward to sick visiting.

He wondered, too, whether Superintendent Petty was aware that Mitchell and Virginia were engaged. His own part in the new arrangement was going to be misunderstood and the situation was awkward for Mitchell himself. Put into words, these objections sounded pretty feeble. They didn't account for his own strong feelings. Suddenly, he wondered if his real objection to the plan was that he had always thought of Mitchell as his own protégé. Was he just unwilling for him to be pushed on by someone else?

The arrival of the four constables he had summoned saved him from having to reach a conclusion but faced him with the problems about which he had been speculating. Dean was angry; even Jennie Smith and Bellamy looked a bit resentful. Mitchell was frankly embarrassed. He was accompanied by a girl, small and slightly built, with bright red hair, a tip-tilted nose and an innocently flirtatious expression. She seemed to be on nodding terms with all the constables and he thought he recognised her as one of the Specials. Mitchell confirmed this, taking her proprietorially by the elbow to introduce her and, Browne suspected, to preempt any possible snub from his erstwhile compeers.

'This is Jocelyn Wade, sir.'

He drew breath to continue but the girl preferred to speak for herself. Browne provided her with a chair as she explained. 'I'm a Special, sir, but I'm also a member of the Choral.'

Browne motioned to the rest of the team to seat themselves as he considered how best to use this volunteer mole. 'Why, precisely, have you come to me?' he asked her.

The red hair was flung back and she eyed him challengingly. 'Well, I shall carry on attending rehearsals. I could watch and chat to anybody you wanted to know more about. You'd have to tell me what you want me to look for.'

'Always provided that Cully carries on with this concert in the circumstances,' Mitchell put in.

She turned to him. 'Oh, he will. He rang me just before I came out to ask whether I'd be prepared to take over the solo in "Mary". He said I'd better realise it's turning out to be an unlucky one.'

Browne's glance round invited general contributions.

'Do the choir members know you're part of this outfit?' Bellamy wanted to know.

She shook her head. 'No, I've said nothing. I talked a lot about it to my mates in the shop at first. I work at Smedley's, the music shop in the precinct. I've got a day off today because I've volunteered to do three Saturdays this month. Anyway, they were so shirty and strange with me that I learned to keep quiet about it. I get the worst of both worlds. Ordinary people can't relax with me because they think I'm a copper spying on them and the coppers I work with are suspicious of me because I'm not.'

'How long have you been in the choir?' Dean asked.

'Three years, since I left school.'

'So you'll be able to tell us about various people including the two victims?'

She nodded. 'A bit, anyway.'

'What kind of duties have you done since you joined us?'

She turned back to Browne, grinning. 'I usually help in the

town centre on Saturday nights, the ten to six shift. I like to see a bit of action.'

Looking at her, Browne could believe it. 'What can you tell us about Denise and Alison?'

The girl shrugged. 'I didn't know either of them particularly well. Denise didn't mix a lot, though she was pleasant enough if you talked to her. She comes from round here but she and her husband worked down south for a while. She was quite good looking but she never took much trouble with her appearance. I don't mean she was scruffy but she hardly ever wore make up and her clothes were comfortable more than trendy. Not like Alison. She always looked like something out of a fashion magazine. That was her job of course. She seemed a bit of a swinger but when you really looked at her you could see she'd done a lot of mileage. I knew her even less well. She was friendly with men rather than women.'

'So the two didn't have much in common or go around with the same crowd?'

She shook her head without having to think. 'No, they weren't the same type at all. The only time they went near each other was when we were actually singing.'

Browne was anxious now to get his team to work. He shook hands with Jocelyn, thanked her for coming and gave her his instructions. 'I want all your usual duties to stop for the time being. Keep right away from here and wait for us to contact you by phone. I'm only happy at your doing this as long as no one connects you with us. At the same time I think one of us ought to be within reach at all rehearsals.'

Jocelyn let her gaze travel round and rest on Bellamy before she nodded enthusiastically. Bellamy blushed; Browne leaned back in his chair. 'Come back Hunter, all is forgiven,' he declared dramatically. 'Can any of you lot sing in tune?'

No one volunteered but Jocelyn thought it was of no consequence. 'Cavan wouldn't accept anyone to sing in this concert now that we're so far on with it. He only took that bass last week because his sight reading is so good that he'll catch up with no difficulty – and even so some of the men are peeved about it.'

She thought for a minute. 'Actually, several of the girls have been saying that if they're going to keep coming their fathers or boyfriends are insisting on coming as well to keep an eye on them.' She eyed Bellamy again, speculatively. 'I could tell them my boyfriend will only let me come if he comes as well.'

Browne smiled grimly as he stood up to show her out. 'I'll see what we can dream up. Just go to rehearsals as usual and we'll see to the rest.'

Mitchell listened indignantly as Jocelyn's heels echoed up the corridor. 'Is that all we're telling her? How's she going to co-operate with us if she doesn't know what's going on?'

DC Dean undertook to satisfy him. 'She's a fairly new Special, isn't she? We hardly know anything about her. We can't have her gossiping to all and sundry the things we're keeping from the press.'

Mitchell's jaw set hard. 'Yes, I see. We took a risk not getting her vetted by you but you were settling even more important matters at the time.'

Browne's glare quelled them both as he embarked on a recital of the main features of their case and they remained silent until it finished. After a few seconds for assimilation, Mitchell summarised it in his inimitable fashion. 'So the second body was found first and after the second letter arrived we looked for the first body. Have we got anything from Dr Ledgard on either of them yet?'

Browne took a single sheet from the file on his desk and pushed it towards Mitchell. 'Just his first impressions. It boils down to the fact that she was strangled from behind after a blow on the right temple and that the middle finger on her left hand was fractured.'

'Could have been done as she was bundled into the car to be dropped off in the park.'

Browne nodded at Mitchell, willing the other members of his team to overcome their resentment and take their usual full part in this preliminary discussion. 'The PM is this afternoon, and now we have two bodies with a connection between them the other one has top priority too. We'll have a report of sorts on both of them after today, though we might have to wait for results on samples they send away.'

Mitchell was well aware of his colleagues' conspiracy of silence but was finding it very difficult not to express his ideas as they occurred to him and play into their hands by letting the discussion become a dialogue between himself and the DCI. 'Are we dealing with a serial killer?'

Browne nodded. 'It looks like it.'

'So, probably, the personal details we're collecting on the two girls won't be particularly relevant?'

'Right.'

'But we'll still have to go on collecting them?'

'Right again.'

There was ten seconds' silence, then, 'Are we taking the letters absolutely seriously?'

Browne turned gratefully to Dean. 'We have to. They read like a practical joke but one arrived before we found a body and we had the second one before either had been given any publicity.' Browne relaxed. He was sure Dean hadn't asked his question from altruistic motives but the ice was broken now.

'So we're following up the singers called John?'

Browne nodded. 'Not exclusively, but Benny has listed them from Cully's register. There aren't as many as you might expect, although there are scores of initial Js with another name written in full. We won't bother with those for now.'

Mitchell produced his list. 'There's Fielden, the accompanist, and a tenor called Simmons. Another tenor, Chance, is listed as Jack and a bass called Searle is known as Jake, but Cully says they're both Johns. Eighteen more of them have J as a first or middle initial.' He handed the list back to Browne who replaced it.

'We'll have to question the whole choir about what they did after rehearsal on the two relevant nights. A daunting prospect but there's no help for it. Of course we're particularly interested in the names on Benny's list and also in the new people who joined on the two nights the girls went missing. Simmons is in both categories. Find an excuse to get a sample of handwriting from the four of them – you might as well include Mellor in that too.'

Jennie Smith, in the depths of Browne's only armchair, was

looking puzzled. With a raised eyebrow, Browne invited her question. 'When the first letter arrived, sir, we thought a child had written it. Didn't Nigel check round all the junior schools?' Bellamy confirmed it with a nod. 'Have we abandoned that idea? These killings could hardly have been done by a young boy.'

Would a retarded adult write like that, perhaps?'

Browne had not considered this explanation. 'You could have a word with the psychologist about that,' he told Dean, 'and check whether there's any such person with a choir connection.' Dean subsided, satisfied.

'Could it be someone who reverted to a childhood mentality at the time of the killings?'

This idea had occurred to Browne. 'It's a possibility, Benny. Richard, you might include that question if you manage to track down your psychologist.'

Dean scribbled in his notebook, then looked up. 'I take it we don't mention the letters in the interviews.'

Browne nodded. 'You take it.' He took photocopies of them from his file and placed them on his desk, noting, as they gathered round to look, that the usual atmosphere of enthusiastic co-operation was becoming discernible again.

'They're neat and painstaking and all correctly spelled,' Bellamy offered.

'Is that significant? There aren't any unusual or difficult words in it.'

Browne wasn't so sure. 'There are plenty of coppers and singers as well, I imagine, who might mis-spell sincerely and there are two apostrophes used in the right places. I'm interested in your idea, Jennie. We'll see if we can dig up some examples of these people's schoolboy writing.'

Jennie, looking suitably gratified and becomingly embarrassed, went back to hide in Browne's armchair. From the safety of it she ventured a further suggestion. 'Even if our man is killing girls apparently at random, because he's off his head, it might be useful to find out all we can about them. They might have had something in common that made them likely victims.'

Browne beamed at her. 'I'm glad that aspect interests you. It's what I had lined up for you. I suggest you begin by chatting further with the red-haired mole.'

'To go back to the letters,' Bellamy asked, replacing a copy on the desk, 'why are we only looking at Johns in the choir? Isn't John the commonest male name in the country? It would be the name that anyone would take if he wanted to be anonymous.'

'I'm not sure that he does, and of course we're keeping all our options open so early in the inquiry, but, in the circumstances, it's only common sense to begin with the choir.'

Bellamy nodded. 'I presume the originals are at the lab. Any idea how long we'll have to wait for their report?'

Browne shrugged. 'I got them in just as the courier was collecting the week's gubbins. I've made sure they know it's urgent. I've been playing with the computer too. There are no reports of anything similar in the rest of the UK so it seems this is a local matter. That makes it all the more frightening if you happen to live in Cloughton.'

Mitchell looked up from the copied letter he was studying. 'Jocelyn seemed to think Cully was going ahead with his rehearsals. Are we happy with that?'

Browne nodded. 'I think so. I shouldn't think banning them would make anyone any safer.'

He dismissed the team to a strictly timed coffee break during which he would write out their action sheets. Mitchell caught his eye as they trooped out and Browne was not surprised, a couple of minutes later, to hear his tap on the door. He rang for coffee for two before giving his new DS his attention.

'I've been reading a bit about serial killers, sir.'

Browne grinned. Since his misspent seven years at comprehensive school, Mitchell had 'read a bit' about a great number of subjects but the fruits of his studies were usually displayed in the presence of his colleagues. Had promotion begun to teach him diplomacy already? 'So have I, Benny. What did you learn?'

'Well, sir, that usually they haven't kept their copybooks unblotted in the past. They're often liars, thieves and so on and some of them have a history of cruelty to animals or have attacked someone before but stopped short of actually killing. They move

55

away from where the trouble was and begin afresh where everyone thinks they're good-hearted blameless citizens.'

'So?'

'So I thought we could see if any of them have got form, sir, and whether they've recently moved into this area.'

Browne nodded. 'Good idea. Like to fill in your own action form?'

Mitchell did not smile. 'No, sir, I'll get it from you like all the others.'

Browne roared with laughter. 'Right. In that case you'd better have your coffee in the canteen like all the others.' He poured his own as Mitchell closed the door.

Chapter 6

Before using the knocker on the rather imposing door in front of him, DC Bellamy paused to check over Browne's instructions on his action sheet. Get Chance's alibi for the two nights when the girls had last been seen, then let him talk – about the girls, about other choir personalities, about whatever he liked. Stay as long as he was offering useful information, at his, Bellamy's, discretion. Bellamy was pleased to be working under a DCI who thought he had some!

Belinda Chance, who answered the door, called upstairs and, when her husband appeared on the landing, explained Bellamy's presence. Bellamy watched Chance as he descended, grabbed a neatly folded dust sheet from the bottom stair and led the way to the sitting-room. Even in a paint-smeared boiler suit, Bellamy categorised him as a well-heeled smoothie, complete with thick waving fair hair, downy skin and attractive smile. Why did rich people never seem to have thin, lank hair and buck teeth? This man looked as if everything would always go right for him.

Having covered his armchair with the dust sheet, he relaxed into it and gave the DC his attention. His wife, about seven months pregnant, Bellamy thought, had disappeared to the kitchen. Bellamy recorded personal details in his book. Chance, John Alexander, age thirty-six, married. Managing Director of Yates Bros., a textile business up the valley in Dean Royd.

Chance expressed his sorrow at the deaths of the two girls, briefly but as though he meant it, then waited, without irrelevant comment, to be questioned. Bellamy established that on November 19th Chance had driven home immediately choir practice ended. He had been dubious about attending at all since Belinda had had a particularly difficult day.

'She's picked up a bit since then, fortunately, but she can't support my account for either of the two nights, I'm afraid. She was in bed and asleep when I came in on both occasions. Actually, last Wednesday I was quite late. I waited around to have a word with Mellor, the new bass. I'm secretary on the choir committee and am expected to sheepdog the new folk. In any case, it's the least we can do if we want people to join us. When I eventually saw him, he was just leaving.' He stopped and hesitated.

'You've remembered something?' Bellamy prompted.

'Well, just that he bumped into Denise on his way out. That's why I caught sight of him. Anyhow, I left straight afterwards. I made good time on the main roads but drifts had blocked the end of the road here and I spent half an hour digging a way through before I could open the gate.' Bellamy remembered the wrought-iron fence and gate he had passed as he entered the private road where Chance lived and imagined the wind might very well pile up the snow behind it.

'Belinda was asleep and I wasn't tired so I sanded down the woodwork in the nursery for an hour before I went to bed. I've just been painting it now.'

Bellamy added briefly to his notes as Belinda came in with a tray. She placed it on a table between the men and then went out again. The coffee, milk and sugar were in heavy silver containers, but Bellamy noted with approval that Chance was dispensing them into plebeian and substantial mugs.

Handing him one, Chance went on apologetically, 'In spite of trying to keep things going socially, I'm afraid I only knew both girls very slightly. I'm not even sure who their particular friends were.'

Bellamy was unperturbed. 'That's all right, sir. The other women will tell us that. What the CI wants from you is some information about the choir in general and about the last two or three rehearsals in particular. Who did what and did anything happen that was in any way different from usual?'

Chance considered. 'It was the rehearsal between the two murders that was different.' Bellamy helped himself to chocolate biscuits and waited for Chance to elaborate. 'It was Cavan's mother's birthday, her sixtieth, I think, and there was a bit of a family do. John Fielden took the rehearsal. It was part of his brief to hold the fort if Cavan should be unavailable.'

'Was that very unusual?'

Chance nodded. 'Yes, quite. I think it's only happened once before. That time John took the rehearsal from the piano. This time someone said it was just as important to have a reserve pianist so Stella Smith played for us. Several people are competent to do it but Stella's going to stop singing soon so if she had the post of assistant accompanist it would be a way of keeping in touch with us.'

'Why is she leaving?'

Chance grinned. 'Well, we're only assuming she will. The choir reauditions its members every three years so that we keep up the standard and don't have a lot of quavery old voices spoiling the sound. Stella knows her days are numbered. She'll probably resign when the auditions come round so as not to embarrass Cavan. We all do it when the time comes. We'll be disappointed but everyone is concerned for the choir's reputation.'

'So, apart from those two differences, everything was as usual?'

Chance shook his head, smiling again. 'Those two differences were fundamental. Nothing was the same at all.'

As Bellamy's mug was refilled he asked, 'All right. How was it with Mr Cully in charge?'

Chance was obviously Cully's disciple but Bellamy watched him make the effort to be objective. 'Cavan's a brilliant musician. He understands choral music, knows what kind of voices he needs to perform it and what he wants them to do. He has a presence. He's conceited and charismatic and charming – and he has a pleasant speaking voice. That's important. So, he can take the choir with him on his flights of fancy. It wouldn't be any good being a visionary if he couldn't communicate his vision. But he's young and still has everything to prove. That's why we've been able to engage him. That plus our willingness, most of the time, to give him a free hand with us. He's expensive. Subs went up when we took him on and some people say he only does it for the money. That's an attitude it's very easy to condemn if no one is willing to pay you for what you can do.'

Bellamy resisted another biscuit and waved the plate away as Chance went on: 'A good conductor is as much a performer as the singers. It's all acting. He exaggerates his pleasure at what's well done and his shock and disappointment at our mistakes. He acts when he's attending to choir business too. When the BBC considered broadcasting one of our concerts and sent someone to listen to us he did a brilliant pretence of picking 'at random' all our most polished and well practised pieces . . . '

'You said some people considered him mercenary. Is he popular with most of the choir?'

Chance frowned. 'As a body, yes. He knows how to handle us, knows when we're tired, when we're impatient, when we need praise rather than criticism. He'll preface a hard slog at a piece that he thinks is all wrong with, "A lot of that is very good but . . . " And, "It's coming," is another standby. It means we're miles away from the effect he wants but he knows if he's to keep the general goodwill he has to say something encouraging. No one seems particularly friendly with him as an individual. In the pub after rehearsal you wouldn't think he was the same man – pleasant enough but quiet and withdrawn, probably exhausted.'

Bellamy had second thoughts and succumbed to a second biscuit. 'How was Fielden different at his rehearsal?'

Chance shrugged. 'It isn't a fair comparison. His first disadvantage is that he hasn't got himself as accompanist so things don't go so smoothly. Stella turns frantically at the end of each page so that you lose a fraction of a beat. John knows his works well enough to play from memory from time to time and turn when one of his hands is conveniently less busy. Stella's reliable and accurate, but with her you're more aware of the piano's limitations in substituting for the orchestra, and because of those limitations you're conscious all the time that she's there. When John's at the piano he withdraws his personality. He knows that he isn't required to impinge on Cavan's performance except as a prop.

'But apart from the piano, the rehearsal went wrong because he was a substitute and everyone knew things would be back to normal the next week. He was brisk and competent and we got

60

quite a lot done, but the atmosphere was different, not so much fun, even though he's possibly an even better musician in his way. He's too ingratiating. He accompanies each criticism with fulsome praise of everything else so that the choir's either embarrassed or amused but against him.'

Bellamy nodded, busily committing as much as possible of the conversation to shorthand, wondering whether this was the kind of thing Browne had hoped for and what possible use he could make of it. 'Can you make any comment on either Denise or Alison as musicians and choir members?' He hoped this might produce something more relevant.

Chance pondered as he stacked their mugs and plates on the tray. 'Denise surprised me. I was there when she auditioned and I didn't think Cavan would accept her. The voice was thin and shaky although the pitch was secure. He could obviously hear her potential. I was amazed when he dropped on her to run through Alison's solo last Wednesday and even more amazed when I heard her do it. The sound was remarkable. It might even have earned her living for her.' He added, his tone changing, becoming wistful, 'I hoped myself, at one time, to sing professionally but things didn't work out.'

'Really? And Alison?' Bellamy was convinced that Chance's frustrated ambitions were irrelevant even to Browne.

'Alison was an able musician. Her voice had an unusual range, though I found it a shade hard. I can't be fair to her because she always irritated me. She was always arriving slightly late to rehearsals. She'd make the splendid entrance of one whose prestigious job excused lack of punctuality. She put a lot of effort into getting her unobtrusive entry noticed and melted with maximum fuss into the background.' He grinned, shamefacedly, at his own condemnation of the so recently dead but was unrepentant. 'When she sang a solo, she snapped her copy shut at the end as though she'd given the definitive performance. If she was asked to go over a section of it again she was deeply offended and she'd find the place with an exaggerated display of patience.'

Sounds overhead suggested that Belinda Chance had taken over her husband's abandoned painting. Or had she needed to retire to bed? Chance was clearly uneasy but Bellamy had another question for him. 'The new lad, Simmons, was in the tenor section, wasn't he? Did you have much to do with him?'

'Oh, yes. Keen lad. Lovely tone. He sits next to me and he learns fast. He was new on the 19th.' The significance of this struck him. 'Here, you're not going to hound that boy over this business, surely? He's got enough problems of his own.'

Bellamy's attention refocused. 'Tell me about them.'

But more sounds from upstairs distracted Chance and Bellamy could get very little more out of him.

Acquainting himself first hand with some of John Simmons' problems, DC Dean felt more annoyance with his DCI for sending him here than pity for Simmons. He knew men in the uniformed branch who, keen to make their mark, had volunteered to work in this area and had worked hard, on the understanding that their posting was short term. Their ambitions lay far elsewhere and so there was no continuity in the force's efforts to make this area less horrendous as a place to live.

He double-checked the security of his unmarked car and mentally located the Simmons' flat in the block beside him, ground floor, third along, facing the road. The youth club building opposite had its windows bricked up and its posters were out of date and in tatters. It was surrounded by an astounding array of litter. The recent snow which had hidden the sea of sweet papers and chip wrappings had thawed and left behind a black sludge of sodden paper on the steps leading to the entrance to the tower block. The roughly cut grass verge was adorned with a smashed TV set, a torn mattress and a split bag of rubbish that spilled soiled nappies and broken glass on to the pavement.

Wrinkling his nose, Dean trod cautiously on the steps and entered the building with considerable reluctance. Looking up the stairwell from the bottom he saw windows with smashed panes and a spray painted alliterative instruction to all fuzz. Stairs leading down to the basement smelt of burning and the banister leading down into the gloomy depths was charred.

Steeling himself, Dean found the Simmons' door, widened to take a wheelchair, brightly painted and surprisingly clean, and rang the bell. He ignored the further instructions to the police sprayed on the wall of the draughty corridor behind him. After a longish pause the door was opened to reveal a huge man in the anticipated wheelchair. Dean was surprised. He had heard no sounds of machinery or of wheels passing over the lino on the floor.

The man, having glanced at Dean's identification, nodded and propelled his chair silently backwards. 'Sorry about the welcome on the walls. I can promise you our John had no part in it.'

Dean nodded and followed the wheelchair up the small hall, realising, as he breathed in its clean freshness, just how unpleasant the smell in the corridor had been. He was led into a sitting-room, sparsely furnished and scrubbed within an inch of its life. Mrs Simmons, whose achievement it was, seated herself in a wooden-armed chair opposite Dean in an attitude that announced that anything he wished to say to her husband he would have to say to her too.

He accepted her terms for the moment and displayed his credentials to her. She repaid this courtesy by offering tea. Dean was surprised until he realised she was not going to make it. She put her head round the door to summon her son, then returned to her chair in time to intercept Dean's appraisal of the tiny room. It seemed even smaller because of the out-of-proportion wheelchair-widened doorway.

'Not the sort of place you'd pay a social call to, is it?'

Dean hoped the remark was prompted by her own attitude rather than any distaste she may have surprised in his expression. Feeling it safer not to answer her he thanked her for his promised tea.

Simmons senior shifted in his chair and shrugged his massive shoulders. 'It could be worse for us if it wasn't for these.' He pointed to his wheels. 'They put us on the ground floor in this end flat next to the ramp. The people above smash the lights on the stairs and pee in the lift but we don't need to use either. They torment the cat, though, and mess up the walls and so on.'

Dean wondered if he was to collect the blame for all this but Mr Simmons was more fair minded. 'The coppers can't do much unless we make a formal complaint and nobody ever dares make

63

one. There'd just be abuse, bricks through the window, tyres slashed and so on as soon as they'd gone.'

Loud disco-type music interrupted him. Dean tried not to look disapproving. 'John's having music while he works?'

He shook his head. 'That's not our John's sort of music. That's from upstairs. We have this racket into the small hours quite often while they have their parties. Don't know where all the folk come from. We don't get to sleep till it's coming light.'

Dean's ears pricked up. He'd heard there were illegal rent parties in this area. 'Do they charge admission for these all-night sessions, or sell drink?'

Simmons shrugged again. 'I've no idea, and I probably wouldn't say if I knew. We'll suffer because of you being here anyway. You aren't in uniform but they can smell coppers a mile off. Anyway, that isn't what you've come about is it?'

Dean nodded and promised to get his uniformed colleagues to keep an eye on things. 'Perhaps you could help me by remembering what time John got home from choir practice last Wednesday.' As he asked, he wondered how much these people knew about their son. They seemed rather old to be the parents of an eighteen-year-old. He'd have guessed they were in their sixties, but maybe hard times and ill health had taken their toll.

Simmons shrugged. 'Since he passed his driving test I've never been sure what time he gets in. He's a good lad and I don't worry about it. We keep early hours. It saves fuel and we can get a bit of kip before the rowdyism starts.'

'He has a car?'

His mother chipped in, 'It's Bill's really, mostly paid for out of his mobility allowance. A great big monster that eats up petrol.'

Dean looked out of the window. 'Is that it?' He pointed to a Citroen 505, parked outside, T registered but well cared for and gleaming. They both nodded.

Dean felt that Mrs Simmons' resentment was unfair. Even without his legs, Bill Simmons must have weighed sixteen stones. He could probably not have got into, never mind been comfortable in, a small car. His father told Dean proudly, 'John keeps it like that. I'm glad to let him go out in it with his nice little girlfriend when he isn't driving me. When I had my accident, Phyllis felt

64

she was a bit old for learning driving and I don't have proper use of my left hand. We had to wait till John was old enough.'

'So, you were asleep when John got in on Wednesday?'

'I wasn't,' his mother interrupted, sharply. 'He didn't go out with that girl. She's at one of her holy-willy meetings on choir nights. I wish you wouldn't keep offering them the car. It's asking for trouble, throwing them together like that.'

Her husband looked shocked. 'Well! I've more faith in our son than that. Anyway, even if he was that way inclined he wouldn't get far with that lass. She's in bother with her church folk for taking up with our John at all, seeing as he isn't in the fellowship.'

Mrs Simmons tossed her head. 'I heard John come in at half-past nine. He put his head round the door and asked me where the writing paper was because he had some thank-you letters to write. It was his birthday last week, his nineteenth. He's always been brought up to send proper thank-you letters, ever since he could write.'

Dean nodded approvingly. 'Most youngsters nowadays think a quick phone call is quite enough.'

She sniffed. 'Chance would be a fine thing. What makes you think we can afford to be on the phone? And if we could, we'd only get the wires pulled down.' She turned as her son brought in the tea. 'I've just been telling Constable Dean how you got in at half-past nine on Wednesday to write your thank-you letters.'

Although he understood the inadequacy of their accommodation, Dean was stung into asking, 'Is there somewhere I can speak to John alone? Otherwise it will have to be the station, I'm afraid.'

Silently, Simmons propelled his chair to the door, leaving his tea untouched. Biting her thin lips, his wife followed him, shutting the door with unnecessary force. Without comment, their son passed Dean his cup and took his own to the chair his mother had vacated.

Dean wondered how these surroundings and these parents could have bred a youth so wholesome looking. He had been expecting a spare, round-shouldered, ferret-faced individual, greasy haired and in grubby clothes. Self admonishment did not come easily to Dean but he chided himself for his prejudices and gave Simmons

65

junior his attention. He recorded his personal details to get the interview under way. Simmons, Barry John. Employment with the Commercial Union Insurance Agency in Bradford.

In response to Dean's catechism, the boy confirmed that he attended his first rehearsal on November 19th. After it he had driven home, helped settle his father to bed, then persuaded his mother to retire early by running her bath and taking a tray of tea to the bedroom, so that he could study for a couple of hours, undisturbed by the television and his father's laboured breathing.

'And, last Wednesday, as your mother was careful to spell out in front of you, you apparently wrote letters to the people who sent you birthday presents.'

Simmons grinned, showing teeth that were a credit to the school dental service. 'I did, actually. She natters at me till it's done so it's best to get it over with straight away. I agree she'd lie to protect me if she needed to because they'd be in a real mess if I got into trouble and got sent away. They were on pins in the summer when I was applying for university places.'

'You didn't get in, then?' Tact was not one of Dean's virtues.

Simmons' chin went up. 'I was offered places at Durham, Bristol and Hull but I knew I couldn't leave them.'

'Surely they'd qualify for help from the social services?'

He shrugged. 'Mum would call it charity and refuse it. She likes being a martyr. But Dad would hate it too.' His voice softened. 'Would you like to be bathed and taken to the toilet by a do-gooding female nurse?'

Dean felt discomfited again. 'Why did you apply if you'd decided you couldn't go?'

Simmons squared his shoulders. 'To prove I was good enough, that I could do it if I wanted.' He paused, then remarked, reflectively, 'I think Dad could get used to the nurse but he wouldn't get used to not having my company. We talk for hours and I take him to the pub and the library and all sorts of places. Mum couldn't and wouldn't. I think she likes having him in a wheelchair. It makes it easier for her to make him do what she wants.'

Dean was shocked into changing the subject. 'How did you come to join the choir?'

Simmons drained the teapot into their empty cups as he

explained. 'A squad of us from school were auditioned after the summer concert. I was the only one that got in.' It was said without pride. 'Mr Cully goes to all the schools' concerts in the area, looking for new singers. In the early autumn, when the choir started its new season, Dad went through a bad patch and Mum had flu and took a long time getting over it so I didn't sing till the middle of November. I was worried that I might miss the chance but Mr Cully took a lot of interest. It was him who told me I could ask for my university place to be held over for a year. He said circumstances might be different by then. I did it but I don't suppose they will be.'

'You don't like your job, then?'

He thought about it, wrinkling his nose. 'Mum always wanted me to be in insurance, although the only reason seemed to be that she once knew somebody who got rich by it.'

'And what would you really like to do?'

The boy shook his head. 'I don't know. I don't seem to know about all the things I could be. I mean, we had careers talks at school but they were just from different firms to try to attract the bright people for themselves. Mr Cully says I'm a natural musician. I don't know how he knows because I find singing in the choir quite difficult and I don't play anything except the piano a bit. My grandad used to teach me before he died but I've had to manage on my own since then and Mr Fielden says I've picked up a lot of bad habits that I'll have to unlearn. Since Mr Cully introduced him to me, he's been teaching me for nothing, but, now I'm working, I'm going to start having regular paid lessons from him. Mr Cully says I couldn't do better at this stage.'

He hesitated, then confided, shyly, 'I've written a bit of piano music. I'm trying to pluck up courage to show it to Mr Fielden. You don't play, do you?'

Dean denied all knowledge of choral and keyboard music. He grinned as his next question was interrupted by the boy's father's raised voice.

'For God's sake, woman, keep out and let them get on with it!'

Dean continued with his questions but, a few minutes later, Mrs Simmons burst in with a cursory apology.

'You'll have to give a hand with your dad's tea,' she admonished her son.

Having obtained what information he usefully could for the time being, Dean retired gracefully.

Chapter 7

Attending post-mortems was not Browne's favourite occupation. They dispirited rather than horrified him. He was not squeamish and the methods by which the pathologist's findings were deduced often fascinated him. Nevertheless, he found it depressing to see a human being reduced before his time to heavy waxen flesh on a slab and he was left in an 'ashes to ashes' frame of mind.

He had indulged himself therefore, after this one, to the extent of going home for tea with his wife at a conventional hour, and Hannah knew this would have to be atoned for. Six thirty found him back in his office, sorting out the various offerings on his desk. Nothing yet from Jennie on the girls' background, nor from Mitchell on the possibly criminal history of the five main suspects.

Dean's interview with Simmons, neatly typed and labelled, lay beside Bellamy's account, less accurately typed but probably containing more useful and perceptive comments, on his session with Chance. Browne scooped up the two documents and his own jottings on the post-mortem and decided to lay them as an offering at Hunter's feet. He was not well enough to be given any responsibility for them but he would have to be at death's door not to find them interesting. Seeing Searle and Fielden and having another chat with Cully could wait till the morning.

He parked neatly outside the Hunters' front gate and was pleased to catch Annette's eye through the sitting-room window. He waited without ringing the bell until she opened the front door, hoping to have a few words about the real state of his sergeant's health. Annette wrinkled her nose as he made his inquiries. 'The fever's gone and his breathing and swallowing are easier but he's exhausted as soon as he exerts himself the least bit. He's no appetite and he's still getting bad headaches.'

'He's probably paying for working through it for so long. He should have given in a week sooner.'

'He's in there.' Annette nodded towards the dining-room. 'And I warn you, he's very fractious.'

Browne hesitated, his hand on the doorknob. 'Does he know about Mitchell being made up whilst he's away?'

She nodded again and disappeared into the kitchen as Browne tapped on the door and opened it. Hunter was sprawled in an armchair with the radio on. It emitted the shapeless sound of instruments with no proper tune to play that seemed to Browne always to be on Radio Three. Hunter turned as he heard the door close, then dragged himself to his feet to welcome his visitor.

Browne was shocked at what he saw. Hunter's six-feet-four-inch length seemed his only dimension and his pallor had been replaced by a yellow-eyed, jaundiced look. He made his pointless inquiries and accepted the invalid's, 'Fine, picking up well.'

Hunter reached out to switch off the music but Browne shook his head as he sank into the opposite chair. 'I've been in a musical bubble ever since this case broke. I don't quite know where I'm going in it but if I come out of it I'll lose my bearings altogether.'

Annette came in with bottles of beer and glasses. The music stopped and a voice began to comment on the completed performance in a public school accent, sharing its opinions with a small élite that understood the terms it was using and excluding Browne. He nodded his thanks to Annette and wielded the bottle opener. Hunter seemed too languid to make the effort but at least he seemed to enjoy the beer when it was poured. Browne drank deeply from his own glass. 'I don't listen to Radio Three any more,' he announced, wiping froth from his upper lip. 'The announcers give me such an inferiority complex. When you've listened to their introductory lecturettes it makes the music seem too much trouble. I only switch on to enjoy it.'

Hunter grinned. 'They're only reading it. Maybe they understand and care less than you. Though they do take the trouble to pronounce foreign names correctly which is more than sports commentators can be bothered to do.'

70

Now Hunter did switch off the radio and Browne made no further objection, asking instead, 'Want to hear about the case?'

Hunter nodded, sliding further down in his chair and Browne wondered where to begin. He chose the post-mortem as it would include no mention of Mitchell. Hunter perked up as he described his afternoon. 'Did Ledgard do both girls?'

'Yes, the second body made the case top priority.'

'And?'

'Cause of death, manual strangulation, so it's certainly murder. Not that we were in any doubt. Half-inch rounded bruises on both necks. They weren't clear on Denise's skin but Ledgard said he could see them in the tissues underneath. There were more marks than fingers so the grip must have been relaxed and then reapplied.'

'Deliberate murder, then, not an attack meant to subdue for attempted rape or done in a quarrel or panic without the intention of actually killing.'

Browne nodded. 'No scratches from self-defence, so the tap on the head they each had was enough to stun them. The fingermarks were on each side and at the front with thumb-marks at the back where the skin's thick and the tissues tough. Ledgard says great pressure must have been applied.' He read rapidly through the rest of the sheet. ' "Fracture of the superior cornu of the thyroid at its base . . . a little extravasation of blood round it . . . hundreds of minute Tardieu spots in the facial skin . . . " Typical strangling.'

Hunter was sitting upright. 'So what now?'

'I haven't finished yet. Each girl had the third finger of the left hand broken. There was bruising, dead vessels torn. Blood had seeped passively into tissue spaces but didn't extend far. No cellular reaction – in other words, it was done after death.'

Hunter whistled. 'So, with that and the letters we've got ourselves a nutter with a new hobby.'

Browne was pleased by the 'we'. 'That's right, a serial killer.'

'Your new sergeant's probably sitting up in bed in the wee small hours, reading it all up.' Browne glanced at Hunter sharply but the expected gibe had come with a grin and no obvious bitterness. The post-mortem having proved a less than safe subject, Browne

71

plunged into a brief summary of the present state of the case, Hunter's comments being brief but in his familiar style.

Reaching the end of his account, Browne reverted to the topic of serial killers. 'I've been doing a bit of background reading myself – an interesting tome by an American who thinks this is a public health rather than a police problem.'

'That's one way of getting this case off our backs.'

'And with a lot to recommend it. He also has some interesting theories about the physical characteristics of what he calls "thrill killers".'

'For instance?'

'According to him, a large proportion of the chaps he's talked to in American prisons have an elongated middle toe, longer than all the others. You think it's stupid to look for a physical type?'

Browne was slightly offended by Hunter's grin until his sergeant removed one shoe and sock to display an arrangement of toes of the kind described. He replaced his footwear and refilled their glasses. 'What else does it say?'

'All the usual things. That psychopaths don't appear callous but intelligent and charming, quite capable of showing all the outward signs of love and affection. That the police are dealing with a damaged mind or personality, so any speculation about how a normal person would think or behave is irrelevant. Then it goes on to try to analyse what does the damage, what kinds of aberration it can cause and the role of the psychiatrist. He, of course, is one.' Browne's hands gestured his frustration. 'I don't scoff at psychiatrists but their work is too long-term and individualised to be of much help to the police, valuable though it may be to their patients.'

He shook his head. 'If a killing is apparently motiveless, the victim chosen at random, we can't work outwards, logically, from him or her.'

'Are you confining your search to the Choral? Perhaps that's his game, to keep you looking there for a connection when he's really completely unmusical and has picked those girls for no other reason than to fool you.'

Browne shook his head. 'With the compulsion on him, he has to be choosing this group either because killing musical people

72

gives him special satisfaction or because these are people he's amongst all the time and he strikes at the nearest girl. I might be wrong, of course, and we're certainly looking further afield than the society, but we've no leads outside it. We don't know enough about this kind of mentality to theorise with any assurance. We just have to plough ruthlessly on with routine and hope to trap him in some practical detail.'

Hunter transferred his gaze from the empty bottles which he had been contemplating with some disappointment. 'He might not be a local. There are plenty of big towns within easy reach and good roads and motorways to make a getaway easy.' He suddenly looked alarmed.

'What's up, Jerry?'

'Tim and Fliss are out at choir practice – up at St Oswald's. They finish about now. It's such a short distance we don't usually meet them if they're coming home together.'

Browne thought the youngsters were in little danger but was unwilling to let Hunter worry. 'It's time I went anyway. I'll pick them up for you and then I'll go home.' He departed speedily, glad he'd come. Hunter looked exhausted by the brief chat but he also showed more than a hint of his old animation.

Nine o'clock on Saturday morning saw Browne's team once more assembled in his office. Mitchell had ushered Jennie Smith into the fat armchair and they had waited with an uneasy cameraderie for Bellamy who was last to arrive. Mitchell was being very careful not to offend. In return, the others, with false heartiness, made feeble and unfunny jokes. Browne felt sorry for them and proud of them in equal degree and rescued them, as Bellamy entered apologetically, by beginning the session officially and revealing the post-mortem findings.

Bellamy followed with a report on his visit to the Chances, then gave place to Mitchell.

'I didn't have time for much, sir. I was in court for part of yesterday afternoon. What I turned up was quite interesting though. Mellor was in trouble years ago for pinching from his classmates at junior school. He was unlucky because he was only just ten. There's a social worker's report that says he was being bullied and when he was dared to do it he was frightened to refuse. Most of the things he took were of no use to him, games kit that was too small and so on, though there was some money involved as well. The report says he'd handed that over to his tormentors. He was cautioned. There's been nothing official since.'

'That's certainly interesting.' The tone was sarcastic. Browne had expected that Dean's goodwill would be the first to break down.

Mitchell kept his eyes on his notebook and made no response. 'I drew a blank with both Chance and Fielden. Simmons has only been in trouble for truancy. He skipped school whenever he hadn't managed to get his homework done, which was fairly often until he was about fourteen, but not after he started his exam courses. And anyway, by then his parents had been threatened with action and were keeping an eye on him.'

Dean opened his mouth again but shut it when Browne glared at him.

'Searle's been in trouble with an under-age girl.' Now Mitchell had everyone's attention. 'He said she lied about her age.'

Jennie sat forward. 'He was probably right. They usually do. Anyway, our girls haven't been sexually assaulted.'

Mitchell nodded. 'Mellor's the only one who's moved into the district recently. The others have always lived fairly locally as far as I could check, though Chance has travelled a lot on business at various times.'

He closed his book. Browne signalled to Dean to take the floor, then sat back to listen expectantly. Dean's report had surprised him by its success in obtaining the flavour of the boy's background and by the amount of personal detail he had persuaded him to reveal. He was not usually sufficiently sympathetic to any witness to draw more than facts from him. Dean gave an efficient summary of his report, adding, as he reached the end and looked up, 'There was a carol book propped on the piano, open at "Deck the halls with boughs of holly". "In the bleak midwinter" would have been more appropriate for the Simmonses. The boy realised that I'd taken exception to the way his mother prompted him. It

74

was canny of him to admit openly that they'd be prepared to lie for him but then to confirm what they'd said.'

He caught Mitchell's eye and waited for his question. 'Did he volunteer anything about his feelings for his girlfriend?'

'Not exactly. Not about how he felt. He said the relationship hadn't progressed very far because he's needed at night and their flat is never empty. He said you couldn't establish a relationship with someone you only saw in the company of other people. He seemed to mind more about his lack of singing and piano lessons and the need to catch up now he's earning. He spoke as though he'd missed out musically and it was too late, though he's only just nineteen. I think his father understands both his problems and feels very bitter about being the cause of them, though his manner's pleasant enough.'

When no more questions were forthcoming, he changed the subject and turned to Browne. 'I rang Birmingham, sir, and talked to the forensic psychologist about the possibility of a disturbed adult reverting to childish handwriting.'

'And?'

'He'd never come across such a thing but he said that didn't rule it out. He suggested that it might be deliberate, an attempt to protect himself.' He added, thinking as he spoke, 'I'm sure I'd find it more difficult to copy the way I wrote as a child than to copy someone else's writing.' There was general agreement.

'He suggested that we try to get some samples of suspects' schoolboy writing and send them for comparison.'

Browne said: 'Right. You'd better all do it then. We won't get anything back on the letters till Thursday. Right, Jennie, what have you come up with?'

Jennie emerged once more from the depths of her chair. 'It's all bits and pieces, I'm afraid, and nothing very substantial.'

'Bits first and pieces afterwards then.'

She grinned. 'Denise Kemp worked in the lab in the same textile firm as Jack Chance. She's well thought of there and had been steadily promoted over the last eighteen months after she'd finished her part-time degree. Chance is the man in charge, by the way, and they all seem to like him. I talked to a Sheila May who was Denise's friend. She doesn't sing but lives in the same area. She should have given Denise a lift into work on Thursday. She got out of the car and rang the bell but went without her when it was obvious that she wasn't there. Then I went to see Joss.'

'Jocelyn Wade?'

'Yes, sir. She reminded me that Alison was singing a solo at the concert which was given to Denise at last Wednesday's rehearsal. We looked at it together but we couldn't see why singing it should make someone want to kill you. Joss hopes not because she's doing it now. Another thing they have in common musically is playing the flute and they all have the same teacher – again, Joss as well. He's nothing to do with the choir but he is called John Phillips. I haven't talked to him. Joss has learned since she was about twelve, though only for the last year or so with him. The other two have only gone to him recently.'

'If that's not significant it's a very strange coincidence,' Bellamy observed.

Jennie disagreed. 'In a musical group, if one of them found a good teacher, they'd recommend him to the others.'

Dean added, 'In a place the size of Cloughton there must only be enough work for one good teacher in each instrument – except the piano, of course.'

'Why is the piano different?'

Dean answered Mitchell impatiently. 'Because it's the instrument every child begins on.'

Browne shook his head. 'A generation ago, maybe. I'm not so sure now.'

'Joss was talking about Jake Searle.' Jennie resumed her narrative and drew their attention back. 'He considers himself the choir Casanova but most people either laugh at him or ignore him. He had a crack at Alison Meredith though, in the pub after practice a couple of months ago. He'd had a few too many, which he does pretty frequently, and was making a nuisance of himself. Alison wasn't the sort to put up with it and she snubbed him fairly viciously and very publicly.'

'Don't tell us the same thing happened to Denise.'

'Not exactly. He has tried it on with Denise – he has with all the women – but she had more sense than to take any notice. But

76

then somebody made a joke of it when her husband was around and he went round to sort Searle out.'

'Was there an incident with Joss as well?' Mitchell wanted to know.

Jennie shook her head. 'No, Joss sticks to men her own age.'

'How old is Searle?'

'Pushing forty, I gather. By the way, sir, Stuart Kemp got back from France last night. I couldn't raise you but Superintendent Petty said it was all right to go round. He says Kemp has a rock-solid alibi in France for Wednesday so he can't possibly be a suspect.'

Browne scowled. 'So what did he have to say?'

'Not a lot. He hasn't a clue about her movements since he last rang her on Tuesday night. He knew she'd be out on Wednesday so he rang again on Thursday. He was puzzled when she didn't answer but the French police got to him late that night. He talked about her in general. Said he encouraged her to use her talents and was glad she sang with the choir and enjoyed their company – at least, he was till this happened.

'He was very preoccupied with the cats. One of them wouldn't eat unless she stroked it first, sort of giving it permission. It mewed all the time I was talking to him. The poor thing was starving but neither of us could persuade it to eat. It stopped him thinking about the murder, I suppose, so it was useful for that.'

Browne's phone rang. He lifted the receiver and listened, his lips tightening. Petty had now seen fit to acquaint his DCI with news of Kemp's return. He gave ironic thanks and replaced the receiver quietly. 'Anything else, Jennie?'

Her little start of alarm told him to change his expression. 'There's just a bit on Alison. It wasn't a compulsory course she was going on so no one made a fuss when she didn't arrive. Then she'd booked a week's holiday so no one at the shops missed her. They thought she was doing her Christmas shopping. The neighbours were used to her travelling about a lot and I don't think she mixed with them much anyway, from the way they talked. I got the impression with everybody that she was well respected but not much liked. Everybody said she had plenty of men friends but no one came up with any names.'

'You had quite a day. What time did you go off duty?'

She shrugged. 'I saw Alison's GP but not Denise's. Alison was very healthy but for the last six months she'd been having treatment for depression. Apparently she'd had a woman friend to stay in the summer and one of her children swallowed a lot of iron pills that Alison had left on a bathroom shelf. He died. He was only three.'

'Sir!'

'Yes, Benny?'

Browne knew what he was going to say. No one else had made the connection but they caught his excitement. 'That means both victims are connected with a child death. Do we know of anyone who's got a hang-up about that?'

'We don't but we're going to do our damnedest to find out.'

'And,' Mitchell went on, speaking his thoughts as they occurred to him, 'we'd better check for any other woman who could in any way be considered responsible for harming a child. It would make her a very likely victim.'

'You could be right. I'll consult Cully first and take it from there. Right, action sheets, unless there's anything else?'

Bellamy blushed. 'Sir, if the person we're after is picking victims completely at random . . . '

'He isn't necessarily. There's maybe a reason from his point of view. It just seems random to us.'

'Well, either way, could it be a female killing females?'

Browne sighed. 'Anything's possible, Nigel, but I don't think so. If you want a bit of physical evidence for that opinion, the fingermarks were probably too big.'

Bellamy subsided and Browne gave the day's instructions. 'Fielden for you, Benny. Searle for Nigel. Find out what he has to say about the under-age girl and what the girls have to say about him. You keep talking to the women, Jennie, as many as you've time for.' He handed out the sheets and they filed out.

He kept Dean's till last and motioned to him to sit down again. 'I want you to track down and talk to this Phillips character who teaches the flute. You did well with Simmons, Richard. How did you get the boy to be so forthcoming?'

Dean thought for a minute. 'It wasn't because I was sympathetic, sir. I think he's had a bellyful of sympathy and understanding from a largely middle-class choir, even though he's grateful for their help. I think he found me a bit abrasive and that gave him the freedom to express some of his fear and resentment without seeming to be asking for anything.'

Browne began to have great hopes of Dean.

Chapter 8

Browne was interested in seeing the setting that Cully had chosen for himself. He locked up his car and looked around him. Most of the landscape was still covered in a frosting of snow so that it was difficult to make out the exact line of the horizon, especially as the dip of the hills in front of him were screened with a black lace of branches. The sun was shining through a thin cloud cover so that there were no shadows but a general brightness.

Beside him, between a church hall and a small general store, a narrow ginnel led him into an enclosed courtyard, smallish, intimate, stone-flagged. Two iron posts in the archway where the ginnel ended blocked the entry of vehicles. The flags were old and weathered, their surface uneven. Here and there one had been removed to make room for young saplings, thin and leafless. The ground had a slight slope so that the houses on the far side of the yard, low and stone built, had steps up to their doors. A church tower rose above the roofs of the furthest houses and seemed to bless them.

Browne wondered whether this was an expensive seclusion or whether Cully had been lucky enough to find this pleasant hideaway before the speculators. The houses to his right were built alongside the churchyard. In front of them, tubs that would contain plants in summer were now snow capped and looked rather like huge iced buns. Browne supposed that the television aerials on the chimneys were out of place but every building, old or new, had them now, and they no longer irritated him as an anachronism. His eye accepted them as normal.

Cully's house appeared to lean against the churchyard wall. It had a white PVC front door that seemed in keeping with the cottage from a distance but which offended Browne with its nasty plastic texture as he drew nearer, especially as the stone lean-to extension in the angle of the walls had what was probably the original door, freshly painted. There was a first-floor French window with a little iron-railed balcony outside it, so low that Browne thought it would be quite safe to jump to the ground from it. There was a snow covering on the dustbin with melted holes in it, so that the lid appeared to be adorned with a paper doyley.

Browne rang the bell and waited to be let in, his eyes resting on next door's hanging baskets, neglected after the summer and now trailing a sad, blackened tangle of stalks. Cully, looking longer and thinner as he stooped in his low doorway, was welcoming.

'I've come myself,' Browne told him, as he settled himself in a reproduction rocking-chair, 'because I don't know what questions to tell my team to ask or what answers I hope to get. I just hope I'll recognise them when I hear them. Just talk to me about yourself, your choir, its members and what it does – but, before you begin, there's just one specific point. Is there anyone to your knowledge who has, or is believed to have, harmed a child in any way?'

Cully was quick to understand him. 'Besides Denise, you mean?' He did not mention Alison's tragedy. 'I can't think of anyone, but you'd better ask the gossips.'

Browne rocked himself gently. 'We intend to ask everyone. What else do you do besides direct this choir?'

'Direct two others in Bradford and Leeds.' He gave Browne details, addresses and times of practices.

'Does that make you a living?'

'That and some private teaching and a little lecturing.' He gave the required details again.

Browne put his notebook away. 'How did you become involved with Cloughton Choral?'

'My predecessor took a teaching post at a school in London.'

'He wasn't making it pay, then?'

Cully grinned. 'He wasn't trying to. He was doing a full-time teaching job here. He conducted the choir for love and expenses.'

81

'But they agreed to pay you?'

'I'm rising in the musical world.' He announced it as an unremarkable fact. 'They wanted to rise with me and I thought I could do something with them. The spice goes out of a creative job when the need to earn by it is obviated. Earning money confirms my ability. And I'm giving them value for it. We're making a recording in Manchester in the summer and there are one or two other schemes in the melting pot.

'People buying tickets for Covent Garden and the Edinburgh Festival don't realise that, up and down the country, music of so nearly the same standard is being practised and performed for the sheer joy of it by doctors, policemen, housewives and the dole queue.'

He rose in response to a click and Browne realised that he had turned down the volume of the music he had been listening to when the doorbell rang. He removed a record from the deck and put it carefully away. 'Cloughton's small for a choral society, only about eighty. It's going to be smaller still now for a while until this business is cleared up. Let's hope that the timid ones will be evenly distributed through the parts so that the balance stays right.'

Somewhat taken aback, Browne asked, 'How well do you know your members?'

He shrugged as he reseated himself. 'I can fit names to the faces and what voices they all are. The only ones I know personally are the committee and the ones that come to the pub after practice. I'm making a point of getting to know all the new members now though so the proportion that I know fairly well is growing.'

'Do you know John Simmons reasonably well?'

His face lighted up and he was silent until Browne repeated the question. 'Sorry. I was remembering the concert at his school where I met him.' He smiled to himself. 'Tender young tenors, downy headed and lipped with their cheeks all puckered with anxious concentration – and sopranos, sweet and clear and weak, well scrubbed and dewy even through the acne. The basses were more substantial and self-conscious – the back row of the school choir and the school fifteen. The altos, as always in school choirs,

82

were lost and hesitant, below their comfortable range, though stiffened by their music mistress from the keyboard.'

His flamboyant appearance made the words fitting, neither melodramatic nor ridiculous. 'Yes, I'm delighted to have John.' He rose suddenly and went through to the kitchen.

Browne heard the sound of a kettle being filled and his heart sank. Not more coffee! He called through, 'Does Mr Fielden play at concerts as well as practices?'

Cully came through and perched on a chair arm. 'Depends what we're singing. He'll play for three items at this concert that need a piano accompaniment. For the main work we've an orchestra coming from Manchester. There's a similar group in Cloughton but less accomplished. It feels passed over and sulks. Never mind. The choir's worth any aggro it causes. The orchestra's important for this piece. It's relatively easy to sing though it sounds complicated. The discords are mainly in the accompaniment. It's by Geoffrey Bush, quite a mixture of styles, bits of it like a Medieval carol, bits rather like Vaughan Williams and bits almost like film music.'

He departed as the kettle switched itself off and Browne had to shout again. 'There's a terrific amount of work involved. Do you give just the one performance?'

He reappeared in the doorway. 'I know what you mean. So few to hear, even fewer to appreciate and it only lasts a couple of hours, if that. But the learning and rehearsing is the purpose not the concert. We do have our extroverts for whom the performance is all important but, for many of us it wouldn't really matter if every concert were cancelled at the last moment. There has to be a projected performance, though, for rehearsals to be directed towards, to hold it all together.'

'You mean it's the working together, the social life that's important?'

'No, it's the musical life that's important. It consists of living with a piece, wrestling with it, letting all its different parts speak at different times.'

He disappeared again for some minutes, then came back with a coffee tray and a qualification of his sweeping assertions. 'Of course, the concert is important in as much as it's the only occasion when the choral sections, the orchestra and the soloists all come together to give an idea of how the composer intended the whole work to sound. But only the performers who've worked at it hear it like that. Most of the audience just hear a confusion of sound. And then, sometimes, when everything's right, a concert has a magic quality that can't be analysed even by the most musical, but is recognised, when it happens, by a lot of people who aren't musical at all.'

His face was alight. It seemed inappropriate that his hands were occupied by something so mundane as pouring coffee. He handed Browne his cup, then abandoned his own and drifted to the piano, seating himself and playing a series of chords and arpeggios and throwing his remarks over his shoulder.

'There was a bit of bother over the choice of programme for this concert. The choir has never been a democracy – since I took over, anyway. No performance can have more than one director and you can only direct well something you're enthusiastic about, that you want to do. I can't imagine how two people can collaborate to write a book. But I usually give way a bit at Christmas. They all want to wallow in traditional carols, sing them this year because they sang them last and the year before. It brought them up short when I told them I wanted to do this piece by Bush and another by George Dyson and that there wouldn't be room for anything else in the programme.'

Browne could tell from his voice that he was smiling. He indulged himself in some more arpeggios. 'At least it stopped them arguing amongst themselves about what they liked and didn't like. They all united against me, at least to begin with.'

He swivelled round on the stool. 'I only really wanted to do the Bush, so when I said I'd withdraw the Dyson they thought I'd made a great concession and let me choose most of the carols without any hassle. I quite like the Dyson, actually. Might do it next year.

'The committee decided unanimously that my choices weren't "Christmassy". For goodness' sake, one's all about the Virgin Mary and the other's a setting of poems about the Nativity! When I asked them what they did think was Christmassy they came up with pieces that were poles apart from each other in style and subject but which they'd been singing every Christmas since they could walk. It's all a matter of association.'

He faced the keys again and underlined this view with a few bars of 'Good King Wenceslas'. 'They want their lollipops. Of course they're all choral singers. They weren't asking for "White Christmas" or "Rudolph". Their favourites are by Joubert or Willcocks or at least arranged by Rutter. What matters to them is that they should be soggy with nostalgia. The buzz they expect Christmas to give them can't be got from one year's allocation of turkey and music and tinsel. It has to be mixed up with the memory of all the Christmases they've ever had, wrapped in the rosy glow of memory.

'Their minds are closed to new pieces. They'd rather show that they know their *Messiah* well enough to sing it right through without a copy – and, believe me, some of them can do just that. There was a lobby to do the "Christmas bits". No way! As far as I'm concerned the *Messiah*'s out as a filler. It's a work. You can't have selections from it as though it's a box of chocolates!'

He paused to play a series of softly placed chords. Browne triumphantly recognised them as the introduction to a tenor solo. 'It's "Comfort ye",' he told Cully with satisfaction, 'but I won't render it when you've been good enough to make coffee for me.'

Cully laughed. 'At first, they all walked out humming bits of the "Hallelujah Chorus" after we'd spent all night practising the Bush, just to show me where their hearts really were. I knew that they had come round when Jake sauntered out one night carolling "A Maid Peerless" instead. I don't think he did it on purpose. It had just taken him over and he liked it in spite of himself.'

He came back to his armchair and grimaced over his cold coffee. He was unable to help Browne with any specific information about who left with whom at any particular practice and the rest of their conversation didn't seem for the moment to get him any further forward. Cully rose to see his visitor out, pausing before he opened the door for Browne. 'It's one thing to face the idea that someone in the district is killing young girls who have to be protected. It's something else again to realise that that killer is probably someone I've been working with for months, who's been

85

helping to make music and magic. It's not the danger; it's the desecration.'

Whilst Browne had been seeking admission to Cully's house, Mitchell had been ringing the bell, not at Fielden's, where he had been sent, but at the DCI's own door. He had hoped it would be opened by Virginia who had returned from Oxford for Christmas the night before, but he had known that it would be her mother who answered him. She'd asked no questions, though, and left the pair of them together in the kitchen for a good forty minutes.

Now Mitchell was enjoying a free cup of coffee at a small café, whose fat, comfortable proprietress he'd assiduously cultivated in readiness for the winter months. He was also analysing his and Virginia's conversation and his own feelings about it. He hoped Hannah Browne wouldn't mention his visit to her husband but he hadn't been able to bring himself to ask her not to.

Virginia didn't seem much changed. A bit thinner, perhaps, though she'd never been fat. The same dark, springy, curly hair – but it was a bit longer, more feminine, very much more expertly styled. She'd been wearing denim dungarees, less scruffy than the jeans she'd worn in the summer – and would she have put on that pink fluffy sweater before she went away? He could tell from the smell of her that she hadn't started smoking; he was glad about that.

She had spoken to him with her usual forthright vigour. He smiled to himself, remembering her flashing eyes that had said more than her tongue. 'Just one crack,' she had warned him, 'about Oxbridge accents or people who think they know it all . . . ' On the way to the house, he'd wondered how much they'd still have in common and whether they'd be able to talk to each other with the old openness. He needn't have worried. He'd ended up being pretty forthright himself when she'd tried to become philosophical about the case.

'Murder is one person preventing another from fulfilling his destiny.' Her forehead had wrinkled as she felt for the words. 'Some people might call it God's purpose for him.'

He'd laughed. 'But if you believe in a God or a destiny that plans people's lives for them in advance, it must know that some-

86

one's going to be murdered. That's part of his destiny too. If Oxford makes you think like that I've gone off graduate entry into the force. You'll get nowhere. You get promoted in this game by nicking people.'

'Are you still enjoying it, Benny?'

He'd nodded, enthusiastically. 'I like being called out to a murder in the middle of the night or sitting in observation posts waiting for something to happen. There's not much else like it. It's an exciting job. If I couldn't do this I think I'd have to be a soldier.'

She'd made no comment, but asked instead, 'Who've you been wining and dining, then?' The tone was light but she knew him and his need for feminine company.

He hadn't struggled against his attraction to Joss. Not that there'd been anything in it. It was his vanity that needed a woman, not his baser urges, though he was not short of those. He felt alarmed at the seriousness of the response Joss had made. He didn't want her. Choosing between Ginny and Joss was no contest. He'd skived off to see Ginny this morning, feeling that if rumours reached her he'd somehow be on safer ground if they'd already met than if she heard them when she'd hardly seen him for two months.

He had ambivalent feelings about Ginny having indulged in similar diversions. At least she was still wearing his ring.

She'd been pleased about his leg up in the force, however temporary. 'Keep at it, Benny. Didn't you say that my getting a degree equalled your becoming a commander?'

He stared unseeing into his empty cup. Perhaps he should have got up to Oxford oftener, but the work had piled up; and anyway he felt out of place there, as though the students Ginny introduced him to were casting around in their minds for subjects of conversation that were suitable for discussing with a mere copper. This sort of self-doubt was a totally new experience for him. In the past he'd taken girls out, and if they hadn't admired him, fitted the required mould, he'd got rid of them, with varying degrees of politeness. He wondered if Ginny would sleep with him before she went back in the New Year and if so where. He didn't think she would have done if he'd asked her before she'd gone but he wasn't sure what attitude she'd have now.

The fat proprietress appeared suddenly in front of him, breaking his reverie. 'Things quiet, then, at present?' He got up hurriedly and set off to see Fielden.

Chapter 9

The street was cold after the steamy café. The sun was shining, but in a menacing way, Mitchell decided, softening him up before the weather did its worst. He hurried along the single track which was all that was left of the pavement by the seemingly permanent unmelted heaps of snow.

He soon found Fielden's house in the middle of a substantial but unassuming Victorian terrace. The premature holly wreath on the door, huge and adorned with bows and baubles, was irritatingly out of keeping with the reason for his visit. He knocked, being careful not to prick his knuckles.

A child's head appeared at the fence. 'Did you want Mrs Fielden? Mr Fielden's playing the piano so she won't hear you in the kitchen. You'll have to go round the back.' She obligingly led the way round the bottom of the row and through a gate into a flagged yard. Washing in the stiff wind threatened to escape from the line. In spite of the sunshine, Mitchell thought it would freeze before it dried.

The wind suddenly dropped, so that as he waited for his peremptory rap to be answered he learned from white text on a bright red cotton background that 'Welsh National Opera refreshes the ears that the other arts cannot reach'. Clever! As the door opened, the T-shirt resumed its wild dance.

Mitchell listened for opera but he was greeted by the voice of a folk singer who he suspected to be Bob Dylan, telling him that John Wesley Harding 'was never known to hurt an honest man'. His expression of recognition and appreciation earned him the approval of the blonde woman before him. 'Come in and listen to the next one before the kids realise I've taken Kylie Minogue off. They're watching a video in the dining-room so they haven't noticed.'

Mitchell shook his head regretfully as he put away his ID. 'Wish I could but I'm late already. I'll just hear the end of this one.' The combination of guitar, wailing harmonica and outrageous but beguiling voice obliterated the shouts of the neighbour's children.

Mrs Fielden switched off as the song came to an end. 'I suppose you want to see John. He's in the sitting-room.' She opened the door into the hall which led past three other rooms before it reached the front door. What a length the place was from back to front. No wonder she couldn't have heard him from the front.

Faint sounds of gunfire and horses' hoofs came through the first door. Mitchell savoured the heat from the radiator on the opposite wall. There had been none in the sun and in spite of his hurried walking he felt chilled. The sitting-room was door three and, as the woman opened it, the notes of a rippling waltz tune licked his ears. They ceased as the woman announced, 'A policeman to see you, John.'

Fielden put his music into a gaudily braided stool and closed the piano before coming forward. He looked for the most part unremarkable, of middle height and slight. His dark hair had a side parting. It was neatly cut, thick but fine and long on the crown so that a heavy lock fell over his forehead. He looked very clean.

Mitchell wondered why this thought had come to him. It wasn't as if the other people he'd met in this investigation had been dirty. Fielden had a broader face and darker colouring but he reminded Mitchell of Hunter with his neat brows and faintly academic air, reinforced by his silver-framed spectacles. His face was not expressionless – it was politely inquiring – but it gave little away. Mitchell was not clear whether the narrowed eyes and tightened mouth denoted a lingering concentration on the music he had interrupted or caution in the man's whole approach to life.

He accepted Fielden's invitation to sit down and began his questions.

Fielden's voice was clipped and his replies prompt. 'I remember November the nineteenth quite clearly because of the day before. On the Tuesday I was invited to attend a concert given by a

90

university friend. We both planned a concert career in our student days. He's making it.' He sounded philosophical, neither disillusioned nor jealous. 'I drove to Leicester, setting out straight after my last pupil left at four, had supper with Harry after the performance and travelled back after that. I got back here pretty late, then had to be up for another pupil who wanted an extra lesson pushed in before school. She was taking her Grade Eight in the afternoon. It was too late to teach her anything more – just a confidence booster.

'Anyway, I was pretty tired by the end of the Wednesday practice. Not many people realise what concentrated work it is for Cavan and me, even though we both enjoy it. I decided not to go to the pub with him and Jack.'

'I believe they didn't go either. So you came straight home? Did you leave with anyone – or give anyone a lift?'

He shook his head. 'Not quite straight home. There were two notes sticking a bit in the bottom octave. They had irritated me all night. I took the front off the piano and sorted them out.'

'Did anyone stay with you?'

'I'm afraid not. I was less than ten minutes but the pub called and my crowd knew I wasn't joining them so they went straight off. The heating was on the blink that night as well as the piano so the place cleared pretty quickly.' Mitchell nodded. This tallied with what Cully and Chance had said. 'I was the last to leave. Cavan left the key for me. I dropped it back to him the next day.'

'You didn't see Alison Meredith leave?'

Fielden dropped from the chair arm into its seat and held out his hands to the fire. Mitchell had expected them to be white with slim, square-tipped fingers and was disappointed to notice they were muscular and broad with the prominent veins he would have expected to see on an older man. The left hand was scarred although the silvery line was half hidden in dark hairs.

'Actually,' he remarked, removing his hands from the heat and rubbing them, 'I knew Alison was catching a train after the practice so I saw her beforehand and offered her a lift to the station.'

'Did she refuse?'

'Said she'd accepted one already.'

91

His half smile annoyed Mitchell. 'Does the grin mean you know who offered it?'

His face straightened. 'Was I grinning? Sorry. I was just wondering if it might have been the new lad Simmons.'

Mitchell was startled. 'What, pick up a woman nearly twice his age at his very first rehearsal? He's only just out of school!'

'But they weren't strangers. John was in the sixth form with some young relation of Alison's that he's taken rather a shine to. It's just that Alison looked rather amused when she was telling me and young John does love running people around in that aged limousine. He keeps it beautifully and likes to show it off. I think Searle's some connection of the girl's too. Emily something she's called.'

Mitchell's pencil flew. 'Can we move on to last Wednesday? Did you leave before or after Denise?'

Fielden looked blank. 'I've no idea. I certainly left fairly promptly, didn't stop to see who was doing what. The weather was foul and my car has rear-wheel drive. It doesn't behave very well on snow.'

Mitchell grinned in sympathy. 'I take it your wife can confirm your early arrival home on both occasions.'

'I'm afraid not. Wednesday is the night the girls stay with their grandmother. Jacqueline takes them and they stay the night each week, then she goes on duty. She works at Riverdale one day and two nights a week. It's a private nursing home. The girls go to school on Thursday mornings from their grandparents' house.'

He glanced at his watch, then apologised as Mitchell glared at him. 'I have another pupil at eleven thirty.'

'I'd like you to put him off, please.'

Fielden shrugged and complied, using the telephone beside him and omitting to mention Mitchell's presence. He received the next question with a faint resentment.

'I understand that you were in charge of the rehearsal between the two we've talked about, the one on November twenty-sixth.'

Fielden nodded. 'That's right. It wasn't very exciting. My brief was just note bashing. Hammering out on the piano,' he added as Mitchell looked puzzled, 'the lines that most of them were still getting wrong. It's necessary and it's boring – and Cavan usually finds an excuse to duck the rehearsal when it falls due. Not that it matters what I'm given to rehearse. Cully's such a favourite, everyone enjoys the entertainment he provides. It takes more than half the rehearsal time for them to forgive me for not being him.'

Mitchell asked who Fielden's particular friends were in the society and was surprised when he named Chance and Searle. 'Jack realises how much actual work gets done when I take a practice. We have quite a lot in common, including our humble origins, though he's risen further from his. He's taken very easily to the good life, as though he's always been promised it. He's not like people usually are when they've become rich after being poor. He's not greedy for more, doesn't feel compelled to parade all the proofs of his achievements.'

Mitchell was surprised to hear that Chance was not the public school son of the upper-middle-classes. He went on listening.

'He never tries to conceal what he's come from but nor does he play the part of a self-made man. I suppose it's partly being married to Belinda. It was she who started calling him Jack, as though a new name made him into another person. He's very generous, you know. That's unusual in someone who's known poverty.'

Mitchell moved him on to talk about Searle. Fielden's attitude to him was more charitable than most people's. His amorous adventures were laughed off. 'Every choir's got one. He's harmless and basically good-natured and that voice is worth any kind of temporary upset he might cause.'

'Like the incident in the pub with Alison Meredith?'

Fielden looked annoyed. 'The silly woman encouraged him – and her voice wasn't worth the ill-feeling she caused, in my opinion anyway.'

The door opened and Mrs Fielden came in with a tray and her daughters. She dispensed coffee from the former and introduced the latter with some pride. 'This is Kim, our big girl, and this is Kelly, our baby.'

Mitchell cringed but the girls were unmoved. The humiliation was not in front of their own friends. The age difference seemed too small to justify the contrasting roles their mother assigned to them. Mitchell estimated them at twelve and fourteen. Identically dressed in designer jeans and sweaters, they were both as plump and blonde as their mother. Mitchell imagined that their names were their mother's choice. Fielden struck him as the type to prefer either plain old-fashioned or possibly literary names.

The whole house seemed to reflect two distinct personalities rather than a compromise. Fielden, he imagined, had chosen the house itself, the picture over the fireplace of a group of monks sitting round a table in what looked like an old library, the plain old-fashioned standard lamp beside the piano. His wife was no doubt responsible for the luxurious kitchen full of gadgets, the children's trendy clothes, the lamentable, beribboned holly wreath and the desecration of the piano stool. Then he modified his opinion of the poor woman. She was, after all, a fellow Bob Dylan fan.

He thanked Mrs Fielden, nodded to her offspring and asked, 'Whose T-shirt is it out on the line? The one about the opera?'

The older girl shrugged. 'We bought it for Dad but he doesn't wear it so Mum sometimes does.'

'Mr Cully said the company was cheapening itself,' volunteered her sister. 'He was wrong. It was jolly expensive. Dad, can I borrow your calculator?' The mother departed, highly diverted by her daughter's wit. Fielden looked resigned. 'If you're careful. It's in my bedroom.'

She went to fetch it before he changed his mind. The child remaining, Kim, announced, 'Dad wrote that piece he was playing.' So this was a district where you could boast that your father was a musician rather than keeping it a secret.

'No, I didn't,' Fielden rejoined. 'Chopin did.'

'Well, he's written a lot of music. He plays it on Sundays in church. It's good.'

Fielden looked pleased. 'Well, it's nice to have family support. That's more enthusiasm than the faint praise of the parish.'

'You're a professional musician, then?' Mitchell asked.

'I earn my living from playing and teaching it, yes. I did it in schools at first but I didn't get on very well. I'm not an outgoing person. I hadn't got what it took to impose my will on a roomful of indifferent children.'

'Indifferent in attitude or ability?'

'Usually both. I have a maths degree so I turned to accountancy, did a brief spell of training and worked for Jack Chance's company for a time. I came back to music through Jacqueline's encouragement. My mother mentioned to her that I used to play well, so when the choir advertised for an accompanist she persuaded me to apply. Then the local vicar approached me when his organist left and I got several inquiries about private lessons so I took the plunge and gave up the accounts. I get by.'

Mitchell looked around him. The man did more than get by. He asked, curiously, 'Don't you get tired of just playing along whilst people sing – all week and on Sunday too?'

Fielden looked shocked. 'But the two things aren't the same at all. In the church choir, when they know the notes, they stop practising and sing the service. Knowing the notes is just the starting point for the Choral.'

Mitchell recognised the glitter of a fanatic in his eye and decided to extricate himself. After a polite handshake, Fielden let him out through the front door. At the end of the garden, he encountered Kelly, perched with the child from next door who had directed him on the wall and pushing the buttons of a calculator.

He winked at her. 'I gather you were away for the night last Wednesday.'

She pushed her waist-length hair behind her shoulders. 'Yes, we go to Gran's.'

'Do you like it there?'

She considered, then nodded. 'Yes, she's all right. We don't like him taking us out though.'

Mitchell closed the gate behind him, reflecting that the poor old man most likely enjoyed it even less than his granddaughters.

Approaching Searle's house, Bellamy remembered Browne's opinion that he would be the best gossip, 'probably the least discreet of the people we're considering'. Bellamy's brief was to encourage Searle, once the routine questions about the two rehearsals were out of the way.

A noisy and energetic piece of choral music was being played in a neighbouring room when Mrs Searle let him into her kitchen.

Bellamy did not recognise it but was glad that it had masked the sound of his own arrival and given him a chance of a brief word with the mother.

When he was escorted to the front room, Searle switched off the tape with no reluctance. 'I love the precision of Bach in something slow, but when he's going hell for leather like that he sounds like a well-organised machine shop in the middle of a shift.' He flung himself into a chair and hooked a leg over one arm.

Bellamy, uninvited, seated himself in the opposite one. 'You work in a factory, then?'

Searle made an exaggerated gesture of distaste. 'God forbid! I'm an academic.'

Bellamy hoped, if this were so, that the man kept his mind in better shape than his body. The high voice and affected manner ill matched the bulges over his jeans which the trendy T-shirt failed to conceal. Bedraggled permed hair hung to his shoulders. Bellamy smiled to himself as he imagined Searle in a hairdresser's chair adorned with curling pins. 'What do you do then – for a living?'

Searle gave a melodramatic sigh. 'Demands that you do something with your life usually mean that you reject the general enjoyment of it and exploit one talent to the exclusion of the rest. I'm trying against tremendous odds to develop my musicality, but, when I'm desperate for money, I do some freelance journalism. My mother is fond of telling people that her son is a writer.' After a pause for Bellamy to absorb this, he added, 'I could never decide on a career. Having a huge tolerance makes decision making difficult. You can always see another point of view.'

Considering this line in gossip unproductive, Bellamy fell back on routine questions and found them more successful. 'We hardly needed to adjourn to the pub last Wednesday,' Searle told him. 'John Fielden had taken a deadly dull session the week before, teaching long runs, tediously, one by one, so that Cavan could let us have a clear run through getting drunk on the sound of them all correctly interwoven. Cavan got a bit worked up himself, hot and excited. Took his tie off first, then his jacket, then his

96

sweater. By half nine, he had his shirt unbuttoned and his sleeves rolled up. He called a halt soon after that, fortunately.'

'So, Mr Fielden took the rehearsal the week before?'

'Oh, yes. It's all right for our revered conductor to miss a practice with a concert three weeks away – he has plenty to say if I do. But Mummy beckons and Cavan drops everything and runs – mustn't miss her birthday party!'

'Why was Mr Fielden's rehearsal boring?'

'I've told you. Cavan played the dirty trick of leaving all the parrot-learning for John to pick up. Mind you, anything would be pretty deadly with John in charge so it might as well be the tedious stuff he's given to do.'

'You don't like Mr Fielden?'

Searle stretched in the chair, revealing an off-putting roll of white flesh. 'He's all right. Just not very entertaining or inspiring and certainly not a good director. He tries too hard. He stamps out rhythms and shouts out beats in a bar as though we were all school children. I don't know why I minded so much. Cavan does it sometimes but that's different. He reminds me of a caller at a square dance when he does it and that's quite amusing. John can't be beaten as an accompanist though.'

'So I've been told.'

'He's a prissy little man. Has a special place at the back of the piano for his music case and special places on the top of the piano for all his stuff. If anyone moves it slightly, everything has to stop till he's put it back. He has to get himself ready before he starts playing. He folds his jacket up and puts it on a chair, then he unbuttons his cuffs and folds them back, just once, not up to his elbows. Then he sits down and closes his eyes for several seconds and we all have to wait till he looks at Cavan to show he's ready. He's impressing us with a bit of temperament.'

'But he's good?' Bellamy encouraged.

'Oh, yes. Anyone who knows anything about music respects him. It's more than they do at home. Well, Jackie thinks a lot of him but those girls are ruined and make his life hell. The place is always resounding with abysmal deafening pop music. He says they'll find their way to a more genuine appreciation of good music if they are free to find it by their own route. Everyone else says he can't control them.'

Bellamy brought Searle back to the previous Wednesday's rehearsal. 'Oh yes, Denise sang the Bitch's solo.'

'Alison Meredith's, you mean?'

Searle gave a mock bow. 'You catch on quickly. Well, that made it a good rehearsal too. There's an ascending scale in the solo of "Lully" and Alison always drove it from in front. Denise just rode on it. It was delightful.'

His delight seemed genuine. Bellamy dispersed it with his next question. 'I believe there was a recent incident involving you and Miss Meredith.'

He scowled. 'Don't start on that again. Silly cow struts around asking for it. Then when I give her a whirl to satisfy her vanity, she turns nasty. Women are all the same!'

This had not been so in Bellamy's experience. He smiled to himself, remembering some of the differences.

A minute or so later, he brought his mind back to Searle.

' . . . all that money and his parents still stuck in a grotty little council house in the middle of Wakefield. Says they don't want to move from their old familiar surroundings. Doesn't want to put his hand in his overloaded pocket more like. Getting his own back for his miserable childhood out of sight of a blade of grass.'

Bellamy thought quickly round his new circle of musical acquaintances. 'Would you be talking about Mr Chance?'

'I said so.'

Bellamy wondered what he'd missed during his brief spell of inattention and kept his wits about him for the remainder of the distasteful interview.

Chapter 10

It had begun to snow again and the drivers parking their cars at the end of the ginnel leading to Cully's courtyard were hoping that they wouldn't have to dig them out before driving them away.

Cully, whose car was safely in its garage, had other problems. He would not allow some psychopath the pleasure of watching the choir disintegrate, whether or not that was his purpose, or whether or not he was a member of it. He had prepared as cheerful a welcome as possible for his committee. In the old fireplace, usually filled with dried flowers, there was a huge log, not yet glowing red, but being busily licked by flames from the twigs and firelighters underneath.

He had his fingers crossed. The chimney had last been swept some years ago when he moved in but he could remember less than a dozen fires being lit since then. Provided no birds had taken lodging there should be no trouble.

He had considered decorating his Christmas tree but decided this would be tactless and not suitable. He had seen no reason, though, not to display such greetings cards as he had so far received. Written good wishes could hardly be out of place. Red and white wine and glasses were on the table and the room was lit by just three table lamps. He was aiming at informality, at cheering up the members of this extraordinary committee meeting whilst they discussed all the practical difficulties which had arisen because of the killings.

He knew that some members were irate because he had vetoed the cancelling of the concert and the suspension of all rehearsals. Pamela Smith, whose young daughter had joined the sopranos in the spring, would certainly be one.

The doorbell rang and Cully opened it to find a group of five on his doorstep. He'd expected them to arrive in large groups. There was safety in numbers and none of the girls seemed to trust any one man to escort her any more however well she knew him. He was overcome by the pity of it. How could the killer be one of themselves who loved and valued music? It was quite impossible and totally inconsistent.

He welcomed the first arrivals and pulled chairs up to the fire. They exclaimed over it and reached forward to warm their hands. That at least was a success. Then there was an uncomfortable silence as everyone wondered what could safely be said, broken by Iain Fraser, the driver, his voice artificially hearty. 'I thought we'd save some petrol. No point in bringing four or five cars when one will do.' There were embarrassed murmurs of 'Very kind of you,' and 'Very sensible.'

Cully began to pour wine and Fraser carried glasses across to the two women as the doorbell rang again. Anthony Markland, still unencumbered with a glass, let in the rest of the committee. Cully breathed a sigh of relief at the sight of Chance. Now the worst of the awkwardness would be over. Jack could be relied on to make the atmosphere easy and comfortable. He wondered whether it was part of his nature or part of his business training and practice. Whichever, he was grateful for it.

Having helped to serve the ladies, Chance took his own glass and the least comfortable chair and the company automatically gathered round him expectantly. He gestured to Cully, giving the leadership back to him and Cully cleared his throat. 'I thought we needed a meeting. Not that we can make many cut and dried arrangements in the circumstances but there might be things we can do to help and protect ourselves. In any case, we need to clear the air.'

Embarrassment and uneasiness made themselves felt again and Cully continued, hurriedly, 'We haven't got an easy job ahead of us, but presumably the choir elected this committee because they felt there was something special about us that makes us stand out from the others, so we'll have to do our best.' He paused, appalled by the inanity of his own words, and the embarrassment increased.

Christabel Canning rocked her enormous body in the chair

100

Browne had occupied and rescued him. 'That's right. I'm black. I was elected to prove there's no racial prejudice among the members.' It was probably true but she spoke without malice and there was a ripple of laughter.

Cully nodded to her gratefully. 'Let's hope that whatever they picked us for, between us we've got what this situation needs. All our altos and sopranos are in danger and there are too many to ask for police protection for them all. If we're to go on calling them to rehearsals, we've got to do what we can to ensure their safety.'

Fraser's organising talents had ensured that choir trips abroad and social events at home had all run smoothly. He was ready for this challenge too. 'We could soon get escorts organised, pair off all the women with the men for travelling.'

Fielden shook his head. 'That wouldn't be any good. The police think it's one of us. The girls would be better escorting each other.'

'Seven of us aren't prepared to risk it,' Cully announced, flatly. 'Penny, Jean and the Fletcher twins in the altos, Susan, Maria and Pam's daughter, Karen, are the drop-outs.' He saw from Pamela's face that this was an unwise choice of terminology, and hurried on. 'It's good that they're evenly distributed between the two parts, and they're not the strongest voices . . . ' He realised he was making things worse.

'What are we discussing?' Keith Donnell interrupted. 'Having a perfect concert in spite of all odds or keeping the girls safe?'

Cully blinked at him. 'Both, I hope.' He had not yet appeased Pamela Smith. He'd better try harder. 'Of course, no shame or blame attaches to these girls . . . '

'You wouldn't have said that,' Pamela snapped, 'unless people were criticising already. Those girls are the sensible ones. Those of you who are ploughing on regardless are just making work for the police, making things extra difficult.'

Cully looked at her and she wriggled back into the shelter of her winged armchair. 'The police have made no requests for any of our arrangements to be cancelled,' he told the assembled company.

Fraser hastened to support him. 'If there's a nutter around who

101

wants to concentrate on choir girls, he's going to find them, even if they don't conveniently gather on Wednesday nights.'

In spite of his foreknowledge of Pamela's attitude, Cully felt betrayed. 'Do any of the rest of you feel as Pam does? We'd better have a show of hands about going on.' He looked round as Fielden and Chance immediately raised their hands. Christabel slowly raised hers as she sat, huge, smiling, placid, and yet with a latent energy that made her vital.

Stella Smith looked about her diffidently, hesitating to vote, knowing that it might be her last chance to do so, unless reserve pianists were made ex-officio committee members. Then she decided and raised her hand too.

Pamela Smith, too insignificant, both physically and mentally, to look aggressive, glowered resentfully at what she considered to be harassment. Jill Perry stared at her scarlet fingernails, as Cully watched her and thought what a surprisingly mature and powerful alto she had for a twenty-two-year-old. She had placed herself next to Markland. Come to think of it, she'd shown a marked preference for his company over the last few months. A nubile blonde like Jill was probably a likely candidate for their killer. His spirits lifted as she raised her hand, further when Markland followed suit.

Cully favoured him with a grin and a raised eyebrow. He was that mixture that young girls always find irresistible – a he-man body, tanned even in December, a fair reputation as a sportsman and melting spaniel eyes that made him appear vulnerable. Whether he was or not, Cully didn't know.

Fraser was still debating with himself. Only when the police had drawn Cully's attention to the lists in the choir register had Cully noticed the spelling of 'Iain' and that Fraser's second name was Angus. His accent was as local as the others'. He must have aggressively Scottish parents. Fraser raised his hand.

Now most eyes rested on Donnell who was stocky, middle aged and a father of four girls. They were all however well below an age when they might be considered for the choir. He looked ordinary, kindly. He was some sort of skilled manual worker, wasn't he? Cully felt ashamed that he knew so little about the unmusical aspects of these elected representatives of the different sections of the choir. Donnell raised his hand hesitantly, lowered it, then resolutely thrust it up again.

Terry Pearce quickly did the same. He was new to the committee, the possessor of a budding, immature bass that would become a full, rounded roar as he got older. His membership was the result of another of Cully's school concert visits, still a schoolboy and amongst them tonight because Cully liked this sixth form element in the choir to be represented and considered an integral part of it.

Pamela glared round, nonplussed. Cully saw she had expected support from Stella and Keith Donnell. Was she afraid for herself? Surely she was comparatively safe. Perhaps she felt that only by getting the rehearsals cancelled could she be certain of keeping young Karen away. He realised he was staring at her and looked away as she shrugged.

'Well, I'm outvoted.' She transferred her angry gaze from Stella to himself. 'You'd better have my resignation from the committee.'

There was an uncomfortable silence as they waited to see what he would do. No one would be sorry if she went but this hardly seemed a good way to be rid of her. Eyes crept to Chance who habitually resolved difficult situations but it was Fielden who spoke. 'I think you should consider whether you want to leave the committee when you're calmer and we're all under less stress.'

'Cavan's allowing a free vote on this non-party issue,' added the irrepressible Christabel and there was relieved laughter. Cully circulated the wine bottle again and Chance, uninvited, took a log from the hearth and mended the fire.

Fielden regarded Cully seriously. 'Have you thought this through from your own point of view, Cavan? Most of the energy and initiative comes from you. It won't be easy under the conditions.'

Cully smiled at him, touched by his concern. 'Oh, yes. When I go into my act I'm on automatic pilot.'

Chance looked up, the poker in his hand. 'You mean all the backchat's ready planned?'

'Oh, no. I don't know what's going to happen so I don't know what I'm going to say, but I switch from being Cully the bloke to

103

Cully the conductor and back again. One doesn't affect the other once I'm under way.'

'That's all right, then.' Having got the fire roaring comfortingly again, Chance returned to his chair. 'Right, having decided we're carrying on, we'd better return to how we're going to take care of the girls.'

'What's the point,' Markland demanded, 'if they don't trust us?'

'We'll look after ourselves.' They turned to Christabel. 'All it needs is a bit of organisation, man. More than a quarter of us have cars. All it needs is for all the mobile women to be allocated a few passengers who live reasonably near. Then I'll ring round and check that everyone's willing and there you are!'

'You must claim something for your phone calls,' offered Cully, weakly.

'Put me down,' Stella offered. Jill added her own name to the paper Christabel had taken from her handbag. Pamela remained silent.

'What's next on your list?' Christabel had obviously decided to take over.

Cully was quite ready to let her. 'They'll release the bodies for burial or cremation before too long. Is the choir going to sing at the services? Are we all going or would the families prefer something quieter, more private?'

'We can't discuss that,' Fielden remonstrated. 'We'll have to ask them.'

'Denise's mother has asked for a bit of the Mozart,' Cully told them. 'I've checked that it's all right with Stuart.'

'Is he still going to print the programmes for sale at the performance? We'll lose a few pounds we were counting on if he doesn't.' Markland, the treasurer, felt chastened by the silence that greeted this question until Fraser remarked, 'It'll give the poor devil something constructive to do.'

'Alison's nearest relatives are her aunt and uncle, young Emily's parents. I'll go to see them, if you like, and see what they want.'

Christabel was tireless, thought Cully. He suggested coffee, and when there was general enthusiasm for it departed to the kitchen to make it. He boiled water and set up the filter, wondering if there was any significance in his receiving no offer of help from any of the women. He decided he was being paranoid and whistled as he completed his preparations, realising after a while that the tune was the soprano solo from 'Lully'.

The conversation as he re-entered the living room with his tray displeased him. 'Well, you must admit young Simmons is a fine, strapping lad, quite capable of overpowering any girl if he wanted to.' Chance gave Cully an apologetic shrug, having failed in his efforts to divert the flow of gossip, and they both glared at Pamela Smith.

Cully placed his tray on the table and invited her to dispense the coffee for him. Having occupied her, he joined the circle round the fire, determinedly guiding the discussion back to the subject of concert publicity. Slightly shamefacedly, the committee put its mind to considering the choir's present notoriety and what steps they could take to attract an audience that only wanted to enjoy their music.

The coffee and business lasted only a short while longer, then the atmosphere became tense again as Cully's visitors contemplated their journeys home. Markland's half-hearted suggestion of an adjournment to the local pub was not taken up and the company departed to climb back into the cars that had brought them.

The snow had stopped and no digging was required. Finding that Fielden and Chance had driven themselves with no passengers, Cully asked them to stay on for a few minutes. They stood and waved as the three cars departed. Fraser's, with four passengers, turned back towards the middle of the town. Stella Smith's, with Terry Pearce in the front, continued up the valley. Jill Perry, who lived some distance from any of them, drove off alone.

'I wish,' Cully remarked as they recrossed the slush-covered courtyard, 'she hadn't got such a bloody good voice.'

'Who?' Fielden stamped his feet to restore his circulation as Cully fumbled with cold fingers at the lock.

'The delicious Pamela, of course. What sort of trouble was she trying to stir up whilst I was in the kitchen?'

They resettled round the fire, after Cully had removed glasses and a whisky bottle from the cupboard.

Fielden grimaced. 'She's got more ammunition than usual at the moment.'

'She might pick on someone more able to defend himself. Why the Simmons lad?' Cully poked the fire, to its detriment, then relinquished the poker to Chance.

Fielden toasted his feet at the flames Chance was resurrecting. 'Because Alison disappeared on the night of his first rehearsal.'

'But Simmons has lived in Cloughton all his life.' Cully was indignant. 'She can't suspect him of murder because he's come to a choir practice. He hasn't disposed of any girls before. At least, if he did, he buried them deep.'

Satisfied with the fire, Chance returned to his chair. 'She had some tale about John's girlfriend, Emily. She's Alison's cousin and Alison was a bit short on relatives and quite attached to her. She used to give her fancy clothes from the shops she dealt with. She's a pretty girl, Emily, I mean, and Alison probably enjoyed dressing her up. But, apparently, she's recently started attending the Plymouth Brethren meetings. "Got religion" was how Pamela put it.'

'Does she go round in sackcloth and ashes now then?'

'Of course not. It's the usual jeans during the day. It's just that she doesn't need all the fancy evening clothes Alison gave her because she says she no longer wants to go to the "worldly" places where they were suitable.'

Cully looked concerned. 'I shouldn't have thought John Simmons could have afforded to take her to such places.'

'Recently he could. It's quite a good job he's got. Pam's theory is that Emily became less accommodating in all sorts of ways and John blamed Alison for his frustration.'

Cully's glass banged on the table. 'So, having knocked Alison off, he got a taste for it and disposed of Denise? My God! Why didn't we accept her resignation?'

'Because,' Fielden soothed him, 'we all feel about her as you do so she can't do any real harm. And, as you've just pointed out, she's got a very useful voice.'

Chance drained his glass and put it down. 'Anyway,' he observed, 'I don't think this chap is sexually frustrated. Stuart

106

said Denise hadn't been interfered with, though I don't know whether the same was true of Alison.'

'Several of the others,' Fielden put in, 'remember Mellor bumping into Denise last Wednesday.'

'But he hadn't joined us when Alison was killed.'

'And his name isn't John.'

They both turned puzzled faces to Cully who reddened. 'I wasn't supposed to mention that. I've no idea why, but the police asked me right at the beginning who in the choir was called John and asked me not to discuss it. It's too late now.'

Chance looked worried. 'Now you mention it, have you noticed which of us the police are concentrating on? We've all been questioned, of course, but the real grilling has been saved for me and you, John, Jake and young Simmons.'

Fielden sat up suddenly. 'Well, Mellor used to be called John! He was talking to me last night after church choir practice. He joined us about a month ago. We're doing the Christmas parts of the *Messiah*.' He ignored Cully's tutting. 'He was asking me why we laughed when he sang at his audition. He's got a lovely old copy that I was looking at. His father's name was in the front, "John Howard". He told me when he was fourteen he got tired of the muddles caused by having the same name as his father. He was seeing his first girl and thought he might have his letters opened and so on. So he decided only to answer to Howard and it caught on.'

Chance glanced at his watch and drew in his breath sharply. Belinda had been on her own for four hours. He rose to go and Fielden too remembered his domestic responsibilities and began to gather his belongings. They all crossed the slippery yard again and Chance, trying to conceal his anxiety, climbed into his car, raised his hand in salute and turned his key in the ignition. Nothing happened. He tried again. Nothing. And again, despairingly.

Knowing Fielden lived in completely the opposite direction, Cully felt in his pocket for the key to his garage. Before he could make his offer, Jill Perry's red Mini drew up in the position it had left twenty minutes before. She wound down the window, looking relieved. 'Thank goodness you haven't gone to bed, Cavan. I'm afraid I've left my handbag behind your rocking-chair. I can't go to work tomorrow without my office desk keys.'

As Cully went back to fetch the bag she noticed the raised bonnet of Chance's Saab. He reappeared from underneath it, shaking his head.

She hesitated only a moment before asking, 'Trouble, Jack? Want a lift?' After all, she would have to pass within a hundred yards of his house. She could hardly trail Cavan all that way and back when she could drop him off so easily. And she'd certainly be safe with Jack Chance. Wouldn't she?

Chapter 11

As Cully's guests were arriving, Browne pushed away his plate and stood up from the supper table. 'I expect Benny beetled round here before he went to Fielden's,' he observed to his wife's back as she carried dirty dishes to the kitchen. Hannah was saved from having to betray her prospective son-in-law by the telephone.

She answered it on the second ring and Browne departed to the cellar in search of home brew. As he returned, a bottle in each hand, Hannah covered the mouthpiece to tell him, 'Annette says thank you for visiting Jerry and he's much more cheerful.' Browne's dislike of Annette abated a little. He resolved to keep Hunter abreast of the developments in the case, especially as discussing things with Jerry helped him too.

He heard a car draw up outside and went out to welcome Mitchell who was a few minutes early for his seven thirty summons. Mitchell remained in the car, waiting for Browne to tell him where to drive them.

'We're going just as far as my study. I always discuss my cases with my sergeant over a few beers – and, if you're looking around for Ginny, forget it. She's out.'

He led the way to the grandly named but tiny office under the stairs with its two chairs, one desk, one bookcase and a lamp. 'You're fatter than Jerry but your legs aren't so long. You should fit in.'

Mitchell paused in the doorway. 'Would there be room for us both, sir – if he's well enough, that is?'

Browne had been asking himself just the same question, though not about the room's physical capacity. He was glad the suggestion had come from Mitchell. 'If you've enough respect for your elders to sit on a hard dining-room chair, which is all I can get in for a third seat, I'll give him a call.'

They each dispatched a pint of the home brew whilst they waited for Hunter to turn up. Mitchell reached for his tankard and sipped gingerly, prepared to grin and bear it, but he found the murky liquid surprisingly palatable, though his thoughts less so. Where had Virginia gone, and, what was more to the point, who with? And why hadn't she told him? If he hadn't been closeted with her father he would have expected to take her out somewhere. Wasn't that what courting couples did on Saturday nights? She'd probably known that Browne would be needing him but she could still have let him know where she was. If their positions were reversed, he would certainly . . . Wouldn't he? Browne was waiting for an answer. 'I'm sorry, sir. I didn't quite catch . . . '

Browne grinned. He had watched the passage of Mitchell's thoughts across his face. 'I was speculating,' he repeated, 'on how long I can stand every house I visit in this case blaring classical music at me. I've been on cases before when all the people involved had some interest in common but never before has that interest been quite such an obsession with them all.' The doorbell rang and Browne smiled. 'He must have been all ready, waiting for his invitation.'

He went to open the door. Hunter's car was parked, empty, in the drive. So Annette had allowed Jerry to drive himself? He looked at his sergeant again and absolved his wife. Jerry was losing that jaundiced colour and looked altogether brighter. He ushered him into the study and into the armchair which Mitchell had obediently vacated.

If Browne was pleased at the improvement in Hunter's appearance, Mitchell, who had last seen him at work, was shocked at the deterioration. If the bloke wasn't wearing clothes you wouldn't know he was there. And his features were sharper and more skeletal than ever.

Hunter smiled and settled himself into these familiar surroundings and Browne plunged into the evening's business before Mitchell said something well meant but tactless and demoralising. 'Well, we've pretty certainly a serial killer diagnosed, so we can't go on

110

any longer, half recreating the girls' lives and half following up their men friends, and assume that will bring results. The good news is that it's got us another half-dozen DCs to help with the deadly routine. It's not helped that I'm without my trusty sergeant and lumbered with this dunderhead in his place.' He favoured Mitchell with a rare wink.

Hunter accepted a brimming tankard. 'Cheers. I'm sure Benny will do us proud.' Neither of his companions failed to note this first ever use of Mitchell's forename. 'What's been going on in the nick, then, whilst I've been holed up?'

'The nudes have gone back on the walls.'

Browne felt that Mitchell was pushing his luck but relaxed as Hunter laughed. 'All right, down to business. We've a bit more on Chance, some of it from an alto-singing nurse who's been taking a professional and sympathetic interest in Belinda Chance's pregnancy. Not only has it been difficult, dangerous even, but apparently it's not their first child. They had a daughter who died a couple of years ago after a routine operation. I haven't any details on that. Mrs Chance has difficulty conceiving – just the two pregnancies in nine years of marriage and in these circumstances. The daughter was a beautiful, healthy child, what the witness called "the reason for their existence".'

Hunter put down his half empty tankard. 'So, one of your Johns is worried about the health of his wife and his unborn child, sexually frustrated, even if only temporarily, and has good reason for a hang-up concerning anyone who's harmed a child.'

Browne looked to Mitchell for a response but Mitchell just frowned in concentration, his eyes on his beer. 'Well, Benny?'

The scowl deepened. 'I don't know, sir. What I've read doesn't suggest that our man would have such a – well, logical reason for what he's doing. And if he was unbalanced for such a reason, I certainly don't think he'd send a note of apology for what he'd done. He'd see it as righting a wrong, bringing a wrong-doer to justice.'

'So, what does your learned tome think is the reason for ritual murder?'

'It says these blokes are hitting out blindly because a repressed childhood has dammed up their talents, frustrated their ambitions and stopped them having an outlet for their emotions. And then they're triggered off to get their own back on society by something that a sane person considers quite trivial.'

Browne tried to conceal his amusement at this deadly serious exposition from Mitchell's textbook. On the whole he agreed with what it said and with Mitchell's conclusions concerning Chance.

'Going back to Chance,' Hunter interrupted, 'quite a number of these people seem to be connected with his firm. Is there something to look into there?'

Browne shrugged. 'Could be. Cully didn't know of any other girl in the choir who had anything at all to do with harm coming to a child. Nor, when I asked him, did he connect it with the Chances losing theirs – always supposing he knew about it. I imagine he does. He seems fairly friendly with them.'

'Another thing against it being Chance,' Mitchell offered, hesitantly. 'The book says psychopathic killers are always introverts. I wouldn't say he was.'

'I'd agree. What about the others?'

Mitchell, surprised at not being teased, considered. 'I'm not sure what one is,' he volunteered, after a few moments. 'I mean, I know what the dictionary says but I don't feel qualified to separate all the people we've interviewed into the two types.'

'You're coming on, Benny,' Hunter told him. 'You'd have been quite happy to do it this time last year.'

The two men smiled at each other as Mitchell went on, 'Fielden is quiet, intelligent, very knowledgeable about himself. If that's being introverted, then I suppose he is. Simmons is quiet too, but I think he just keeps a low profile because of his circumstances from what Dean's report says. He's probably going to have sausages for his Christmas dinner and the last thing he wants is for everyone to find out all about him and be sorry for him. It's a crazy coincidence that all the Johns we're looking at have serious problems to live with that might have driven them to flip like this, to do with their careers or personal or sexual lives. Simmons is tied to his family and can't do what he wants and his girlfriend's turned goody-goody and won't give him a good time. We've turned up all this stuff about Chance and his wife. Searle lives this fantasy life and all the girls think he's pathetic. Only Fielden

112

has healthy kids and a normal set-up and he's eaten up because he wants to be a pianist and composer.'

Hunter was shaking his head. 'If we checked out the Freds or the Peters with the same suspicions and looking for the same factors, we'd find them. It's a pretty frustrating society we all live in.'

Browne refilled the empty tankards, looking gloomy. 'We've looked at all these people and they're all tied in knots. Any one of them could have flipped. Only routine's going to sort this one.'

'Or luck?'

Browne scowled. 'No such thing. When conscientious routine work turns up what we want, some folk will have the cheek to call it luck and others will overrate it and attribute it to our deductive powers, but really it will be the machine, grinding on to the end of its task. There'll be no joy about this one. One of us will turn up the conclusive piece of evidence and won't need to speculate. It'll just be settled as simply as that – but it might take for ever.'

Hunter patted his hand in mock sympathy. 'For Pete's sake don't cry into the beer. It's too good to dilute. I had another thought. This chap is probably under some sort of compulsion when he writes the notes – always supposing they're genuine and not sent by some criminal idiot jamming up the works – but he might still have an eye to self-preservation. He might have signed them with a false name.'

'That's unlikely. It wouldn't assuage his guilt.'

'Well, what if he used a middle or unused name? It would still be his but it wouldn't be so incriminating.'

Mitchell looked despairing. 'That means detailed questioning of another sixteen.'

Hunter shrugged. 'So be it. In fact, to throw it really wide open, are we sure that the Choral isn't just being used as a red herring?'

Browne wearily pushed the hair out of his eyes. 'I thought I was sure. I really don't know any more but I just have a feeling. What use that is I can't tell you. I've never dealt with – even met – a psychopath. Petty, greedy, unprincipled little people, yes; daring, imaginative, equally greedy big people; people temporarily insane because of circumstances; arrogant people who

113

wanted to change the world to suit themselves and never mind the cost to anyone else – but I've never come across mindless deaths that give no pleasure or gain to the perpetrator, who probably wishes as much as I do that he wasn't doing it.'

There was a depressed silence for some seconds. Mitchell was aware that his buttocks on the hard chair were becoming numb and wriggled unobtrusively. 'Why didn't Alison Meredith drive herself to the station?' he asked suddenly. The others looked at him. 'She was well set up. She must have had a good car.' Browne nodded an acknowledgement. 'So why did she need a lift?'

'She might not have wanted to leave her vehicle in the station carpark all that time. It's not cheap any more and it's not safe either. We've had two disappear from there.' Hunter and Mitchell nodded.

Mitchell continued to ruminate on Alison's departure. 'Both Fielden and Simmons say that they offered her a lift and she told them both she'd already got one. She didn't say who. That seems odd. Wouldn't she be likely, if it was another member, to say so and so's already offered?'

'Perhaps.'

Mitchell had found a theory he liked. 'What if she'd met Howard Mellor somewhere else and got to know him. He hadn't joined the choir then but he was living near by. He could have been calling to pick her up. She wouldn't have suspected anything for a while. The graveyard isn't far from the station. Perhaps he found it turned him on to talk about music with someone he was going to strangle. So, then, he joined the society so that it would happen again. His first name is John. He's one of the sixteen.'

'Sounds a bit far fetched, Benny, but I agree with Jerry that we'll have to have a closer look at the sixteen. You can have Mellor as your pigeon if you like but be careful not to ask him any leading questions.'

Hunter had no comment to make and Browne saw that his look of alert interest had faded. In fact, he looked exhausted. Browne had known Mitchell was maturing. He had only to catch his eye for Mitchell to yawn magnificently. Browne gave him a delighted grin.

'These youngsters have no staying power, Jerry. We'd better call it a day whilst there's still time for his beauty sleep.'

Mitchell's magnanimous gesture was not over yet. 'Sorry, sir. Can't keep my eyes open. I'm going right now if you've finished with me.'

He deserved a reward. He should have it. 'You'll miss Ginny and Alex then. They're always late when they visit Hannah's mother. The old girl's got more staying power than the lot of us put together.'

Hannah switched off the reading-lamp and wriggled between the cold sheets, shivering. One of the few respects in which she and Tom were incompatible was over this question of heat in the bedroom. She snuggled up to him. 'It's your fault I'm cold so you can get me warm. What were you looking so pleased about? Made a breakthrough?'

He rolled over to face her. 'No such luck, but it was quite an entertaining session and it might lead to progress. Jerry's quite a lot better, bored to tears and, now that he doesn't feel so ill, is accusing himself of malingering. He's been begging for a specific job connected with the case.'

She extended one leg into the icy region further down the bed and withdrew it quickly. 'You can't use him if he's off sick, can you?'

Browne recoiled with an exclamation as Hannah placed her frozen feet on his back. 'Desist, woman!' Feeling martyred, he entwined his nicely warmed limbs with her cold ones. 'If Jerry entertains himself on Wednesday evenings by sitting with the various guardians and escorts at the Cloughton Choral rehearsals and chatting them up, I don't see that I have any right to prevent him. It'll keep him cheerful and help to soothe his conscience. I've made the condition that he reports to me here, though, in person or by phone. He's not recovered by any means and I'm not having him upset by someone down at the station hinting that he should be back on duty.

'Benny's as solicitous as I am. He abandoned his macho image when he saw how tired Jerry was getting and broke things up by yawning extravagantly himself and then beating a hasty retreat so that Jerry and I could have a final few words. He almost overdid it. I was sorry I'd teased him when he first arrived.'

'What about?'

'I half gave him the impression that Ginny was on the razzle with someone else.'

'That was unkind, Tom. They're having enough bother readjusting after two months' separation.' She turned her back on him. Browne grinned to himself. Now he knew Benny had been round earlier in the day.

'Jerry must have been tired if he let you drive him home.'

'Oh, he wasn't tired enough to agree to being driven. Just tired enough for me to be worried about it. It wasn't a problem. I got the whisky out, poured him a good double and then told him he was over the limit.'

'And you weren't?'

'I'm on call, aren't I? I had to make do with another scant half pint.'

Hannah turned back to face him. 'Tom, if you won't have the bedroom radiator switched on, you're at least going to have to put up with another blanket.'

He grabbed her, smothering the rest of her protest. 'I'll soon warm you up, woman. Just try this.'

The telephone rang. Muttering unendearing imprecations, Browne reached for it, identified himself and listened. 'What? Oh God! What time did she leave Cully's? What distance was she driving? All right. I'll be there in ten minutes.'

He replaced the receiver and turned to Hannah who had switched on the lamp again and was sitting up. 'Not another one?'

'It's a possibility. Switch the radiator on whilst I fetch you another blanket. You're going to have to keep yourself warm.'

116

Chapter 12

The half-hearted, wet snow that had fallen in the early evening had frozen towards midnight. As Browne drove towards the station, thick clouds that blotted out the stars were beginning to empty themselves in fat flakes, forming a treacherous cover over the ice. In spite of his extreme caution, Browne's Cavalier skidded twice before he parked, unscathed, in his usual spot. He spared a moment's thought for the traffic police, coping with the Saturday-night revellers who would have treated the conditions with less respect.

The station sergeant, who had spoken to Jill Perry's father, came to greet him and put him in the picture. 'He's frantic, of course, sir, in all the circumstances.' His gesture took in the atrocious driving conditions as well as the murder investigation. Browne's anxiety was not allayed when he heard that a choir committee meeting had been held and that Jill Perry had given a lift to Chance. 'He's blaming himself,' Sergeant Tuckey went on, 'for letting Jill drive instead of taking her and fetching her himself.'

Browne nodded. 'Rung the hospitals?'

'Yes, sir, just the two local ones. If there'd been an accident between Mr Cully's house and Mr Perry's, they wouldn't have used any other.'

Browne thanked him and retired to his own office to ring the Perrys and the traffic police himself. The Perrys had heard nothing and his colleagues in the traffic division spoke, as he had expected, of scores of collisions and injuries, both major and minor . . . Extracting a promise to pass on immediately any relevant information, Browne left them to get on with their affairs and wondered what it would be best to do next. A further search of the parks and graveyards would be useless in the dark, but by dawn the snow would have covered everything they would have looked for.

He would not, until now, have put money on Chance as their man, and he did not seriously think, even if he were wrong, that Chance would harm Jill Perry tonight, when so many people knew that they had driven off together. He had read that most serial killers eventually wanted to be caught, but surely not so early in their careers. Should he ring the Chance household? He hesitated to alarm Belinda but he had little choice.

After a moment's consideration, he sent PC Falk, renowned for and proud of his excellent driving, round to the house, then he rang for coffee and reached for the case file. If he couldn't sleep, he might as well work as he waited – but not until his coffee came. He drummed his fingers resentfully on his desk, feeling sorry for his team. The grinding routine he'd spoken of to Hunter was busy grinding. It was exhausting at the best of times but in these conditions it was doubly stressful. Each car journey began at best with clearing the bonnet and de-icing the windscreen and at worst with a major dig. Travelling was over treacherous roads and the glitter of their icy cover made headlamps seem feeble and powerless.

Getting out of the car meant a change of footwear and each step sank you into a sucking depth from which your boot had to be hauled so that your calves ached after the shortest walk and you moved all the time with muscles tensed against slipping and falling.

After a tap at the door, a hand appeared and placed a cup of coffee beside his file. Recognising the freckles and the bitten nails, he muttered, 'Thanks, Karen,' without raising his eyes. He drained his cup quickly, then settled to his file until his telephone rang with a message that Falk had found a distressed Belinda Chance. She had woken to find her husband not returned and could offer no optimistic suggestions about what might have delayed him.

After another hour, the pinkish-greyness at the window had begun to compete with the striplight above the desk. Browne switched it off, stretched and went to look outside. The white outline of hills on the horizon made the sky look dirty and shabby and the houses below had a strange uniformity with common white roofs, sills, wall-tops and gardens. He saw that in snow the roof dominated a house, the rest of it huddling under its white cover.

He shook himself. It was time to send out the searchers. The phone rang again.

'Brenner, sir. Traffic Division.' Browne remembered Brenner. 'We've found your people. Jill Marian Perry and John Alexander Chance were in a Mini that collided with a VW. Nasty incident. Both your customers kept in the infirmary overnight with slight concussion. It's merry hell down there – and here too. We'd twenty-two OTLs before midnight.'

'Details? About our incident?' Browne demanded, tersely.

The voice ignored this rudeness and obliged. 'Don't know yet how it happened, sir. The two adults in the VW have shock, cuts and abrasions. They had a baby in a carry cot on the back seat.' Browne groaned softly. 'Some folk haven't the sense they were born with. They fastened the cot to the seat, firm as the Rock of Gibraltar, then dropped the infant in it and assumed she'd be safe. The cot stayed put and the child went straight through the windscreen. They were travelling at night to avoid traffic, delivering Christmas presents and seeing the woman's parents before they went abroad for the holiday.'

'What about the infant?'

'Critical, sir. In intensive care.' Browne groaned again. 'Beg pardon, sir?'

Browne pulled himself together. 'Thanks a lot, Brenner. Sorry to be a bear. I haven't been to bed yet. Keep in touch if there are any more developments.' As he went to the canteen for breakfast, he willed the baby to live for its own sake and for Jill Perry's.

Bacon and tomatoes had put Browne in a more receptive frame of mind than he had expected for the remarks of his team when they assembled some time later. Their resentment at an early start was always greater on a Sunday morning but their fairly cheerful grumbling was hushed as Browne related the night's events. Mitchell, inevitably, was the one to point out, 'We've another girl who might be connected with a child death now, sir. Are we going to give her any particular protection?'

Browne shrugged. 'I gather she isn't going to be out of her father's sight until this case is solved. We'll see what we can do though. I've read your report on Searle, Nigel. Any points you want to make to the assembled multitudes?'

Bellamy tried to look alert. 'He has an alibi of sorts. He always goes on a pub crawl after practices. First to the Three Feathers with the others where they all have a couple of drinks and go home. Then Searle starts his tour round. Some staff and customers remember him in some of the places he mentioned but everyone's vague about times and his mother's always in bed and asleep when he gets in.'

'Did you talk to her at all?'

Bellamy nodded. 'She became quite irate when I brought up the matter of the under-age girl. He keeps her pretty ill informed. She thinks he doesn't drink much or smoke. She's clean and tidy, keeps the house reasonable and does most things for him. She says he adopted his current name when he was about nine and there was a character, "Jake the Rake", in one of his comics. He was John before that. She says he is very popular with all the girls in the choir.'

'Joss says,' put in Jennie, 'he's been out with all the ones that aren't too fussy. And Stella Smith told her that when his father was alive he was smart and attractive and generally much more together.'

'What happened to the father?'

Jennie subsided and let Bellamy answer. 'He was killed in a steelworks accident. Searle says they got on well together and stood up for each other against the mother's nagging.'

'Cully rates him as a musician,' Browne told them. 'He plays quite a selection of instruments and takes pupils for piano lessons. Stuart Kemp and Carolyn Ryder, Denise's sister, were two and there were others from the choir. They were loyal to him but he can't keep his child pupils. Their parents get fed up because the lessons often start late and finish early and he sometimes cancels.

Cully says he does bits of freelance journalism when he can't scrounge enough from his mother.'

Bellamy grinned. 'She told me her son was a writer.'

They were still looking at Browne who went on, 'He began like that, hoping to become a performer but never practised enough and was too lazy to push himself and seek out opportunities. Cully says he enjoys Choral because it comes easily to him. He behaves himself there because he knows Cully means business and will throw him out if he gives too much hassle. Did you get any handwriting samples, Nigel?'

Bellamy pulled out several pieces of paper covered in a flashy scrawl, and a dog-eared photograph, and passed them round. The photograph was of schoolboys arranged in conventional fashion, the front row kneeling, centre row seated on a bench and the back row standing. Behind them was a prefabricated concrete-block construction with a corrugated-iron roof which may have been the school itself or one of its outbuildings. A youth on the front row, bashful at the honour thrust upon him, nursed a slate, ruled with three guiding lines for the elaborate chalk script: 'South End Boys. Std.2. 1960'.

The boys were a motley array in outdoor garments ranging from new-looking belted school gabardines to a crumpled and ripped sports jacket, several sizes too big for its wearer, that looked as if it had been lent by or purloined from his father. One knobbly front-row knee exhibited a spectacular graze. The boys had in common a spark of interest in what was happening to them. Maybe it was pride in their school or interest in the workings of the camera, but the look of glazed boredom, characteristic of modern school photographs, was absent.

Browne examined the picture carefully and picked out a tall, well-made boy in the centre row who had the sort of strong features that could have developed into the face of the forty-two-year-old Searle. Then he turned it over. Three rows of names, all in the same regular schoolboy script, presumably Searle's, identi-fied the members of Standard Two. He saw that the youth labelled 'The Fantastic Jake!!!' was not the boy he had selected but an attractive child with smooth hair, neatly cut, dark eyes alert and

121

amused, knee socks neatly pulled up and blazer fastened. He slipped the photograph and scribbled sheets into his case file.

'Can't we eliminate Searle,' Jennie wondered, 'on the grounds of having no transport? Surely it must have needed a car to get the girls on their own after the practices and to dump their bodies later.'

'He has one.' Bellamy looked apologetic, as though it was no part of his brief to implicate his interviewee any further. 'Lent by an uncle who's on business abroad. He comes back just before Christmas. In return, Searle has to drive him to and from the airport, keep an eye on his house, water his house plants, et cetera. Searle seemed to consider that an imposition. Wanted the car with no strings.'

About to invite the next member of his team to make his personal, unofficial comments on his last interview, Browne suddenly changed his mind. He let his gaze rest on them each in turn as they slumped on chairs, cupboard tops and window sills that offered varying degrees of comfort. Their rounded shoulders and carefully expressionless faces told him that it was Sunday, their day of rest that was being denied them. The weather was atrocious. The progress of the case was not encouraging. He broke the meeting up.

'You'll owe me your evening instead,' he warned them. 'We'll have a brainstorming – in the Fleece. I'll arrange to have the back room and get them in for eight. Meanwhile, let's hope another day's routine manages to throw up something interesting.'

Backs straightened and smiles returned. Action sheets were distributed and, clutching them, the team left their DCI to his 'Browne study'. He smiled to himself as he reached for a sheaf of reports. After a couple of pints, Bellamy and Mitchell at least would not hold back their tentative opinions or the more preposterous of their ideas, for fear of being wrong or being accused of 'showing off'.

In the meantime, having deprived himself of their individual impressions of their various suspects, he'd better take a look at their reports again and try to read between the lines. He noticed that Dean's account of his interview with Simmons, like Bellamy's with Searle, had a photograph pinned to it.

The background to Simmons' picture too was a prefabricated building, in this case, some kind of nonconformist church. Notice boards flanked the main door, and in front of the left-hand one stood a pretty, dark, freckled girl, smiling into the lens. Her slim shape obscured the end of a brightly printed Bible text. The viewfinder had cut off its beginning, but, partly hidden by a mass of curly hair, Browne read in red block capitals, NO PLEASURE . . . IN DEATH. He was reminded of his own words, offered to Mitchell and Hunter, along with the home brew. They were dealing with deaths that seemed to bring neither pleasure nor gain to their perpetrator.

He turned the picture over. Blue ink, in a careful schoolboy script, not unlike that of 'John's' apologetic letters, informed him that the girl was Emily and that the picture had been taken after the meeting on November 12th. Another hand, writing with more of a flourish in black ink, gave him the full version of the text from Ezekiel. 'I take no pleasure in anyone's death, says the Lord: Repent and live.' The words in blue ink seemed to reveal less the character of the writer than the style of letter and word formation taught at his or her school.

This, then, was Simmons' Plymouth Brethren girlfriend. He wondered how far the relationship and the girl's indoctrination had progressed. Could he assume Simmons had a satisfactory outlet for his adolescent ardour? He checked back through Dean's carefully typed notes. The lad had his mother's affirmation that he had arrived home as soon after the end of both relevant rehearsals as he could reasonably get there. He reflected on the mother's insistence on a written acknowledgement for the boy's birthday gift. Still, it would be a pity if every manifestation of old-fashioned courtesy in this case had to be suspect. And Simmons' age was against him, in Browne's book. It seemed to him that this killer's hatred, bitterness and frustration must have built up over a long period. Had John Simmons lived long enough yet for this to happen?

He laid the report on Simmons aside and took up Mitchell's on Fielden. Fielden's family were conveniently out for the whole of Wednesday nights and on neither of the relevant occasions had he followed his usual practice of adjourning to the Three Feathers for a quick pint. On the other hand, if they were looking for a disturbed personality, probably sexually and personally frustrated, Fielden seemed to be the one 'John' who wasn't.

Comfortably married, this one, with two pretty daughters. Simmons had a girl with scruples and nowhere to take her. Chance had a wife at the end of a difficult pregnancy. Searle, apparently, hadn't got what it took to get a girl interested.

Mitchell had obtained samples of Fielden's writing by asking for the names and addresses of his old schools. Browne noted with interest that Fielden seemed to form the same letter in several different ways. It gave his script an oddly immature appearance. He looked back at Fielden's account of his movements immediately after rehearsals on the nights of the two murders and made a mental note to ask Cully whether he noticed any improvement in the keyboard at the next practice.

Nothing was clipped to Bellamy's account of his interview with Chance. An initialled postscript mentioned that Chance had seemed to avoid having to write anything in his own hand. When asked about his schools he had mentioned a small church school in Wakefield. 'It has no address and probably no records any more,' he had told Bellamy. 'It was demolished for road widening two years after I left. After that, I went to QEGS.' When Bellamy had exclaimed that so had he, he could hardly ask for its postal address. He'd asked, instead, for choir details which Chance, as secretary, would be able to supply. Chance was not only able but anxious. He turned them up, immediately, on his computer screen and printed out a copy. Browne needed to turn no pages to remind himself that Belinda Chance had been peacefully sleeping during the digging out and decorating that Chance purported to have done after the significant rehearsals.

For another two hours, Browne pored over lists, reports and notes. He'd told Hunter that grinding routine was their only method of catching this killer. He'd condemned his team to it. He wouldn't excuse himself.

At twelve o'clock, he rose, stretched and wandered across to his window, contemplating his view over the town with his usual satisfaction. He was fond of Cloughton in all its manifestations but he enjoyed it most in winter. He liked visiting houses full of rows of drying boots, being met by the smell of damp wool and the sight of festoons of bright anoraks, gently steaming. The snow was inconvenient but it generated its own atmosphere of goodwill. It was only partly the imminence of Christmas, more a sort of wartime spirit, living in difficult circumstances in which all had to pull together. Old people were shopped for. Cars were dug out by communal effort. Queues of people, who would normally stare into space, conversed brightly about their travelling adventures.

Whiteness and wetness impartially covered everything before him, so that deprived of colour his eye became aware of shapes and patterns he usually ignored. His private view was that heaven would be similar to this. Nothing would be different but those who attained it would see with new eyes what they had always ignored or taken for granted. Everything would thrust itself on his attention with a permanent freshness of impact.

He shook himself, walked back to his desk and began to worry at the case again. Cloughton had made the front page of the *Independent*, he noticed. He sighed as he read the column through. Journalists loved to write about constables doing finger-tip searches, inch by inch, crawling shoulder to shoulder. Browne knew that most of them only went through the motions. Uniformed officers, who got stuck with most of the searching, had things they'd much rather do. They didn't believe they were going to find anything, or even that there was anything to find. In many cases they were right. Browne realised he was getting maudlin. It meant he needed food, and then his bed!

Chapter 13

By a quarter to nine the brainstorming in the pub was well established and Browne knew it had been the right move. His team was well primed with liquor, and the conversational ball was rolling merrily. He fished another note from his pocket and slid it across to young Carson, one of the extra DCs that Petty had procured for them when the nature of the case became apparent. He was in a better position than Browne to extricate himself and go to the bar.

The team had come in light-heartedly looking like a new sort of uniformed branch in the duffles which were now piled in a heap with his own in the corner. Most of them were dingy, ranging from navy through khaki green to muddy brown. Only Dean had been dashing in a ski jacket, emerald, scarlet and white, worn with a white bobble-cap that took away his usual rather priggish look. Their demeanour showed their realisation that, however many tiresome tasks he might dream up for them as a result of their discussion they would be postponed to another day. Whatever went on tonight, at closing time it would be home from the cheerful open fire in the pub's back room through fairytale snow to their cosy beds, where they could sleep the sleep of the intoxicated.

Browne had decided not to invite Hunter. He was supposed to be ill. He could hardly be sent home, less than sober, twice in a week, and though his personal work was very valuable he did tend to inhibit the DCs – except Mitchell of course. Nothing was going to inhibit them at this stage of the evening. Firelight flickered on horse brasses. A cheerful hum came through from the public bar together with a hamper-laden raffle-ticket seller.

Browne looked around him as his men fished for pound coins and chose colours and numbers from books of cloakroom tickets. No Christmas decorations had been put up yet but posters on the walls, advertising seasonal events, were appropriately illustrated so that there was at least a suggestion of robins and holly and carols and cribs.

He had been both amused and proud to find that all four of his regular team had read up something on serial killers. At first they had been reticent, but after the second round, had vied with each other to supply the most theories.

'One per cent of the population is psychopathic, genetically fearless, people users, manipulators, antisocial but clinically sane. They feel no remorse, assume no blame . . . '

'They're often fascinated by police work, sometimes even get involved in the investigation and offer suggestions. They clack beer mugs with off-duty cops.' They pretended to look round for imaginary spies and laughed raucously.

'I still think it's somebody who's sexually frustrated.'

'But neither of our girls has been raped.'

Mitchell banged down his tankard. 'They daren't rape any more. They know all about DNA techniques. They've read up that case in Leicester. If they leave semen behind it can be traced straight back to them.'

Bellamy, probably the soberest apart from Browne, spoke more quietly. 'I don't think, under his compulsion, a psychopath would reason like that.'

In the pause that followed, Jennie Smith's hand went to her mouth.

'Sir, I've just remembered. I talked to a nurse in the second altos today who knows all about Belinda Chance's condition. She's got what's called cervical incompetence, aggravated by a *placenta praevia*, and it's meant no sex for Chance since they found out about it months ago.'

Bellamy had interviewed Chance and considered himself the authority here. He got their attention inadvertently by choking on a mouthful of beer in his anxiety to speak.

'Chance wouldn't need to kill for kicks. He wouldn't even have to rape. He'd be offered it willingly wherever he looked. He's the sort of smoothie who could talk the knickers off a nun!'

Browne blinked. Maybe Bellamy wasn't as sober as he'd thought. Jennie chipped in again, voicing the sad conclusion they'd all reached. 'All this stuff about what serial killers are like isn't much help with people you don't know. You can hardly ask them questions like "Do you practise any obsessional rituals?" or "Do you talk out loud to people who only exist in your mind?" or "Were you extremely cruel to animals or excessively violent with other children?" '

Browne nodded sympathetically. 'True, but you can keep your eyes and ears open and keep on ferreting around, especially among past teachers, school-friends or neighbours. How did you get on with Mellor, Benny? I've skimmed your report but that's all I had time for.'

Mitchell pulled a face. 'He's got to be included. He was a John till he took to his second name when he was fourteen because he was tired of being confused with his father. He's fifty, comes from Worcester Park in Surrey. Moved here months ago to lecture at Bradford University – geology department. I suppose he's been going without it too. His wife had a hysterectomy almost as soon as they arrived and presumably something wrong with the vital parts before that to make the op necessary. He rushed back to wait on her last Wednesday and says he hasn't the faintest idea what he did on November 19th. There's nothing in his diary so he supposes he stayed in and watched TV.'

'Denise wouldn't have gone off with Mellor last Wednesday. She didn't know him.'

'She made a point of being friendly with new members apparently. Didn't he barge into her on the way out and start a conversation?'

'If she did go with him, what was his contact with Alison? Had he met her since he moved to Cloughton?'

Jennie put her hand up like a schoolgirl. 'Stella Smith told me this afternoon. She and Alison were queueing in the library and heard him asking about local choirs. They started chatting and he told them he was nicely settled now and it was time he had some music again. They told him about the Choral and the chamber

128

choir that Sergeant Hunter's in, and the madrigal and light opera groups. Then Alison offered to lend him some tapes to give him an idea of the sort of thing the Choral does – just ones they'd made themselves at rehearsals. I think it was in connection with those Manchester people who are arranging a broadcast. He said he'd call for them and Alison gave him her address.'

Browne pulled a face. 'Not very wise of her. Did you manage to see John Phillips, Richard?'

Dean shook his head. 'No, sir, but he's agreed to see me first thing tomorrow.'

Jennie sighed. 'There's just more and more proof coming in that any of them at all could have done it.'

Browne smiled at her. 'Let's try another angle then. Anyone have any ideas about why the killings should have begun on November 19th?'

They tried to oblige him. 'Someone just out of hospital?'

'Or prison?'

'Or had just suffered a traumatic experience of some kind?'

Browne shrugged. 'Ask away then. I'm curious, too, about the finger-breaking. Does the killer have a hang-up about hands? Is he a sadist, getting at their hands because they both played the flute?'

'Or,' Mitchell wondered, 'is there anything about that particular solo that sets him off?'

'What I want to know is . . . ' They all looked at Dean. 'Where the hell Carson's got to with the DCI's twenty quid. We've all had time to sober up again since he disappeared.'

On cue Carson turned up, bearing his tray on one huge hand, mopping his brow with the other and controlling the door with his enormous boot. Willing hands distributed glasses as a wave of juke-box noise drifted in.

'Thank the Lord for some normal music as background to all this business.' Mitchell buried his nose in beery froth.

The conversation became less general and the men and Jennie talked to their immediate neighbours. Browne sat back, closed his eyes and let it all drift over him. In one corner another copy of Emily Turner's photograph was apparently circulating. 'She's certainly a looker but then young Simmons is quite a prize.'

'Do you think he'll get religion too?'

'That's unfair. You're hardly a religious nut because you're serious-minded enough to break contact with an aunt who's built her whole career on buying and selling dance frocks.'

'Cully says he was amazed how proficient Fielden was when he auditioned. His letter said he hadn't played for years and Cully nearly didn't bother to interview him . . . '

' . . . so we should be asking about who's acted out of character in the last few weeks . . . '

'That's easy. What about Super Bloody Petty?'

'Well, we know why. Three of his concubines sing first soprano.' Raucous laughter.

'Sing baritone you mean.'

'No, that was before they had the op.' More raucous laughter.

'Are you telling us something about bloody Petty?'

Browne roused himself. It was time he sent them all home.

Dean reported in sick the next morning. Browne sympathised with no hard feelings. The drinking session had been his own idea so he'd have to accept the consequences. Phlegmatically, he transferred Dean's session with John Phillips to Mitchell's sheet.

Following the instructions given him by Jocelyn Wade, Mitchell ran John Phillips to earth in a boarding-house in a run-down suburb of Leeds. His room was the attic of a house in the middle of a dilapidated terrace. The atmosphere was not sleazy. Rather, the street had an air of desperate, respectable poverty. The gardens were dark, sodden patches in the December chill but very few were rampant and overgrown and none was a repository for rusting and unwanted prams or bicycles. The door of number 23 was peeling but carefully washed, in earnest of a promise to paint it when time and money allowed.

In Phillips, Mitchell found he had a witness who actually welcomed him. Having placed him in the room's only chair, his host disappeared into a curtained alcove to fetch a coffee tray, leaving him several minutes in which to study his surroundings. The attic was a fair size though the sloping ceiling made it impossible to use the corners for anything but storage space. Phillips had filled them with neatly stacked cardboard cartons. Leaning forward, Mitchell saw that they seemed to be full of scores and sheet music.

A faint smell of fresh paint mingled with that of the coffee. The room's woodwork sparkled white and the existing wallpaper had been painted over in silver grey. It had not been possible to deal similarly with the unfortunate carpet, hideous in its original design and not well treated by generations of previous tenants. Bare floorboards surrounded the carpet, and curtains, even drawn and hanging in folds, still let the light through, and presumably the heat out. Not that there was much heat to lose. Mitchell thought the slight relief from the outside chill might be from heat rising from the rooms below.

A brave attempt had been made to disguise the divan. If Phillips was obliged to use the attic to give lessons to young women it would be unsuitable for it to look like a bedroom. There was one bookcase, old and well polished. Mitchell had no idea what was valuable in music, and books about it, but those in the bookcase looked venerable, expensively bound, well used but well cared for. Cases, presumably containing Phillips' flute and clarinet, lay on a folding card-table. Beneath the window stood an imposing-looking and nicely made desk, not an antique but a good piece of furniture, obviously cherished. On the opposite wall a small modern piano somehow managed to live happily with the rest of the pieces, its stool covered with plain grey fabric that matched the walls.

Phillips reappeared, placed the coffee tray on the corner of the divan and switched on an oil-filled heater. Mitchell saw that he had been deemed worthy of the same creature comforts as Phillips' pupils.

Phillips sat on the bed beside the tray, rocking it but managing not to spill anything and Mitchell watched him as he poured. An unhealthy pallor was his most striking characteristic. His mouse-brown hair was short and neatly cut, his shirt and sweater not in their first youth but clean and tidy. He wore cord jeans of which only the parts that were neither knelt nor sat upon still had velvet ridges, but these too had been carefully washed and pressed.

Mitchell put the man at his ease by inquiring first how he had made the acquaintance of Jocelyn Wade. His face lit up. 'It was

131

at a Leeds Philharmonic concert at the beginning of last winter.' The cultured tones were much at variance with his appearance and surroundings. 'I was with an old friend of mine, also a flautist. We both played with the Hallé at one time and he'd just been taken on by the LSO. He was treating me in the bar as part of his celebration when Joss came in with another girl.

'He offered them a drink too. Joss said she'd nothing to celebrate. She was losing a damned good teacher. Ralph knew I was looking for work and knew I was good so he suggested she considered transferring to me. We arranged to meet and discuss it and I've been teaching her ever since.'

Mitchell dropped three sugar lumps into his coffee. 'What about Denise Kemp and Alison Meredith?'

'They came to me in the same way. Joss told them she was doing well with me, so they both came, together, initially, for a session where I worked out exactly what stage each of them had reached. Actually, next week, Joss is bringing a young man with her. He's a complete beginner but musical and keen on the sound of the instrument. I . . . '

Mitchell cut him short. 'What happened to your job with the Hallé?'

Phillips seemed offended by 'job'. After a reproving silence he stated briefly, 'I gave it up.'

'You weren't happy?'

Phillips considered. 'Yes, I was, reasonably, but I knew I had to see whether I could make it as a solo performer.'

Rashly, Mitchell persisted. 'Did you manage it?'

Phillips shrugged. 'There was nothing doing in England. I was offered a short series of engagements in Europe, nothing very high-powered. My wife thought I was crazy and refused to go with me. Imogen thought playing a flute was a funny sort of job for a man anyway, and she absolutely refused to countenance throwing up her own regular income to trek across Europe living out of a suitcase and with no promise of security at the end of it.

'Mummy being defunct, she had to go home to Daddy – the only slightly original act she ever performed.' He slammed his cup down on his saucer. 'As it happened she was proved quite right, wasn't she?'

Mitchell thought he'd better change the subject. 'So Joss, Denise and Alison have been coming here for lessons for the last few months?'

He shook his head. 'These premises aren't very suitable. I have a car.'

'What kind?'

'A Mini, A-reg, red where it isn't rusty. I taught Denise and Alison at their homes, both on Thursdays, Alison first.'

'What was your impression of them?'

'As performers?'

'If you like.'

Phillips put the tray on the floor, kicked off his shoes and lay on the bed, staring at the ceiling. 'Alison played like a computer – good technique, everything right but no soul. Denise played much more sensitively. She loved the instrument and the sounds she could make with it. I considered she had the potential to be useful as an orchestral player . . . '

Phillips had shut his eyes and Mitchell raised his voice to command attention. 'When did you see each of them last?'

The answer came promptly enough. 'I saw Alison at her lesson, over three weeks ago now. I knew she'd miss two weeks because of her course. I went to her flat this week and found a policeman there, keeping me out. It was a shock, although I'd known about Denise from the television news. Denise had cancelled her lesson last week because Stuart was away. She flattered herself 'if she thought she wasn't safe with me, but it's more likely she was giving the neighbours no cause for gossip.'

Mitchell begged for more coffee, chiefly so that Phillips would have to sit up again and look at him. As his host poured lukewarm dregs, Mitchell demanded an account of his movements on December 4th.

'I was here at six, teaching Joss. At seven I gave her a lift to Cloughton so that she'd get to choir practice in time. She's well worth the trouble. She's brought me in a good number of pupils. I owed her a few favours.'

'Why didn't you do the Cloughton trip earlier and teach her at home?'

'Because her grandmother lives near by. Thursday is Joss's half-day. She comes over during the afternoon most weeks and has tea with the old lady, checks that she's all right, then comes on here at six. It sets Joss's mind at rest but gives her an excuse to get away from the interminable gossip.'

Mitchell nodded. 'I see. Was this the pattern for the nineteenth as well?'

'As far as I can remember. You could check with Joss.' They were both silent for a moment, then Phillips offered, tentatively, 'I'm very sorry about the girls. Not just because I've lost two regular pupils, but personally too. Denise, in particular, I liked very much.' There was another silence. Feeling that more was forthcoming, Mitchell let it continue until Phillips remarked, 'Bed-sit life is pretty lonely, Sergeant.'

'Only acting sergeant, I'm afraid.' Phillips smiled.

'Sergeant, acting sergeant – it's all the same. Your face obviously fits.'

Still Mitchell left the initiative with his host.

'I suppose you don't fancy a few jars at my local with your lunch?'

Mitchell nodded, turned up the collar of the leather jacket he had not removed, and followed Phillips downstairs.

Chapter 14

Browne accepted Mitchell's report with raised eyebrows, inviting comment. Mitchell pulled up a chair and obliged. Briefly he summarised his morning's interview and his lunchtime drinking.

'It seemed a bit fishy sir, especially after what was said last night about matey wanting to hobnob with the police and keep a check on how we're getting on. He was a bit too hospitable as well – wanted to buy all the drinks.'

Browne grinned. 'Can't be bad. What did he have to say for himself when he'd got 'em in?'

Mitchell considered. 'Well, he asked a lot of questions. He tried hard to make them sound general and casual, as if he was just making polite conversation. You know, things like how, in a fingertip search, do we know what to seal up in little bags and what to leave. But then he pressed for details of what we'd actually found. Then he asked if I found it depressing, knowing that nearly three weeks have gone by since Alison was killed without us getting any further. Then he asked if we actually were further on than the papers say. He wanted to know if the girls' injuries revealed anything about the killer – oh, and he asked if there was any way he could help us. I said he seemed to know an awful lot about our methods and he laughed and said he once had a policeman in the family.'

Mitchell reached for his report, found the place and read from it.

' "No, he isn't defunct. It's just that I don't belong to the family any more." '

Browne pursed his lips.

'Well, well. So what do you want to do about him now?'

135

Mitchell's answer was ready.

'Go back to the computer, sir, to see if we've got anything on him. This diving off to Europe sounds a bit odd, unspecific anyway. I just wondered if it might be a small area of Europe known as Armley or Strangeways, and what exactly he'd done to be invited to perform there.'

Browne grinned.

'Right, get on with it then.'

Mitchell rose to go but paused in the doorway.

'By the way, sir, I've suggested to Joss that she gives her lessons a miss for a while.'

'Quite.'

Browne's expression was quizzical. As Mitchell's footsteps echoed in the corridor outside, he reached out for the report and began to read with his usual concentration.

A lengthy court appearance prevented Mitchell from checking his suspicions about Phillips until late on Tuesday afternoon. He attended it grudgingly, marvelling as he remembered the pride and excitement that his first few opportunities to offer evidence there had afforded him. What the computer revealed to him when he managed to consult it renewed his excitement and restored his good humour. He made copious notes which he was clutching when he arrived ten minutes early for Browne's Wednesday morning briefing. Maddeningly, Browne continued with his own paperwork, refusing to let Mitchell speak until the complete team was assembled. Then he relented and allowed his new sergeant to open the proceedings.

Mitchell described his extended interview in a few sentences, then moved on to his latest findings, needing no reference to the scribbled sheets in his hands.

'I was right. He has been inside, in Armley. John Phillips is what he's calling himself now but his real name is Jonathan Philpott. He did actually play with the Hallé but there was no concert tour, high powered or otherwise.'

Dean felt Mitchell was making too much of a meal of what should have been his own interview and report. 'So what was he sent down for?'

136

Mitchell considered a dramatic pause but Dean's expression warned him against it. 'Attacking his wife, Imogen, for one thing. There was a charge of attempted murder but they couldn't make it stick. Also for rape and assault of one Jacqueline Jennings. There were a couple of other incidents in the area at the time, women grabbed round the neck, but neither of them was seriously harmed and neither made a positive identification.'

They considered this information in silence. Bellamy was the first to break it.

'Any broken fingers?'

Mitchell shook his head. 'Not on record. No letters either, as far as I could find out.'

'Sir . . . ' Jennie hesitated then plucked up courage. 'Do you think we might be giving undue significance to the letters? Couldn't they just be a coincidence?'

Carson, who seemed to have attached himself to Browne's usual coterie, lent Jennie his support. 'Bodies are always turning up, sir. Couldn't we have a joker who's counting on his letters being thought to have a connection with the next one found?'

Browne shook his head firmly. 'No, the timing of them means they're definitely relevant to this case.' He picked up the sheets of paper lying on his desk. 'I want to swap a few ideas on what we've picked up about the early years of these various people. These are the specimens of their schoolboy handwriting you managed to collect, photocopies of course. The genuine articles have gone to the lab for comparison.' There was silence for a few moments as they perused the papers.

'They all look like the writing in the John letters to me,' Dean said, gloomily, passing on the last of them.

'Little boy, big imagination,' said Jennie, handing Browne a masterpiece by the youthful Simmons entitled 'The Best Day of the Holidays'. 'We had just got home from Paris,' it began, 'and we disided to have tea on the terrus, looking out on the lawns and flowers. My mum made pancakes because my freind Paul was there. He said he wished he had a model railway like mine . . . '

Chance's effort was much more mature. 'He was right,' Bellamy explained, 'about his demolished junior school. The nearest I got to it was seeing where it used to be on an oldish map in the library. Then his grammar school could only dig out that one account. They have a folder in the library in which they keep any pupils' original work that they consider worth preserving. Chance managed it the once but he was fifteen by then so it's not much use to us. QEGS considered him a model pupil.

'I got a different reaction when I asked about Searle. Only one teacher had been there long enough to remember him and he said they couldn't get rid of his scruffy work soon enough. It's a good job he wrote on the back of his photograph. Apparently he behaved fairly well in a negative sort of way. He was always the twelfth man or reserve in the school teams. He was considered very musical and was in the choir and the school band but he let them down once or twice. His parents were very pro-school, this chap said. They seemed to find him a disappointment.'

'Poor lad.' They looked at Jennie in surprise.

'Pushed into fulfilling his parents' ambitions for him. Perhaps he'd have worked with more enthusiasm if he'd been left to choose his own activities.'

'Cully doesn't think so,' Browne told her.

'Did you find any early works of promise by Fielden, Benny?'

Mitchell indicated the sheet that had been his contribution to the collection. 'Just that. Every class at Fielden's school kept a log-book, a sort of diary. They still do it now. Each child in the class writes up a day in turn. They've got them going back into the Dark Ages and they let me look at them. Some entries are hilarious. No one at the school now remembers Fielden as an actual boy but one of his entries in the log-book is a school legend. He'd played the piano in the end of term concert on the day it was his turn. He described his piece, then wrote, "Mr Sugden" – that was the headmaster – "didn't listen. I could hear him talking while my recital was going on." His teacher wanted to strike this out but the head, to his credit, insisted that this record of his bad manners must stand, and apologised to the lad for good measure.'

Browne chuckled. 'I like "my recital". Does Fielden take himself just as seriously now, would you say?'

Mitchell thought about it then nodded. 'Yes, I would.'

Browne glanced at his watch and brought the discussion to a close with the distribution of yet more action sheets.

As he reached the door, Dean asked, 'What was the name of the young woman John Phillips raped?'

'Jacqueline Jennings.' Dean nodded.

'Fielden's wife is called Jacqueline.'

'So? It's a common enough name.'

A little less common, Browne mused, when they had left, was the name Imogen. And that was the name of Superintendent Petty's daughter, now returned to her father's house after an unhappy and short marriage somewhere in Leeds.

Browne's thoughts moved forward to the Choral Society's rehearsal that night. He intended to address the choir as a body at the end on the subjects of taking unnecessary risks and of their responsibility to tell the police everything they knew. He hadn't the manpower to escort all the women home, even in groups, but he had arranged for a discreet watch to be kept on the vehicles of the people they were specially interested in. He added a rusty red Mini to this list and wrote out an action sheet for Carson. He could spend tonight up on the Leeds road, stopping motorists and asking which of them had noticed the same red Mini travelling to or from Cloughton a week ago.

Seven twenty-five found Fielden halfway through his customary pre-rehearsal procedure, cuffs turned back once, metronome, notebook, pencil and music more or less in their appointed places. He moved the notebook half an inch, leaned sideways to arrange his coat in folds more to his liking, then glanced at Cully, giving the signal that he was ready.

Cully sat as usual on his high stool, feet hooked behind its ledges, looking totally relaxed and unaffected by the silent tension around him. He was pleased with the display of solidarity before him. Only the seven women who had notified him seemed to be missing. The rest sat waiting, some from time to time glancing nervously up to their escorts in the narrow side balconies, glad of but made awkward by their presence. Every so often, someone had ventured a comment and a wave of embarrassed giggles passed along the row. As the hand on the electric clock to his left juddered the last half minute to seven thirty, Cully stood to begin the usual routine of scale singing. Force of habit had its part, but

139

the force of his personality in restoring the atmosphere of a normal rehearsal was paramount.

Mellor was prepared for scales this week but discovered they were not a repetition of what he'd heard before. This time they were in D major, he thought, and were sung in unison on different vowel sounds. He asked himself how, given only Fielden's opening chord, everyone knew how to proceed. He had obtained his copies and done his homework during the week, knowing that Cully would be aware of any disasters he caused, and that the men on either side of him, whilst not exactly hoping he would make mistakes, were certainly listening out in case he did. The one on his left swayed to the beat, almost as though he were disco dancing. His right-hand neighbour had a forward stance, like a long-distance runner waiting for the starting gun. They put him off equally.

He noticed that last week's hanging flake of paint had descended from the ceiling and another was beginning to detach itself. Looking, unseeing, at the patch of bare ceiling, he reflected on the grilling he had received from DS Mitchell on Monday morning. How had the police found out about that trouble at school? What else had they discovered about him to spring on him later? Jean was depressed already. If she found out about all this she'd be unbearable. It wouldn't do the kids any good either.

The singing stopped. The basses had displeased Cully in some way. Mellor prayed that he was not the offender.

'The bottom of page five is quite sufficiently intricate without the bottom line composing. Sing it by yourselves from letter C but listen first.'

Fielden hammered out the correct version of the offending bars, then, with both hands, played the four parts together, with the bass line emphasised. As the basses tried it, Cully smiled ironically. 'Yes, I thought there was a game of musical Blind Man's Buff going on down there. The trouble's in bar eighty. Listen again.'

After a couple of minutes, Cully was satisfied. The disco dancer whispered to Mellor, 'Sing that bit looking my way. You got it and I can't get the hang of it.' Mellor glowed and obliged. He began to relax slightly.

Searle smiled as Cully removed the scarf which until now he'd left tucked into his open-necked tartan shirt. Stripping was going to take their leader longer tonight. He'd heard Chance apologising because he'd forgotten to switch on the heating till it was almost too late.

Cully's meticulous criticism was irksome to Searle. He'd come for the exhilaration of romping through the pieces they now knew fairly well. It was not in his nature to make himself concentrate and he let his eye travel idly along the backs of the heads of the rows in front. The ends of half of Pamela's lank wisps draggled over her collar and the other half seemed to be gummed to her neck. Next came Stella's sculpted coif that didn't look as if it consisted of separate hairs at all, then Jill Perry's blonde thatch and Donna's close curly crop that reminded him of his grand-mother's chenille tablecloth, which was almost the same gingery tobacco colour. At the end came the white floss of that second alto, mussed up to try to hide the sebaceous cyst that drew his eye till, revolted, he forced himself to look away. He wondered if one of them would die tonight.

Now the tenors had offended, though Searle knew that he himself was blameless. Cully regarded them sternly. 'This is the piece we've been rehearsing, you know! What really needles me is the smile that goes round when you've got it wrong. I wouldn't mind if it was a smile of embarrassment.' Searle knew that the tenors were seldom dealt with too severely. They were the small-est section and the most difficult to recruit. 'Before you steal a breath you strike the note before a resounding blow – a curious part of the English Choral tradition.'

To Searle's satisfaction, he suddenly relented and allowed the choir to sing the piece straight through.

'Off we go. Good luck! I'll see you at the end.'

Chance, too, enjoyed a good 'sing through', though at first his pleasure was not so great that he failed to be critical and he noticed the thin sound every time they hit an accidental as some of the section ducked out of singing it. They finished the short unison passage that threw into relief the magic weaving of the strands of harmony that followed. The sound rose round him and suddenly overwhelmed him. It was like the moment, he thought, when you stop drinking wine for its taste and intoxication takes over. He watched Jake in the row below and marvelled at the refining quality of the activity that caused this talented but silly and self-absorbed man to lose himself and participate totally.

The piece drew to a close and Cully regarded them solemnly. 'Years ago I conducted this piece with another choir and they made the same mistakes as you're doing.'

'They had the same conductor!' was the immediate response. Cully grinned and gave them a break, inviting Chance to give the notices. Chance strode to the front and stood for a minute with his back to them reading what was on the wall. Then he raised a laugh by exonerating all the choir committee of any blame for the recipes for 'low-calorie Christmas goodies'. 'Either the well women or the slimmers want us to believe that when we've tasted *fromage frais* we'll prefer it to cream. May their desperate efforts to convince themselves be successful!'

Cully blessed him for the light relief and tilted his stool back against the wall, willing the tension to drain out of him.

In the side balcony, on his narrow wooden bench, Hunter was uncomfortable but well entertained. He realised with astonishment that, until this pause in their efforts, the choir had totally forgotten the circumstances in which the rehearsal was being held. The music had been all, and now Chance was holding their willing attention quite effortlessly as he dealt with the sale of concert tickets, the 'right' kind of publicity and the suggested choral contributions to Denise's and Alison's funerals at whatever point the police allowed those ceremonies to take place.

After five minutes or so Chance gave place to Cully once more. Hunter was glad to see the director held the pink copy of 'In Praise of Mary'. The work was new to him and he listened with interest. 'I'll just remind you of a few things and then we'd better try it through. Can you cope, Jocelyn?' Hunter saw the auburn head of his charge nod confidently.

'Right then. "Hail Mary, full of grace." The words tell you to shout but the accompaniment tells you the singing must be restrained – full of awe, not patronising her. Last week the angelic chorus sounded like a shaky rendering of the "Volga Boat Song"! The music builds up an atmosphere. The voices mustn't dissipate it. The drums will suggest importance, the strings will suggest mystery. "Hail" is a greeting but muted, showing respect not a shout from the rabble.

'And, for pity's sake, let's have everyone singing "All was for an apple" in section four. I've noticed the fun you've had, substituting various different fruits and veg. I can only conclude that such infantile humour taken up by such a surprising number of otherwise sensible people is due to a dose of Christmas hysteria.'

The first section was embarked on and Cully was sufficiently satisfied to let it continue to the end. Hunter liked it. It had unexpected intervals and a harmony that wasn't sweet but never quite became discord. The sound produced was remote, cool, academic and yet not unemotional. They proceeded to section two and Hunter listened, curious, as Jocelyn rose to sing her first solo lines. The voice was adequate rather than inspiring, but then, Hunter conceded, the girl was Cully's third choice, and nervous and under-rehearsed at that.

'There is no rose of such virtue . . . ' Hunter thought the very modern-sounding setting of the ancient stanzas was probably more fun to sing than to listen to. Still Cully allowed the choir to continue, unreproved. With the unconventional figures of the third section Hunter began to warm to the work. The soprano solo led. 'A maid peerless hath borne God's son': and the choir echoed in wonderment: There was menace in the underlying rhythmic chords that the melody took no account of. The fourth section, a setting of 'Adam Lay y-Bounden', was dramatic and energetic with a hint of humour, the 'Deo Gratias' much repeated.

At this point, Cully could contain himself no longer and glared at them over his tapping baton. 'Your "gratias" is too obsequious. You sound like an over-tipped Spanish waiter.' They grinned. 'And sopranos!' (Did the sections really offend in turn, Hunter asked himself, or was it just that Cully wished to be seen to be fair?) 'Think about the words. Colour it in. It sounds like a black and white drawing!'

The sopranos looked puzzled. Cully tried again. 'Smile into the notes; sing as though you're spinning a web.' He raised his eyes

143

to the ceiling as they attempted to obey. 'Mm, it sounds very French – slightly out of time, slightly out of tune!'

They were getting tired. Some of them looked offended. He let them go on. The last section appealed to Hunter least. There seemed a lot of palaver musically for the simplicity of the words, though the magic returned for the final, ethereal 'Alleluia'. It was a strange piece, Hunter decided, something and nothing, just less than a quarter of an hour long, not an oratorio the choir could get its teeth into but with more body than even a lengthy single piece. He shook himself suddenly. He wasn't here for a diverting musical experience.

He let his eye travel over the women and girls in the rows below him and wondered whether his colleagues had taken all the measures open to them to get all these women safely home. There had been advice and warnings about travelling together to which the *Clarion*, in its usual obliging manner, had given prominence. Maybe attention from the press and the excitement of the police investigation had stimulated the killer and he would strike again tonight. He looked to each side of him along the balcony at the other 'minders'. There seemed to be a good number of them but how could the police, or, for that matter, the girls, be sure that the killer was not amongst them?

Suddenly Hunter smiled at their glum faces and was convinced that all the ones in sight were genuine. They had found nothing whatsoever to enjoy in the evening's activities and had attended merely to assure themselves of the safety of someone dear to them. Though he was very much on the fringe of this case and would have found it difficult to justify his view objectively, Hunter was convinced that the man they sought was some kind of musician.

Chapter 15

John had been glad when the choir gathering in the pub had broken up early. None of them had felt any more enthusiasm for a convivial get-together than he had himself. They'd only been showing the flag. The atmosphere had been different tonight, partly because the more timorous of the regulars had fled home as soon as they were released, whilst the escorts of the braver spirits had introduced some new blood.

He knew that none of them had been particularly pleased when he joined them. None of them really liked him. It was strange, when he felt such contempt for most of them, that he should feel a sort of desolation at not being one of them. They were polite to him, of course, even, from time to time, made much of him, consulted him, but they'd never accepted him into their easy fellowship.

Not that that was where he wanted to be. He didn't need the likes of them. One or two of the escorts looked more interesting. He wondered if that uncle of Jocelyn Wade's would end up by becoming a member. With his kind of speaking voice it seemed likely he'd have a natural tenor though probably not a strong one. He'd said very little but he'd talked intelligently about tonight's music. He must have felt the odd one out, up on that balcony.

Fumbling his key in the lock, he suddenly became aware of his frozen fingers and the general chill around him. He switched on the fire before filling the kettle and stretched his hands towards the warmth as he waited for the water to boil. He hung up his coat in the hall cupboard and stood sideways before the mirror considering the slight bulge of his stomach. He'd better increase the number of sit-ups he did before he went to bed. Maybe his trousers weren't the right cut. She'd bought his clothes when other people his age were learning what suited them.

On a wave of fear he realised that he didn't know what was right for him because he didn't know anything about himself. He wished he could explain it to somebody who wouldn't think he was mad. By average standards he'd had his successes but he couldn't enjoy them because, as a person, as his own self, he wasn't really there. He couldn't make friends with anyone because although he could get to know them he couldn't reveal himself to them. There was nothing there to show them. Nothing he ever achieved was enough to make him feel real. At one time he'd tried to get into religion but he'd been unable to feel any shame, any real need of forgiveness. His sins didn't have enough substance. It wasn't that he felt there was no God to hear him. It was as though he wasn't there for God to talk to.

Tonight, it had amused him for a short time to join in the speculations about his own possible identity and probable next move. How stupid they were to be puzzled about why police activity seemed to be concentrated on people called John. Surely anyone with a grain of sense could work it out for himself.

His smile widened. Two policemen now had apologised to him, sympathised, though not sincerely, because it was unpleasant to be questioned. They were quite wrong. He enjoyed talking about himself. He always had. He liked being interviewed – by sixth-form masters, for jobs, by the police. It didn't matter. He had achieved plenty to impress them with.

The kettle switched off and he went through to make tea, bringing his mug back to the chair by the fire. Placing it on the chair arm and being careful not to knock it over, he reached under the seat cushion for the two additional newspapers he had been buying recently. He was annoyed that the *Guardian* had removed him from the front page and even the *Yorkshire Post* had omitted the case from its headlines and relegated it to the lower half of page one.

The *Clarion* still gave the case its proper prominence, though only on the day Alison's body was discovered had he had the whole front page to himself. Today he shared it with trivialities that seemed to emphasise his importance, so that he didn't resent them. 'Water demand falls'. 'By-election date'. 'Fight to control building blaze'. This looked slightly more significant. 'Sixty-five fire fighters battled for more than six hours . . . a blaze which ripped through a Cloughton warehouse . . . within minutes flames had engulfed the building . . . '

What a lot of emotive language wasted on a few rolls of carpet! John remembered the day he'd set fire to the school caretaker's house. The spiteful old crone had stood talking to his mother in the playground. 'A loner', she'd called him, and his music a 'girlish hobby'! He felt the blinding rage that had taken him over. His revenge had achieved nothing. The house hadn't burnt down and the woman hadn't been hurt at all, though it had been some comfort that that braggart, Peter Clifton, who called him a tinner, had been chief suspect.

John perused today's report. It included a serious warning to all women, choir members in particular, not to go out alone, especially after dark. It was going to need careful planning to get the next one on her own. He went through to the kitchen again to collect some biscuits and refill his mug before he resumed his reading. Had Denise really been twenty-six years old? She hadn't looked it.

He was sorry the cat wouldn't eat. He liked cats. Why did her stupid husband tell the reporter that? John felt a wave of resentment against Stuart Kemp. He'd no right to try to blame the cat's suffering on him. Who on earth was interested in the clothes Alison was wearing when she was found? Only the vain woman herself would have cared what she was tarted up in. Trying to whip up his anger against Alison didn't distract him from the cat. It worried him.

In a way, he welcomed the worry. He remembered experiencing similar feelings as he'd watched a newsreel that had shown a bewildered and defeated cormorant trudging along a Kuwaiti beach covered in Gulf oil spilled from deliberately fractured oil refinery pipes. He'd thanked God for the pity he could still feel. He felt panic rising. He mustn't think about war in the Middle East. He'd think about God instead.

As a child he'd had a fixed and definite picture of God, as a stunted and slight old man, wearing a black skullcap and cloak and

147

having the colourless complexion and very thin skin of extreme old age. He'd pictured veined white hands, almost waxen but with no suggestion of impending decay. This figment of his imagination had a mild demeanour and a serious, long-suffering expression. He shuddered as he realised he knew better than that now.

Sometimes he'd taken a pillow into the bathroom and punched and bitten it to ease his panic and frustration, but since he'd first thought about killing Alison he hadn't found release in that any more. He knew God was going to punish him. Forgiveness was for other people. It wouldn't be any use explaining why he'd been right to steal.

He remembered the almost-tenderness he'd felt each Friday night when his father had handed him his pocket-money, a tiny fraction of his hard-earned small income, and the angry resentment with which he'd agreed to let his spendthrift mother 'borrow' it. He'd never told his father because by then he'd acquired his mother's dread of a scene, plain speaking, raised voices, 'unpleasantness'.

An uncle had once given him sixpence to buy an ice cream. When he'd queued at the cart he'd found that sixpenny cornets were the cheapest there were. He'd worried for the rest of the afternoon that his mother would condemn his greediness because he'd offered his uncle no change.

The obligation to bring credit on his mother had caused him unbearable tension. He'd been pushed forward to perform for her, pulled back at every show of initiative, until he'd gone round in circles, biddable but chock-full of anger, bewilderment, self-pity and fear. It hadn't been fear of his mother herself, but of realising that he couldn't function without her. She'd fought his battles by keeping him out of them.

'*Don't do that. You might hurt yourself.*'

If he hurt himself the world would come to an end. Most activities might hurt you so you didn't do them. You didn't leap from one stone to the next. You didn't run, or unfasten the gate, or try to climb the stairs. And he was still afraid. He understood how he'd been hobbled but he couldn't untie the bonds. They were invisible, woven from the forbiddings that went back before memory started. He'd heard about people who bring out the worst in others. What about people who shut in the best?

John wished he could believe his mother had meant to harm him, then he could hate her without those inhibiting overtones of pity and half-understanding. She'd told him about her own early life, exploited by parents and brothers who thought she was their chattel. He wondered how much of what she'd told him was true. He supposed she saw him as her own compensating possession, an extension of herself through which she could have another chance. He was sorry for her, but she'd stolen his boyhood, ruined his career, taken away his purpose in life with one stupid, misguided act of cruelty.

If he could have hated without guilt he might have killed her but he could have left the girls alone. He was doing what she'd done but at least he finished his victims off. He didn't leave them eaten away inside by a wasted genius. He could perhaps have lived with the injury she'd done him if only she'd loved him. She wasn't capable of love or any other emotion and now he couldn't feel anything either, except this frightening, cold paralysis, this aching disappointment with everything, this futility.

As he drove to the station on Thursday morning, Mitchell too was feeling frustrated and depressed, though his sufferings were of a less profound and more temporary nature. He had hoped they would be well on with the case by now, leaving him free to spend his off-duty hours during her Christmas vac with Ginny. The garish ornaments strung across the main streets above him emphasised rather than dispelled his gloom. His spirits fell still further when Browne began the morning briefing by telling them that the infant daughter of the couple whose car had collided with Jill Perry's had died during the night. There was some brief discussion about measures to protect Miss Perry which were abandoned as Browne reviewed his manpower.

The eagerly awaited report from the documents section had arrived but disappointed them with its frequently reiterated 'shows some similarity to' and 'may be consistent with'. In layman's terms it amounted to the two conclusions that the two letters might or might not have been written by an adult reverting back to childhood attitudes, and that the writing of all children taught by the same junior-school system has many common features. None of the carefully collected specimens of the early calligraphy of their suspects had been eliminated by comparison with the letters the police had received. As a small consolation the report stated that the edges of both letters were slightly sticky with caramelised sugar, whilst one of them also bore traces of the rosin used to increase the friction on violin strings.

Dean heaved a deep sigh. 'Now all we need to do is reinterview all eighty-seven of them to check who plays the fiddle and then try to find out which of those rewards himself with a toffee apple when he's finished practising.'

The dispirited team had few constructive suggestions to offer and sensing their mood, Browne dispatched them to their various tasks. Mitchell's first mission was to visit Alison's relations who had been inquiring how soon they might be allowed to make funeral arrangements. The general public had little idea of the time-consuming examination and analyses that might lead the police to track down their murderer. Mitchell was to enlarge on these in a general way, although he knew that the two or three weeks which had elapsed were sufficient for virtually every kind of photograph and sample to be taken. He decided not to enlarge on the offer that would have to be made to the defence, once a charge had been made, of a second post-mortem if they required it. His commission was not a cheerful one, and when Mitchell noticed Cully in the bus queue outside the building society he stopped to offer him a lift. Any choir member's chance remark might offer a clue and any company in Mitchell's present mood was better than his own.

Cully's car had been booked into his garage for a service the previous day. 'It ailed,' Cully informed him, mournfully, 'even more seriously than I feared, so the mechanic's ministrations were not completed when I called for it. I'm hoping to collect it later this morning when I've finished my shopping. How's the case progressing, or shouldn't I ask? I suppose that crowd in the balcony last night included a few of your chaps?' He paused, hopefully.

'We're doing what we feel is necessary, Mr Cully.' Mitchell was shocked at the stuffy tone of his reply. He was beginning to sound like the stuffed-shirt Hunter. Maybe that's what happened to sergeants. Out of the corner of his eye he watched Cully scrabbling in a tatty wallet with its stitching undone. 'Lost something?'

Cully grinned. 'I'm lucky I haven't lost everything. I hope someone produces a new wallet as my Christmas present. Ah!' He extracted a pink ticket and transferred it to his top pocket. 'Had my DJ cleaned for the concert. I'd have had to conduct in a dress-shirt and a denim jacket if I'd lost this.'

A dog darted in front of them and Mitchell braked sharply, causing flaps of leather and dog-eared papers to cascade to the floor. Cully was still grovelling round his feet, retrieving his possessions, when Mitchell drew up outside the cleaners. Before catapulting himself from the car to the shop, he shook his head ruefully. 'You know, we're all beginning to behave as though having a murderer picking off choir sopranos was a temporary inconvenience like the bad weather. What on earth does it matter what I wear?'

The list of instructions on his action sheet complied with, Mitchell felt the need for a substantial lunch and Virginia's company. He drove round to the Brownes' house, found her in and picked her up, feeling that the day was improving. Spruce and trim, she climbed into the car and looked around her with distaste.

'Benny, this car's a disgusting mess!'

Mitchell was indignant. 'I've got to have my duffel and wellies at the ready. It's bad enough having to put them on and take them off all the time without having to lock and unlock the boot as well.'

'Fair enough, but you needn't leave tatty bits of paper all over the floor.'

Mitchell looked at the piece she had retrieved from under her seat. On one side was a child's drawing in wax crayon. Turning it over he saw pencilled rows of boxes containing initials. 'Oh, Cully must have dropped that. I've just given him a lift.'

'Who's Cully?'

Mitchell grinned. 'He's an amiable lunatic who thinks anyone without perfect pitch is mentally handicapped.'

Virginia's nose wrinkled. 'What's perfect pitch?'

'Ah, you see, you're not the only one who's being educated. Apparently, it's the ability to know whether a note is middle C or not without checking on the piano.'

Virginia shrugged. 'Never mind, I'll live with my handicap.'

She sounded like a golfer, Mitchell thought. He dropped the paper into the pocket on his door and turned left towards the town centre instead of right towards the Fleece. 'The Lord knows when I'll be free to have the next meal with you. Let's be extravagant.'

He couldn't quite put his finger on what had gone wrong between them in the last week or two but good food and wine would supply the right atmosphere in which to put it right. Twenty minutes later he was less sure. Virginia had laughed at the lush decor and the self-important obsequiousness of the waiter. She was, however, in the intervals when she wasn't doing valiant battle with duck and orange sauce, making an effort to keep the conversation flowing.

She tried to interest him in a study of the Scottish Chaucerians which her tutor had set as a joint project for her and a fellow student. 'Piers took a year out after leaving school and spent the whole of it just reading so really he's providing the information and I'm just tagging along and doing the writing up.'

'Piers!' Virginia could hear the anxiety in his mockery. 'I suppose his surname is treble-barrelled.'

She disposed of another forkful of duckling. 'Believe it or not, it's Potter.'

By the time Mitchell had established where he came from, how clever he was, how well she knew him and where she'd been with him, Virginia was beginning to diagnose a guilty conscience and to develop a healthy resentment of the catechism she was being subjected to. The expensive food was being chewed angrily and swallowed, untasted, by both of them. He might as well have bought her fish and chips – or better still not seen her at all. Things had definitely deteriorated between them. By the time the dessert arrived they were eating in stony silence. Mitchell wondered how, even if, they would survive eight more terms.

Finally, Virginia drained her glass and stood up. 'Benny, you want me to say I'm having a fling with Piers, don't you? I don't

152

know why and I don't want to know, but, anyway, I'm not.' Not really wanting to walk out on him, she sat down again, awkwardly. 'I'm not going to spend the next half-hour telling you he means nothing to me and you mean everything. You've never needed your confidence boosted.' She raised her hand to indicate the Victorian hoop of opals. 'I wouldn't be wearing this if you did. I don't see that as my role in life. You aren't afraid that I'll prefer somebody else. What I suspect is that you want permission to amuse yourself without recriminations when I'm away. At least Piers can buy me a drink without putting me through an inquisition about you.'

When Mitchell delivered her back home the weight on his mind was in direct proportion to the lightness of his pocket.

Chapter 16

One rehearsal down, Browne mused, and one and a concert to go. Between the two rehearsals the investigation, with its checking and cross-checking, continued. No new lines of inquiry opened up; the house-to-house questioning spread wider, made more discouraging by persistent freezing fog that reduced visibility to a couple of feet. Other people's Christmas festivities, usually justified as 'for the children' seemed irrelevant and unfeeling. The team's mood was bleak as nothing transpired to help them.

Reports were studied for the third and fourth time and anxiety mounted as the rehearsal scheduled for the seventeenth approached. A fortnight had separated the first two murders and now a second fortnight was almost completed. Sometimes Browne almost hoped for a third killing that would supply some fresh evidence. On the Saturday morning he decided to take a half-day break, buy his Christmas presents, and clear his head. If anything came of his team's relentless questioning he could be contacted easily enough.

The weekend passed peacefully, too much so for the officers, anxious for progress. Resentful of his CI's dereliction of duty on Saturday, Mitchell decided to take his own break on Sunday afternoon and invited Virginia for a tramp on the hills that surrounded the town. They'd leave the car in the pub park and if the walk went better than the lunch had done, they'd drop in for a drink and a bite to eat when they came down.

Since Ginny had objected to it on her last ride the condition of the car had deteriorated. After an attempt to bribe his sister, which proved a non-starter, Mitchell washed the bodywork, then attacked the interior himself with his mother's vacuum-cleaner plugged into his father's extension lead. Clearing out the larger pieces of rubbish he came upon Cully's paper with its pencilled diagram and wondered whether it was important. He'd better phone.

Cully was voluble. It was, he explained, a concert seating plan, each rectangle a seat, each set of initials a person.

'How very regimented. Is it to stop them chatting to their friends?'

Cully became still more animated. It was all to do with the balance of sound in a particular acoustic. Mitchell cut through a detailed explanation with an offer to deliver the paper but Cully refused. 'It was only the first rough draft I made in the pub a couple of weeks ago. I've got a neater copy here somewhere and in any case I might alter it when we rehearse in the hall itself. Thanks all the same.'

About to dispatch the diagram, with its backing of lurid purple wax crayon, to the wastebin, Mitchell paused and looked at it again. The paper was coarse textured, with flakes of glue along one edge indicating that it had been torn from a pad. He felt a growing excitement as he slipped it into a clean envelope and set off once more for the Browne household. He had rehearsed various remarks with which to greet his fiancée at their next significant meeting. What he actually said, when she opened the door to him, was, 'I must speak to your father.'

It was unplanned but it got him conveniently over an awkward moment. Browne however was not in.

'He's nipped over to France,' Virginia told him. 'Something to do with double checking an alibi.'

Mitchell put his envelope carefully away and enjoyed an invigorating and restorative afternoon.

When Mitchell reported for duty on Monday morning Browne had still not returned and Superintendent Petty was conducting his briefing in a less than jovial mood. Mitchell was reluctant to relinquish his scrap of paper to a superior known to be less scrupulous than Browne about according due credit to his junior officers for their part in any successes the team might achieve. He decided, knowing there would be wrath to come, to dispatch his evidence to the documents section himself. He filled in and signed the accompanying forms in triplicate, smiling to himself as he taped them to the plastic bag. When he was promoted and such tasks were routine they would become irksome but today signing his forms three times over made him feel pleasantly important and added to the satisfaction with which he looked back on a Sunday afternoon with Ginny that had been just like old times.

The feeling lasted just over an hour. Browne was back in his office by mid-morning and summoned his temporary sergeant to enjoy a cup of coffee and to hear about the CI's Sunday exploits. As a polite preliminary he inquired into Mitchell's own weekend progress and was not pleased with what he heard. 'You take too much on yourself, Benny. I've had to speak to you before about exactly the same thing.'

Mitchell was incensed. 'But, sir —'

Browne dismissed the protest with a wave of his hand. 'I don't deny it was urgent. Superintendent Petty was in the station all day yesterday to deal with matters that were urgent.'

Mitchell's face registered his opinion of Superintendent Petty. Browne, who had a few minutes before been treated to the rough side of Petty's tongue, dismissed his sergeant before he let his sympathy show. Petty had ,reacted badly to Browne's reminder that the French police had checked only that a man calling himself Stuart Kemp had spent the time crucial to the inquiry in Paris. Further telephoned questions had revealed that this was the first time Kemp had made this particular trip and that none of the French computer experts he'd visited had met him before. Irritated by Browne's suggestion that he had been less than efficient, Petty had become almost apoplectic when Browne made the discreetest of inquiries about a possible connection between his daughter and John Phillips.

'Try the social services, Tom,' he had advised Browne before slamming the door on him. 'Maybe that's your real métier!'

Browne drained his own cup, started on the one he'd poured for Mitchell, and went back to worrying about the Choral's next and last rehearsal. He phoned Hunter to double-check that he would collect Jocelyn Wade and requested a telephone message to let him know when she was safely home again.

156

On Wednesday, after helping his wife transfer about a tenth of the contents of the shelves of their local supermarket to their own fridge and freezer, and then attending the carol concert at his eight-year-old daughter's school, Hunter duly carried out his CI's instructions. The rehearsal had been gruelling, but, so far as he was aware, uneventful.

He had hoped the company would be too exhausted to go on to the pub. He certainly was himself but he was unsurprised when, urged by Jocelyn and Jake Searle, the usual adjournment had taken place. He sat with his half of best bitter almost untasted, letting the conversation drift round him and hoping that, if he opted out of all further rounds, he would manage to remain sufficiently alert.

He had noticed as he came in that Dean and Jennie Smith were stationed, gazing convincingly into one another's eyes, in a corner by the fire. Jocelyn had obligingly acknowledged them as her friends, invited them to join the group and introduced them, straight faced, to her 'uncle'.

Hunter was sitting between Chance and Fielden, and sensing his exhaustion they chatted to each other across him.

' . . . absolutely no time for Rutter. He just puts chiffon drapes on other people's tunes.' Hunter smiled to himself, perfectly agreeing.

' . . . obviously have to play at both funerals or neither.' That must be Fielden. 'If there are no facilities to play at Alison's cremation I could make a tape and set up the equipment there. Denise is easy. She'd have wanted Mozart. Do you think the "Dance of the Blessed Spirits" would be all right for Alison? She wasn't very religious.'

Someone Hunter recognised as a tenor, but couldn't put a name to, was speaking from across the table. 'Our first reaction to this piece was unfavourable but then it grew on us. Now we're going to throw it at an audience that's never heard it before, and we'll be annoyed, or at least disappointed, when they're not appreciative and don't want to come again.'

'Unless,' Chance put it, 'they suffer from the misfortune of compulsory attendance because they're related to us.'

Fielden leaned forward. 'We haven't learned what to do with

157

these minor works yet. There isn't the same problem with something like the Mozart *Requiem*. Great works have a power and an authority that are discernible at a first hearing but offer more and more at each subsequent one, so it's worth getting to know them for both the choir and the audience.'

'You have a different relationship with a piece you've learned and performed than you do with one you've only heard, even if it was hundreds of times.' Hunter turned and saw that young Simmons had found the confidence to speak up.

'That's right.' Chance was quick to support him. 'You almost feel you've given it something – an airing – or, if you're really good, an interpretation.'

How serious they were getting tonight. Hunter was ready now to slip in his question. 'I know what I was going to ask when I saw you people,' he announced, as though he'd just thought about it. 'Do any of you folk play the violin? I've a youngster who wants to have a go. She's eight so I don't know whether she'd cope with a full-sized instrument. Where would I get a half-size one from and how do I go about finding a good teacher?'

They were all anxious to oblige him. Chance knew an old lady who was excellent with beginners. 'You'd have to be firm with her though,' he warned Hunter, 'if your daughter turns out to be good. She can't offer advanced tuition but she likes to hang on to pupils when they've grown out of her.' He could not bring himself to offer the loan of Sally's tiny violin. It would probably be far too small for an eight-year-old anyway.

Fielden had a half-size instrument that he was anxious to sell. He urged Hunter to inspect it any time he liked. 'Kelly never really took to it. She just liked the idea after she'd watched Nigel Kennedy play on television. She had no idea of the amount of patience and dedication involved.'

'Jake's an excellent violinist,' Cully contributed, adding, in tactfully lowered tones, 'I can't honestly recommend him as a reliable teacher but he'd play to your daughter and chat to her about what the strings can do.'

Hunter made mental notes on all these replies. They didn't seem to have narrowed the field very much. When, at long last, the company dispersed and he was free to deliver his charge and go home, he had formed the serious intention to broach the idea of fiddle-playing to Fliss. At least it would make a change from Tim's oboe.

Hunter decided that his mind on Wednesday evening must have been working on automatic pilot. He had been thankful, when he rang to assure Browne that Jocelyn was safely back home, that the CI had deemed it too late for conferring. He had been quite beyond thinking straight. Browne had invited himself to the Hunters' house for Thursday morning coffee, and, after a good night's sleep and a late rising, the sergeant found he could recall for him the events of the previous evening quite clearly.

At the same time he felt on edge and vaguely guilty. He didn't feel ill any more and Petty and Browne, leading the hunt for a maniac killer, were seriously undermanned. And yet, yesterday, a shopping trip and a school concert had exhausted him and made his voluntary escort duty in the evening an almost intolerable burden.

To give himself something else to think about, he wandered over to the music centre, surveyed his rows of compact discs and decided Strauss's *Four Last Songs* would be therapeutic. Of the two versions in his collection, he decided he needed the Schwarzkopf rendering rather than Kiri te Kanawa's. He could rely on Schwarzkopf to be technically perfect.

Hunter could not listen uncritically. When confronted with less than perfection in any field, he could not rest until he had worried out and analysed the faults. He could safely let Schwarzkopf get on with it, though, enjoying the sound intermittently, knowing that, if his attention drifted back to his job problems, she wouldn't be letting him down.

Browne arrived at the beginning of the third song, Hunter's favourite. Seeing his sergeant's rapt face, Browne indicated that they would listen together and found, to his surprise, that he too was captivated. 'It's not a silver voice. More like best-quality stainless steel.'

Browne's remark startled both of them as the fourth and last song ended. Browne smiled to himself as he realised that his steel-city background had provided the image he needed to express his

159

response to the music, as Hunter tried to explain why that particular disc had satisfied him this morning.

Browne had noticed before that Hunter could only relax when nothing marred, or needed the therapy of his disapproval. He wondered whether a police career had been a tragic mistake for him or whether it was the only thing that kept him in the real world, able to function as husband and father to less than perfect wife and children. Certainly, Hunter did not have the temperament to be the sort of policeman who rose in the ranks because he knew when to compromise with those not of the same mind. He was an inimitable officer who was often useful because he was so different.

Browne sat back in his chair. 'Well, now that civilised music and Annette's coffee have restored both of us, shall we get down to it?'

'What was wrong with you then?'

Browne described the short shrift Petty had given him when he had suggested a possible connection between his daughter and one of their suspects. 'And Mitchell is getting uppish again.' Hunter forbore to comment as Browne described the finding of the seating plan and its dispatch, without reference to higher authority, to the documents section.

Hunter smiled. 'It'll all be forgotten when he's chief constable – and it is the first lucky break we've had. Let's hope something comes of it and soon.'

Browne helped himself to more coffee. 'Nothing from last night, then?'

'Nothing that strikes me as significant.' Hunter's face puckered in concentration. 'They were all well aware that if the killer was striking regularly then someone else was due to be picked off last night. The atmosphere was pretty fraught, a mixture of anxiety about the girls and anxiety about the concert. It's a sell-out – in support of their courage, I suppose. Giving the concert has become a gesture. As far as the public are concerned, the standard they achieve is no longer important. Cully was saying it's made him even more determined to give them something magnificent and beautiful.'

Browne realised suddenly that, for Hunter as well as Cully, the

160

standard of the concert mattered as much as the safety of the girls. 'Just the usual routine, then?'

Hunter shook his head. 'Not quite. It was the last rehearsal, except for Saturday afternoon, when the main object is to adjust to the orchestra. They dispensed with scales and went straight into the programme after Cully had rearranged them into their concert positions. He changed his mind a few times so there was some pretty dangerous clambering about over seats. Oh – and at the end, all the copies for their concert in March were given out. Apparently they have to spend their Christmas holiday doing homework.'

He took Browne's empty cup and stacked the tray tidily. Browne hid a smile. 'In the pub, they mostly talked music, in spite of Richard and Jennie's efforts to get them to gossip about each other. When they did speculate about the identity of the murderer, they were getting a kind of vicarious thrill out of it, as though none of them felt personally at risk.'

Browne sighed. 'I don't think most of them do. The majority of them are travelling sensibly in groups now but one or two of the girls are still happy to go off with some male singer they think they can trust.'

There was a companionable silence, during which Hunter prowled round the room, his forehead furrowed. Browne knew he had forgotten that he was not officially on the case. Suddenly, he sat down again. 'Would it help to take a break from trying to guess who it is and try instead to get inside his mind, anticipate his next move, work out how long he'll wait before he tries again, how he'll choose his girl . . . '

'How?'

Hunter shrugged. 'I'm not sure. By looking at what he's done already, I suppose. He doesn't seem to favour a particular physical type or personality. Denise was dark and Alison was a dyed blonde. Denise by all accounts was unsophisticated, a bit reserved, whereas Alison was loud, a flashy dresser, a bit of an exhibitionist.'

'They were both drivers,' Browne contributed, 'temporarily without a car. Of course, no one was suspicious the night he took Denise away, because Alison hadn't been found. Now, they all

161

are. Is that the only reason he didn't kill last night – or is it that whatever triggers him hasn't happened again yet?'

'Or will he,' Hunter asked, 'kill any girl he can manage to get on her own? We're good at asking questions, aren't we?'

Browne shook his head. 'Don't knock it, Jerry. If the questions are in the forefront of our minds, we're more likely to notice any answers that float past us. If we can work out what sets him off, we'll have cracked it. I've already told the lads to look hard for somebody whose circumstances changed in early November.'

Annette came in to collect their tray, frowning at the complicated design her husband had created with the abandoned sugarlumps. He popped one into his mouth as the tray was whisked away and asked, 'Do you think it's just coincidence that both girls were singing the same solo, or is Jocelyn now especially vulnerable? We'd be in a hell of a lot of trouble if she was killed when she was co-operating with us, however willingly.'

Browne nodded, grimly. 'Thanks for that bit of consolation. I've been thinking about the *Clarion*. They're being very helpful, willing to print whatever we ask them. I hope we're getting it right. Do you think friend John is pleased or annoyed that his letters haven't appeared on the front page? Petty thinks he's just sending them to torment us but I can't agree. I'm sure they're written under compulsion – partly because of the handwriting. The so-called experts haven't helped us much over that, but perhaps I'm being unfair.'

Hunter had sunk back wearily into his armchair and, glancing at him, it occurred to Browne that Annette's frown might not have been directed at the wasted sugar-lumps. He invented an appointment he was late for and departed.

Chapter 17

Lunch at the Brownes' house on Saturday was interrupted by a phone call. Annette did not consider Hunter well enough to attend the afternoon rehearsal at the Victoria Hall. Browne was concerned. Jerry must be feeling rough to have allowed her to ring. He decided to go to the Vic himself and call for Jocelyn on the way. When he arrived, he found a surprising number of people who, like himself, were apparently taking no part in the proceedings. He wondered why they were there but was glad they made him unremarkable.

Cully came up to speak to him. In spite of the wintry weather and the none too efficient heating of the hall, he wore Jesus sandals, cotton trousers and a short-sleeved shirt, and already there were beads of perspiration on his upper lip and brow. A sweater, tied by its sleeves round his waist, glowed with jewel colours as though it had been knitted with the left-over yarn from a Persian carpet.

He was anxious to explain his objectives. 'It's too late to worry about the accuracy of the notes, so late in the day. We're just adjusting to the acoustic. We need to make a sharper, brighter sound to make up for the soft surfaces of the theatre and its bigger size.' He glared at their surroundings with disapproval and Browne felt guilty for sitting on a soft, well-padded plush seat.

'Then we have to make a few compromises with the orchestra and let the soloists get the feel of things. They're familiar with this place, of course. They're all from the choir – though I don't make a fetish of that. We sometimes invite a guest singer. Good choir voices and good solo voices aren't always the same thing. Sometimes a solo needs a voice with a cutting edge, the sort of voice that would spoil a choir, but today – I only want power and purity. Several of my choir girls had that, as has, unfortunately, been proved.'

Agonised yells from behind him as muscular choir members completed the erection of the tiered seating augured badly for a mellifluous sound at the concert. Metal-tipped chair legs grated as they were dragged across the floor and hoisted to the back of the top tier, where, so far as Browne could see, there was nothing to protect them or their occupants from an accidental descent into the depths behind.

Coils of cable for extra lighting rested at the foot of an incredibly long and shaky-looking ladder reared against the wall. The halogen lights they would supply would keep unhappy company with the monstrous Victorian shades of the existing theatre lights that were like glass imitations of Ali Baba's turban.

Beside the ladder, a card-table held enormous vacuum-jugs of hot liquids. Browne dug his chilly hands into his pockets and wished he had thought to bring one of his own. The members of the orchestra were beginning to arrive, identifiable by the bulbous black cases they carried. As they unfastened them and assembled the various metal tubes from their velvet depths, the choir began to take their places on the newly completed seating, some in danger of their lives, as a man shouldering a rather shorter ladder made his none too gentle descent against the tide of them. The female singers were self-consciously coiffed, the hair-dos created that morning to go with their long dresses looking somewhat at odds with their anoraks, shell-suits and jeans.

Having been banished from the stage the groupies continued to climb, drape, screw and hammer in the well of the building as the orchestra tuned up. Browne looked at the rippling muscles of a youth busy testing the lighting and wondered if enough attention had been paid to these choir extras. The girls might well be at risk from one of this staunch band whose practical exertions made their concerts possible.

The rehearsal began. The row of seats in front of Browne held empty instrument cases that reminded him of strange animals hibernating. The instruments rudely interrupted each other's practice scales for a few minutes and then the choir stood to sing.

Browne was not a concert-goer. His musical tastes were simple and Hannah's predilection for Shostakovitch had persuaded him that the best thing to do if it got too highbrow, if highbrow was what Shostakovitch was, was to let it float over his head. Now, he decided that the difference between a recorded tape and a good live choir – (Were they good? He'd better ask Jerry.) – was like the difference between a test match on television and a match at the ground. No one had told him that singing, too, had its own smell and facial expressions and vibrations that shook his seat.

The orchestra, in their civvies, had looked as though each of them had sent along an incompetent substitute, but now they produced a reassuring, firm harmony. Browne was temporarily entranced.

Looking at the choir, he noticed a preponderance of grey heads on the alto side. He'd heard jokes about altos being worn-out sopranos but he thought it more likely that lower voices lasted longer. Maybe the odd assortment of people around him was the grey-haired ex-sopranos. Cully was obviously giving the sort of performance Hunter had described. Not all his remarks reached into the auditorium, but they were being greeted with ripples of laughter through the ranks.

Browne saw Jocelyn come forward, Cully's third choice. The circumstances electrified the atmosphere as the piece began and as the solo was reached there was smiling, proprietorial approval. Browne felt a painful, disbelieving pleasure. Here was another side to the rather silly, flirtatious girl who had already turned into a rather better special constable than he had first expected. He knew that what was needed to respond fully to the sound she was producing was not within him and the knowledge made him suffer but held him spellbound.

A daring soul entered at this late stage, defied Cully's basilisk stare and waited to devour a sandwich before scaling the heights of the staging and taking his place. Cully punished him by waiting till he was settled, then granting a five-minute break. Browne was amused.

During the interval, Fielden's two daughters passed back and forth along the rows, putting leaflets about the March concert on the empty seats. Two rows were missed out and Browne under-

165

stood when the stalls door opened to admit a couple of dozen children. This would be the boys' choir, of which Cully was also musical director, that was contributing an item to the second half of the programme. When the rehearsal restarted, they sat quietly and tidily, with the exception of one fat, stupidly grinning organiser of insurrection. He was mildly reproved by the young woman who had brought them in, and produced, as Browne had expected, an exaggerated display of innocence and indignation. Browne was philosophical. The boy probably had the poorest voice too, one of life's non-contributors who'd be causing trouble to the force before long.

He transferred his attention to the platform where a bassoonist was looking startled by the sound he'd just made. Cully beamed at him. 'Yes, believe what you've got in front of you!' There was general laughter, during which an enormous black girl jangled her way down to the space beside the conductor's rostrum, waited until her jewellery had stopped swinging, and began to sing 'O come, O come, Emmanuel'.

'They're opening the concert with this,' Browne's neighbour informed him, 'in the dark with candles.' She nodded to herself in complacent anticipation. She was blacker and older than the soloist, probably her mother, Browne decided. The voice was as big as the singer, powerful, almost strident, filling the building. Browne remembered what Cully had said about voices with cutting edges. There was no way that this voice would blend in with the soprano line he had spent the afternoon listening to. He'd ask Cully about it later. At least it would show he was taking a bit of trouble to understand what was going on.

In the middle of the second verse, Cully tapped on his stand and stopped the carol. 'That's fine, Christabel. We don't need to go all the way through it now.' Two ladies took advantage of the interruption to consult their watches and creep towards the door. Browne admired their temerity. Cully let them almost reach the exit before turning and calling to them, 'Let's hope that's confidence, not desperation!' Red faced, the ladies jostled each other in the doorway in their attempt to escape.

Cully had noticed, however, that by now the larger ladies at least were sitting down without waiting for permission. Further

166

demands would detract from rather than improve tonight's performance. He'd let them go now and concentrate on the boys.

By seven o'clock, Cully felt quite relaxed as he stood in the foyer of the Vic, shaking hands with those concert-goers who by reason of their sponsorship expected to be greeted personally. He always abandoned his role of comedian on the night itself, except for an odd nod or wink of encouragement. Concerts had their place but they were not of prime importance. Getting to grips with great music was what it was all about. Concerts and competitions were merely events on which to focus their efforts, short term, reachable goals. Knowing the music well was sometimes too long term to achieve in a lifetime.

The punters were rolling in nicely tonight. It surprised him that they kept on coming when they were treated so badly, despised for their lack of musicality, encouraged to buy tickets, blamed when they didn't, disparaged when they didn't understand what they heard, jollied along to join in the traditional items and talked to from the rostrum as if they were morons.

He thought over the evening's programme as he forced his face into yet another smile. It would do. The singers' northern vowels, which took the edge off their performance of some pieces, were approximately right for the Medieval text of 'In Praise of Mary'. He remembered from the last auditions no excitingly outstanding talent but their voices were sweet and competent and their dedication as total as was practicable. Suddenly, he loved them all, felt a gratitude for their commitment that he couldn't find words for.

''E were right pleased we'd made the effort,' the mayor muttered to his wife as they moved away after Cully's emotional handshakes. 'I saw tears in 'is eyes!'

As Browne moved aside to allow the mayoral party to pass, he was accosted by Annette Hunter. 'I just wanted a word. Jerry's busy settling the children and buying the programmes. I'm sorry about this afternoon. He really overdid things yesterday – passed out last night and I had to send for the doctor.'

Browne was dismayed. 'You should have said. I wouldn't have dreamed . . . '

167

She shook her head. 'No, it's me who's to blame. You know – "You might as well get this fixed whilst you've got all this spare time." ' Browne could imagine it. Her ability to admit her own faults was all that prevented him from thoroughly disliking her. 'As a matter of fact, the doctor thinks that being able to help you a bit has set his mind at rest and done him good. Anyway, I'd better get back.' She disappeared into the crowd surging through the nearest door.

Jocelyn Wade could see, through the eye-level panels of stained glass in the door, a green-tinted image of the DCI and a crimson-tinged Cully. She pulled her wrap more closely round her shoulders, wishing she were in the warm foyer with them, but, in that milling throng, she'd definitely miss Benny. It was getting a bit late but she was quite sure she'd heard him telling Browne that he'd be here and she didn't think she'd missed him.

She saw the Fieldens arrive, minus their daughters whom she knew well in her capacity as baby-sitter, though she was seldom required now that Kim was a teenager. So, the girls had won their battle and been allowed to entertain themselves some other way this evening. For John Fielden this arrival was late, and he hurried off to arrange his copies of music on the piano and the organ. Jocelyn went to speak to his wife who had paused to admire the strings of coloured lights across the shopping precinct.

'Hi there! I like the new hairstyle.'

Jackie Fielden turned, the better to display it, but Jocelyn's attention had been transferred to an encounter taking place on the other side of the glass doors. How did her flute teacher know the Superintendent? Why did he stand challenging him with a stupid grin? And, most curious of all, why had the Super turned on his heel and come out again? To complete her bewilderment, her companion, following the direction of her gaze, and also observing the confrontation between the two men, burst into tears, and, to the detriment of the new hair-do, buried her head in her hands. John Phillips stopped grinning and approached a programme-seller as Jocelyn concentrated on providing her friend with a little privacy.

'Come on, the bar's about empty now the bell's gone. Let's

dive in there.' It was too late to find Benny and arrange to meet for interval drinks. She'd better see if she could sort Jackie out in the five minutes that remained before the performance began.

Jocelyn had failed to meet Mitchell because he had come in before her with the Browne family. Alex having declared, as Browne on reflection had feared he might, that wild horses wouldn't drag him to the concert, Mitchell had volunteered to take his ticket and escort Virginia. He was at present sitting between her and Browne, wearing an expression that read, 'The Things I Do For You!' The Chief Inspector was not sure to which of them it was addressed.

He surveyed his party with some satisfaction, told himself it was at least a possibility that Alex was busy with some revision, then gave his attention over to the, occasion. He wondered why people always felt it necessary, on official or festive occasions, to transport huge chunks of the outdoors indoors. On the sides of the platform, huge banks of gold and white chrysanthemums towered, which by morning would be dehydrated and would look as unhappy and uncomfortable in this place as Mitchell did now.

Unexpectedly, after his afternoon preview of the programme, he was looking forward to it. Browne usually wasted his ticket money at the few concerts he was unable to avoid. He would concentrate very hard at the beginning but before long would be wriggling uncomfortably, solving cases, reflecting on his marriage, wondering where his children were. He would come back to the performances with a start from time to time, wondering what he had missed.

Today, he had learned that live music, its volume not controlled by a button, its cost to be read in the faces in front of him, could be exciting. The choir looked very smart and festive tonight, the men in dinner-jackets, the women in their long dresses. He wasn't sure about the deep coral colour. It made the big black girl look magnificent and suited quite a few of the dark- and grey-haired women but it emphasised the brassiness of some of the blondes and the dowdiness of some of the mouse-browns. How would it go with Jocelyn's vivid red-gold?

His heart missed a beat as he registered that she was not in her place. He conferred in a mutter with Mitchell who seemed

169

unconcerned. 'I had a word with – er – Jerry when I came in. He definitely delivered her safely. It's probably some woman's problem. You know what they are. She'll creep in in a minute.'

Not satisfied, Browne turned round to catch Hunter's eye, but the lights were lowered at that moment and Hunter sat oblivious to everything except the tuning up as each instrument went on an exciting journey of its own, the whole effect a chaotic musical adventure. As Cully appeared at the platform door they all honed in on a universal A which was lost in the polite applause for his arrival on the rostrum.

Christabel appeared, minus her dangling adornments, in a burst of candlelight and began to sing in her black chest voice, not the head voice she used in the choir. Hunter knew he had made a hash of explaining this to Browne. His thanks for his enlightenment had been ironic. The voice reverberated with power and energy, yet managed to retain an element of mystery as it moved in a pitch unfamiliar to the audience. The effect came partly from the music's minor key and partly from the associations the old Advent hymn had for everyone, but the girl was good, Hunter decided.

He recognised the opening orchestral passage of 'In Praise of Mary' with its suggestion that something exciting was about to happen. For the composer it was the Annunciation, for the choir, the introduction of this new work to their audience. The orchestra played the notes that Fielden's piano had made familiar but dressed them in their best clothes. Hunter leaned forward into the sound, oblivious of his responsibility to his charge.

As the passage leading to the first solo began, Jocelyn entered, unobtrusively, by the stage-door and came forward to stand in her place. Browne's relief and Cully's were equal. The coral dress married surprisingly well with the vivid hair.

As soon as the interval released her, Jocelyn stationed herself by the bar entrance and was not happy to discover that Benny seemed to have attached himself to the Brownes. She took quick stock of the DCI's daughter before touching Mitchell's arm. She was like her father and yet very attractive. Strange. Jocelyn was glad to see she was safely engaged and therefore no threat to herself.

Mitchell, she thought, looked less than pleased to see her.

'Excuse me, Sergeant. There's something important I ought to tell you.'

Virginia was gracious. 'If you're doing double duty as police-woman and singer, you need this more than I do.' She handed her untouched G and T to Jocelyn and went to join her parents at the bar in search of a replacement.

Mitchell headed down the main staircase that led to the now empty foyer. 'It'd better be important, Joss.' He settled himself on an ornate gilt and velvet sofa in an alcove away from the few busy officials.

After a glance at his face, she sat at the other end of it and stared, as she spoke, at the expanse of pink fabric that separated them. 'Jackie Fielden's a neighbour of ours. If she and John go out, I've sometimes done baby-sitting for them. The girls are quite big but Jackie spoils them and fusses over them. It was hard-earned money. They were always a pain.'

'Get to the point, Joss.'

Stung, she bit back tears and described the odd encounter between Petty and Phillips. 'Jackie's just told me that John Phillips used to be his son-in-law. He and Imogen, the Super's daughter, had a quarrel about something to do with his job and he attacked her. She was quite badly hurt. He went to prison and they were divorced. Imogen's back with her father.'

Mitchell was interested now. 'So, the Super's been sticking his nose into this case because he was scared that John Phillips was the one sending us the letters?'

Jocelyn shrugged. 'I don't know anything about any letters but I know John Phillips quite well and he's always seemed perfectly normal and pleasant.'

Mitchell disposed of the half of bitter he'd allowed his penniless student fiancée to buy him and admonished himself to watch his tongue. 'How does Mrs Fielden know about all this?'

Sensing a slight lessening of his irritation, Jocelyn moved an inch closer. 'Well, whatever the Phillipses' quarrel was about, it seems to have caused him to have a sort of brainstorm. He left his wife on the floor, slammed out of the house and made another attack on the first woman he met. That was Jackie. He raped her.'

171

'So, if anything happens to Phillips, we'd better look at Fielden.'

She nodded. 'Probably. You haven't heard all of it yet. Jackie wasn't married to Fielden then. She lived in Leeds and her husband was called Leonard something.' The end of interval bell rang and Jocelyn stood up. 'I'll have to get back to my place. I'm in enough trouble already for missing the beginning of the concert.' She ran up the stairs leading to the corridor behind the stage, pausing at the top. 'By the way, if you want to talk to Jackie tonight, her face was all messed up with crying and she couldn't face the concert. She's gone back home.' She disappeared with a flash of coral and a toss of red hair.

Returning to the balcony corridor, Mitchell was not surprised to see Browne waiting for him, having sent the women back to their seats. 'Anything?' His voice was calm but his eyebrows, raised almost to his hairline, betrayed his excitement that things might be beginning to move. When Mitchell had explained he was sent to bring the car round to the front door whilst Browne himself left a message to be delivered to the members of his team scattered around the audience.

By the time they arrived at the house, Jackie Fielden had dealt with the ravages to her face caused by her storm of tears. A fresh mask had been applied in the style that had been fashionable in the seventies when she had been a new bride. She appeared to Mitchell much as she had done when they had listened to Bob Dylan together. Browne realised that she had merely followed the routine of her habitual grooming. She had taken off whatever garment she had worn for the concert and thrown a dressing gown over her underclothes. Frothy lace showed where its skirts parted and at its neckline but there was no attempt to be seductive. The informal garb worried her and throughout their conversation she continually adjusted the folds of the gown for maximum coverage.

Browne apologised in his best fatherly manner for any further distress he might cause her, before asking her to repeat to them the information she had given to Miss Wade. She delayed answering, ushering them into armchairs before retreating to her own.

With her eyes on her twisting fingers, she addressed the wall behind the two officers. 'I wouldn't have told her anything if I'd

172

thought she'd repeat it. We aren't all that friendly. It was only that it was such a shock, seeing him unexpectedly and Joss just happened to be there.'

'She didn't tell us anything about your private feelings.' Browne noted with approval that Mitchell's tone was as sympathetic as his own had been. 'She just explained Mr Phillips' connection with his ex-wife and with you. She only wants, as we all do, these killings to be stopped.'

She nodded, the tears falling again. 'I do too, of course. I didn't explain before because I didn't see that it had anything to do with the case. My first husband and Jonathan Phillpot both live in Leeds. I didn't know that he taught Joss or even that she'd met him.'

'But now you've seen him at the concert you can see there might be a connection? You'll tell us about it?'

She nodded, but then bit her lip, unable to begin.

'Suppose,' Browne suggested, 'Sergeant Mitchell goes over the facts Miss Wade gave us, and you fill in any missing details, put him right if he gets it wrong?' Browne's glance at Mitchell warned him against leading his witness.

She nodded again and sniffed but listened quietly as Mitchell began. Her sobs increased as he came to the assault on her.

Browne cut in. 'Did Phillpot ever write you a letter of apology – either immediately after the attack or from prison afterwards?' Distracted from her distress, she shook her head. Browne followed up his advantage. 'I won't ask you to describe your injuries. I can read the report for myself – but, did he make any attempt to hurt your hands, especially your fingers?'

Again, she shook her head, mystified. There was silence for a moment except for the hissing of the gas fire, then she looked up with a watery smile, her make up ruined again. 'Some good came of it all. I ended up with John.'

'Your present husband? Were you unhappy in your first marriage, then?'

She considered the question. 'I didn't think so at the time. I had the girls. They were only little and so sweet, and Len always brought his wages home and never got drunk. I had nothing to complain about. He wasn't like John, though.' She paused.

Browne waited patiently for more. 'After what that beast did to me, I couldn't bear – well, to have relations with Len. He was angry about it. He made me see the doctor and then a psychiatrist, but when I came home from seeing him he said I'd been talking about him behind his back. When things didn't get any better, we decided we'd come to the end of the road.' She scrubbed her eyes, smearing mascara extensively. 'I don't see him any more but the girls do, every Wednesday.'

'So, it's their real father's mother they spend the night with?'

Browne frowned. He hoped Mitchell's interruption had not stemmed the flow. Mitchell frowned back. He'd met this witness before and established a rapport with her over John Wesley Harding who was never known to harm an honest man. Browne had better learn to trust him.

'That's right. He moved back in with his mother. He's very stern with the girls. They don't like going much. They like John better than their real father.'

Mitchell smiled triumphantly to himself before asking, 'Are things better now?'

She looked at him, sharply. 'Not in that way. I never got any better but John's so understanding. He says it isn't my fault and anyway he's got two lovely daughters that he couldn't love any more if he'd produced them all by himself.' She broke off, a hand to her head. 'Oh God! He thinks I'm in the audience. He'll think I've been taken ill or something . . . He might even think . . .' She couldn't put it into words.

Browne's instinct was to put a comforting hand on her shoulder but he knew she would flinch at physical contact. Instead, he looked at his watch. 'Don't worry. DS Mitchell and I have both left our women in the audience so we'll have to be back before the performance ends to pick them up. Several officers are on duty at the concert. I'll tell your husband you're safely at home but a bit upset and get one of them to drive him back.' They left to carry out the promise.

'In the morning,' Browne told Mitchell as he nursed his cold engine into life, 'I've no alternative to interviewing Imogen Petty, as she's gone back to calling herself. You can come with me. If you're going to rise in the ranks, you've got to learn to cope with

174

embarrassing personal problems within the force.' Better than Petty was doing, he added, though not aloud.

Mitchell's mind was running in a different groove. 'I knew Fielden wasn't the sort to give his children trendy names like Kelly and Kim!'

Jocelyn was waiting in the theatre foyer when Browne and Mitchell swept past. She had taken only two steps towards them before they were through and taking the stairs to the circle at a smart pace. She was not sure whether Mitchell had ignored her or not seen her. She grimaced and had restationed herself glumly beside the booking office by the time Jennie Smith arrived.

'Sergeant Hunter's got a full load with his own folks so I've volunteered myself to take you home. Is it to be via the pub or do you want to put your feet up at my place, having stood on them all night? Good concert, by the way. I enjoyed it.' Then, seeing the girl's gloom was unremitted, 'What's up, Joss?'

Jocelyn hesitated, then decided that Jennie was no gossip. 'What's the matter with Benny Mitchell? He sends out come-hither signals thick and fast, and, the minute you give him the slightest encouragement, you can't see him for dust. Has he got a problem, or have I?'

Jennie grinned. 'He has. A fairly pressing one. He's got both a roving eye and a ring on the boss's daughter's finger. He has trouble reconciling them when she's away at Oxford.'

Jocelyn froze. 'You mean they're engaged?'

Jennie stopped grinning as she realised the other girl was genuinely upset. 'Well and truly spoken for, I'm afraid. Come on, let's go to my place and drown our sorrows in gin. Tomorrow you can . . . ' But the special's face had crumpled and she had disappeared through the swing doors, leaving Jennie talking to thin air.

Putting herself in Joss's place, she knew the last thing she'd want would be company for the next five minutes and resigned herself to waiting. By the time eight minutes had elapsed, Jennie had reassessed her responsibility and become worried. By now, the vast majority of the audience had disappeared into cars, restaurants or the pub across the road. She went through the swing-doors herself and looked up and down the street, but, wearing high heels, mini skirt and brief silk shirt, she soon felt both chilled and vulnerable and common sense reasserted itself.

It would do her reputation as an officer no good but she'd better find Browne in the bar upstairs and tell him what had happened. Browne responded immediately, gathering up Dean and Carson who had been enjoying pints in the doorway, to help him search. 'Find Mitchell and send him after us,' Browne threw over his shoulder, 'but you stay here with my family.' Jennie was very willing to find Mitchell. She delivered the DCI's message, then added one of her own. It was only two sentences long but it caused his ears to burn.

John stood at the top of the grand staircase, slowly withdrawing himself from the busy scene in the foyer below. The evening had flown but now time was slowing down. The crimson-panelled walls of the circle corridor glowed more vividly, the gilt tracery sparkled more brightly for him. All the theatre sounds, chatter from below, the clink of glasses from the bar became music, tuneless, atmospheric and modern. Scents intensified. The bouquets of the bar wines were all-pervading. He could smell excitement on his own skin and felt a pressure wherever his garments brushed against it.

Tonight, he would find another girl. She appeared in fantasy before him, a slim shape in a coral dress, faceless as yet. The theatre no longer existed for him. There was a complete world within his own mind. He moved inside it, following his ephemeral girl, greedy for power over her. Then it began to evaporate.

Now he must find a real girl. He struggled to discipline his compulsion, to channel it, to organise his powers to satisfy it. He could see two girls below and considered them. They were both attractive, one older than the other but both young, slim, vulnerable. Only one of them wore the form-hugging coral dress of his fantasy. He willed her to isolate herself, knowing that his power over her was growing, knowing that she would obey him and leave her companion. He smiled to himself as he watched her turn away. The smile remained as he waited, willing the other girl to abandon her brief search and rejoin her friends in the bar to satisfy her gross appetites, social and physical.

He wasn't sure where Jocelyn had gone but he knew she was

still in his power. She would lead him to her. He descended the stairs slowly, standing aside as her friend rushed past him in the opposite direction. He chuckled to himself as he realised that Jocelyn, too, had sung 'Lully, lullay'. It was sheer coincidence but it amused him that the police saw it as a clue.

Chapter 18

DC Carson was the only member of Browne's team besides Hunter who was a regular church-goer. The nearest he was going to get to it this particular Sunday morning, he told himself, was the short cut he proposed to take through the churchyard on his walk from his rooms in St Chad's Parade to the station. Browne had allowed him a scant five hours' sleep and now he paused, just inside the wall, stamping his feet to get his circulation going and looking around him to savour the awakening day.

He had met one other person since he had set out, a van driver, delivering newspaper stacks to his corner shop. Blowing hard on his fingers, the man had remarked that it was a cheerless morning and retreated to his battered and steamed-up vehicle. Carson supposed that the temperature was fairly low and the sun wasn't actually shining, but the outlines of everything around him were stark and clean. The factories down in the valley had produced neither goods nor noxious emissions since Friday evening and the buildings on the lower slopes opposite seemed almost touchable.

The icy air stung his face and made him feel alive. He decided that the morning was uplifting, even exciting. The churchyard was a study, not so much in black and white as holly green and translucent grey. A weak sun was diffused by thin cloud and gave a pearly sheen to the damp gravestones. There were still traces of snow in the hollows but most of the ground had a cover of thick fleecy frost which had carefully outlined each twig and every blade of grass.

The graves huddled close to each other, so that relatives of the dead who visited them had trouble gaining access to their own plot. They obviously did visit, and often. The memorials were mostly well maintained, the lichen scraped from the engraved headstones and many of the marble vases containing fresh flowers even at this expensive season.

Behind him were large stone houses of the same vintage as the church but younger than their surrounding trees. The place, even in his own boyhood, had been a separate village but now it was linked to Cloughton by the housing estate that trailed down the hill in front of him.

Stirring signs of life in it brought him down to earth again and he thrust his hands into his pockets and strode forward. He was cold, and if he didn't hurry he was going to be late. The voice of his vicar, addressing him by name, halted him. 'Robin, have you a minute?' The vicar was duffel-coated like himself and striding towards him from the corner of the church.

'Not really. I'm just going on duty again. There's another girl missing. The search will have started up again now it's light.'

'I rather think,' the vicar announced, cutting across one of the more imposing of the graves to stand beside him, 'that I might have found her for you.'

Both men used the tracks made by the vicar's footsteps in the frost to regain the church porch. The body lay face upwards but with its knees tucked up to one side, as though making itself as comfortable as possible in this bleak shelter. Carson had never met Jocelyn but he was not in much doubt that the special constable they were looking for lay before him. The girl had red hair and marks on her face just like the ones he'd seen in the photographs of the other two dead girls. There were the same sort of fingermarks on the neck as far as he could see, though the long coral-red dress chastely covered the legs and the cleavage.

The chief difference between this body and pictures he'd seen of the others was in the temple wound. It was in a slightly different place and looked as though it had been administered with more force. There was quite a bruise formed even though, presumably, death had followed soon after. There was a slight abrasion too. Carson could account for this. This time the killer had needed more speed and force. The girl had thoughtlessly put herself at risk, but when approached she would have been immediately on her guard. The killer would not have had the pleasure of luring

179

this one unsuspectingly into his clutches, spinning out his time with her, watching fear dawn only gradually. He had a quick look at the girl's left hand. Yes, the third finger had been damaged in some way.

Carson got to his feet. He had noted all these features quite dispassionately before he remembered that this was his first corpse. He looked at it again and the porch closed in on him. When it receded again, he found himself sitting on the stone bench that ran the length of it, with the vicar's hand humiliatingly pushing his head between his knees.

He struggled to sit upright and, with what dignity he could muster, requested the vicar to summon reinforcements whilst he stood guard in the porch. There was no sign of the girl's folder of music or any other of her possessions. At least this time the objects the SOCO boys sought were not under a foot of snow.

He tried to atone for his temporary lapse with extra efficiency. With his back to the body, he regarded the flagged path from the porch to the gate into the road. It was barely a car's width and there were a good many tyre tracks in the frozen mud at the edge of it. It was likely that the killer had carried the girl in his arms for these last few yards, and even if he had turned in and driven up the path it was unlikely that last night's icy ground would have received any tyre impressions.

The only marks in the furry frost that covered the flags were replicas, going in the opposite direction, of the tracks left by the vicar's shoes that followed his retreat to the vicarage next door. Carson wondered whether to close the churchyard gates or whether they should not be touched. Then he noticed that the wrought-iron frames hung crookedly with their lower outside edges sunk in the frozen mud. A pigeon preened, perched on a marble angel's head and taking shelter from the wind between its stone wings. Carson sat down again on the bench, took out his notebook, and tried to get his stiffened fingers to record his thoughts and observations.

Carson's Sunday was fascinating to him; everything was a first. To the rest of the team, everything was further grinding routine. His case now having first priority, Browne departed to the path lab to watch Dr Ledgard as he double-checked all the findings

180

they had come to expect. Death was by manual strangulation some time between the end of the concert at nine thirty and midnight. There was no sign of any sexual interference. The third finger on the left hand had been broken after death. Carson's observations on the temple wound were confirmed and Browne comforted himself that at least the case seemed to have revealed another promising young DC.

He reflected too that, since there was no longer a Sunday collection, the expected letter of apology would not reach him before Tuesday. Unless, of course, the killer felt compelled to make sure it arrived promptly by delivering it personally. Hurriedly, Browne excused himself to contact the station and request a twenty-four-hour watch on the letter-boxes at both his own section and the substation to which the other notes had been sent. Ledgard continued to smear slides with viscous substances and wondered why Browne was so squeamish this morning.

In Browne's absence, Mitchell had been stationed in his office to collate the various reports coming in. The temporary elevation afforded him neither amusement nor pleasure. Jennie Smith's acerbic criticism was unfelt now as he suffered the corrosion of self-condemnation. He concentrated fiercely on the reports as an anaesthetic, the only positive course available.

He was interrupted by just two phone calls. The first was from Virginia, offering him beer and sandwiches in the pub at lunchtime. He refused. The second was from the documents section and Browne arrived in time to take it over.

'What's ESDA?' Mitchell heard him ask, and saw that the answer, whatever it was, had pleased the DCI, who listened for three or four more minutes before replacing the receiver.

'What is ESDA?' Mitchell repeated Browne's question.

Browne took the swivel-chair at the desk that Mitchell had vacated and waved his sergeant to his armchair. 'It's the big break we need. Electrostatic Detection Apparatus – it deals with indented impressions, marks left under paper when it's being written on that are invisible to the naked eye. Apparently, impressions, however slight, cause lasting effects on paper, probably internal damage to the fibres.

181

'They put your bit of paper into a metal box, sucked there by a vacuum, and covered it with a thin layer of plastic. The top surface was given a high-voltage charge that delineates the impressions with photocopying toner.'

Mitchell was getting impatient. 'So, what impressions were there?'

Even Browne's voice betrayed some excitement. 'Picked out with difficulty from a lot of other stuff was "very sorry about the girl" in a rather familiar style. All forgiven, Benny. Your instincts led you aright and there was no time to be lost . . . ' To Browne's astonishment, Mitchell left the room, slamming the door behind him.

Surprise giving place to annoyance, Browne sent for Dean instead. 'Get up to Cully's place and bring him in,' he bawled at him. 'I'll be waiting.' He paced his office, waiting for his irritation to recede, then watched from his window to make sure Dean's departure was swift. He saw, instead, that Mitchell was emerging from the building and that Virginia was sitting in Hannah's car on the edge of the visitors' carpark. If he'd walked out in the middle of a conference with his CI to settle a tiff with Ginny he'd have lost his stripe when he got back. He soon saw, however, that, until she climbed out of the car and came towards him, Mitchell had been unaware of her presence. He wished he could hear what they were saying.

Virginia had been well aware of the reason for Mitchell's curt refusal of her invitation. She had borrowed her mother's car and come down to the station to give him a piece of her mind. One look at him now though dissolved her aggression and her tone, when she spoke, was quite gentle. 'You were messing about with her, weren't you, Benny?'

He nodded. 'It wasn't important, Ginny. Not to me, anyway.'

She glared at him. 'But that was why it was wrong. It's in your nature to flirt with the nearest woman. I can live with that but not with you enjoying yourself by hurting people who are more vulnerable than you or me.'

His stricken look returned. 'I thought I couldn't sleep till they found her. I know I can't now they have.'

182

She became impatient. 'It wasn't your fault she died. For goodness' sake don't start indulging in melodramatic ideas that you killed her – but you did hurt her and you deserve to feel rotten about that.'

He reached out for her. 'Ginny . . . have you ever . . . ?'

Now she was really angry. 'You'd like that, wouldn't you? That would make you feel better. Well, I certainly haven't lived like a nun but I haven't concentrated on any one individual.' She moved out of his reach and he let his hand drop.

'I'm sorry. I shouldn't have asked. I know . . . '

'Don't say you know I never could. We neither of us know that. And you've no more right to expect a perfect partner than I have. I can't tell you that I wouldn't, only that I haven't.' She went to sit on the carpark wall, her back to him, hunched inside her anorak.

He left her for a minute, then came up behind her. 'You seem to have changed so much since we got engaged.'

She wouldn't turn but answered him quickly. 'I've changed a bit. There'd be something wrong with both of us if we couldn't keep learning and adjusting. You've changed too. You're taking more responsibility professionally and you're making less cheap jibes about Jerry Hunter. But it's your guilty conscience that's spoiled things between us this holiday. It wasn't that I couldn't forgive you for a fling with that girl but that you couldn't.'

He absorbed this in silence. 'Right. Are the beer and sandwiches still on offer?' They went towards the car.

After two pints of beer and two ploughman's lunches, they were quite sanguine about their future together. He hugged her before re-entering the station. 'I'd better make a clean breast of things to your father before he hears about it from Jennie.'

She shook her head. 'Don't insult Jennie. And don't try to offload the burden on Dad or me or anybody. Just learn from it. You were cruel. Don't be again. I'm probably going to like the Benny who emerges from this better than the one who got involved in it.'

'Maybe. I just wish it hadn't cost so much.'

Cully was upset and indignant. He had promised himself a lie-in after his triumph of the previous evening, and the celebration that had followed it. When DC Smith had brought him the shocking news about Jocelyn first thing this morning, he had well understood the urgency of answering all her questions promptly and helping her all he could. He had not obstructed her in any way and had described his movements from the minute he left the rostrum last night until she'd rapped on his door this morning.

He'd repeat it all again now, he told the chief inspector, if that would be at all helpful, but to be hustled along here by DC Dean with no explanation and none too pleasant a manner was totally unreasonable.

Browne realised that Cully had suffered through Dean's annoyance at his own sharp tone and peremptory unexplained order, but was in no mood to soothe either of them. He took them to an interview room, rather than his office, and sat Cully on an upright chair in front of a table adorned with spilled tea and two dead flies.

Dean sulked by the door as Browne drew up a chair for himself. 'I'm interested in a piece of paper, Mr Cully. It has a wax-crayon drawing on one side and some pencilled hieroglyphics, which I'm told are yours, on the other.'

'You mean the one I dropped in the sergeant's car?' His voice betrayed his curiosity in spite of his determination not to co-operate until he was treated more civilly. Browne nodded. 'So what about it? I told Sergeant Mitchell that it was no use and that he could throw it away.'

'I want to know where it came from.'

Cully had had enough. 'And I want to know what I'm being accused of and why it has suddenly become necessary to be so rude. I've tried to be helpful. I'm still anxious to be.'

Browne felt the man had a case. 'I'm sorry, Mr Cully. We don't mean to sound rude. There's been another death. We're all very worried. There's no time for pleasantries. I'm not going to tell you why we need to know about the paper but I assure you it is very relevant to our inquiries.'

He was mollified and scratched his head in an effort to remember. 'It was only a first rough draft of the seating arrangements. We'd been arguing – in the pub – about whether to have all the women at the front and the men behind instead of vertical blocks. Both Denise and Alison had reliable voices that we were going to miss and seven other women had chosen not to go on with this concert. Then Jack said the men were always below strength in numbers, especially on the tenor line, so it was just that for this concert things were evened up.'

'Yes, go on – about the paper.'

'We decided to have the stronger voices in the women's section along the back rows and I fished out a pencil to jot down some names but I'd nothing big enough to write on in my wallet. Someone fished out a child's drawing, folded up, and I drew boxes on the other side.'

There was silence as he tried to recall the scene in detail, then his face lit up. 'Got it! It was Howard Mellor. I remember now. He's new and we didn't know much about his family. We asked him when we saw the picture. He's got twin sons who are thirteen, and then Sheridan, a little afterthought, who's three and promises to be the musical one.'

Browne was already getting up. 'We're extremely grateful for your help, Mr Cully. I'll arrange for a car to take you home. No, Richard, I need you for something else.' Leaving Cully in the foyer with the section sergeant, Browne briefly explained the situation to Dean.

'So we fetch Mellor in now?'

Browne shook his head. 'I think not. It's the other sheets in the block we're interested in. We may have to speak to the child.'

As they set off, the section sergeant called after them, 'By the way, sir, Benny Mitchell's looking for you.'

Browne smiled, grimly. 'I thought he might be. Let him stew!'

Chapter 19

In spite of the low temperature which caused Dean to stamp his feet and flap his arms when he climbed out of the car, most of the front doors on Timpson Street stood ajar. 'Crikey!' Dean continued his warm-up exercises. 'They must be hot blooded down this way.'

Browne, who had been brought up in a very similar street in Sheffield, smiled to himself at the scenes conjured up from his past by this row of doors, opening on to the street and emitting saliva-stimulating smells of roast beef and Yorkshire pudding.

Dean's nose wrinkled. 'Bit late for Sunday lunch, isn't it?'

Browne shook his head. 'No. This is all on schedule. Most of these men work long shifts at Greenwood's mill round the corner. Sunday's their only day of idleness and they make the most of it. Lie in till eleven, big fried breakfast, pub till half-past two, Sunday dinner – not lunch – with all the trimmings at three. It should continue with snoring in the armchair till whatever time their favourite television programme begins. When I was a lad, very few people of this class had television and it was back to the pub for the evening.

'Each street usually had one household that was the pillar of the local chapel, where no one took strong drink and they considered the rest of the street dissipated and damned. We're going to spoil the sabbath for the Mellors, though.'

'He doesn't work in a mill,' Dean objected. 'He's a college lecturer.'

'True.' Browne was scanning the numbers on the doors in search of fifteen. 'I hadn't realised Timpson Street was down here.'

Number fifteen, when they reached it, had its door closed and the only result of repeated knockings was the appearance of the next-door neighbour with an explanation. 'Off to Ripon for the day, they are, though she said they'd be back well in time for the bairn's bedtime. It's because of Mr Mellor's concert last night. The boys didn't want to go and Sherry was a bit too young, so they took them to Mrs Mellor's sister's yesterday morning and they're fetching them back today. Can I do anything?'

When Browne hesitated, she reinforced the offer. 'I could at least brew some tea. By the time you've drunk it they might be back. Sherry's always in bed by six and they'll get back in time to give her some tea and a bath.'

Browne thanked her and, as they entered her tiny living room kitchen, Dean realised why everyone's door was open. All the resources of the gas stove in the corner were doing service towards the meal of the week, the joint in the oven, saucepans bubbling on all four rings and plates warming under the grill.

Their hostess switched on an electric kettle. It had been a tin kettle on the stove for his mother, Browne reflected, but otherwise in just such a room as this he had undressed before going to bed in the freezing room above, done his homework at the table, and discussed world events round the fire with his parents after they had listened to the radio news.

He had accepted the woman's invitation chiefly because, of his six or seven main suspects, Mellor was the one he felt he knew least well. Maureen Stevens was pleased to oblige him with all the information she possessed. 'I don't know them all that well, though it's not our fault. Ever since they moved in in July, they've kept themselves to themselves like they do down there.' In the south, Browne supposed she meant. 'I'd have been glad to watch the kiddies and do for her a bit, especially as she's been ill quite a lot – women's troubles, you know.'

Slices of buttered fruit cake had accompanied the tea and she paused to bite into her second piece. Browne wondered whether she also intended to demolish her fair share of the mammoth meal she was preparing. She pushed the laden plate towards Dean, who, after a piteous glance at Browne, took a piece and glared at it.

187

Mrs Stevens licked her fingers. 'I'd have been happy to baby-sit last night but they'd already arranged to trail the kiddies miles away and didn't want to offend the relations now it was all fixed up. Still, it saved me an evening of towing with them. The bairn's spoilt to death and the lads are young tearaways. Kevin's in some bother at school, from what I've heard.'

She refilled their cups. The tea had been strong to begin with and was so black now that Browne expected it to have thickened and was surprised that it still ran freely from the pot. For the first time there was an edge to Mrs Stevens' voice. 'Mrs Mellor seems to think he got led into bad ways round here.' She tossed her head. 'She couldn't be more wrong. There was no trouble with teenagers in this street till they moved in.' Fairness compelled her to add, 'Mind you, my own two were a pair of young devils till they had the badness walloped out of them. Still, they're good enough lads now. Gone to stand their dad a couple of pints before they go off with their girlfriends after dinner.'

Dean was considerably relieved when a blue Consul drew up next door, rescuing him from a second piece of cake and a third cup of the black brew. He offered Mrs Stevens less than sincere thanks and the two officers stepped into the street as two fair-haired adolescent youths erupted from the back seat. The two adults climbed out more slowly, talking in lowered tones, Mellor sounding placatory, his wife impatient.

Mellor approached Browne. 'Were you wanting to speak to me, Chief Inspector?' Jean Mellor glared at the three of them, then pushed the key in the lock and led the way indoors, calling over her shoulder, 'Bring Sherry in, one of you, and try not to wake her.' One twin ignored her and wandered along the kerb to inspect Browne's car. The other quietly opened the back door of the Consul and gently began to disentangle the sleeping child from the strappings of her safety seat.

In spite of his care, she roused and stared at the two officers, half awake and unseeing. Browne studied the enormous black eyes and sleek dark head. The little girl bore no resemblance to her brothers nor to either of her parents. Cully, he remembered, had said that Mellor referred to her as an afterthought; but whose, Browne asked himself.

The adults moved indoors as the two boys shot off up the street, and Jean Mellor, having removed her outdoor clothes, began to prepare a meal for her now-tearful daughter. Mellor took the two officers through to the extremely chilly front room, where they broke the news to him of the third murder.

Mellor seemed shocked. 'I didn't know anything about it, Inspector. We left the Victoria Hall last night as soon as the concert was over and spent the night with Jean's sister. We'd taken the children . . . Still, you won't need me to tell you. You've been next door so you'll know all about it and everything else about us that she's been able to unearth.'

Browne merely asked him for their time of arrival in Ripon and the address and telephone number of their relatives. As Dean wrote them down, Browne asked Mellor to confirm that he had given Cully the piece of drawing-paper on which he had made a preliminary seating plan.

Mellor readily agreed. 'Sherry couldn't make up her mind what she'd drawn. At one point she said that it was me, then later that it was herself.' He grinned. 'It didn't flatter either of us but I was evidently meant to be extremely grateful for it. I made a great play of folding it carefully and putting it in my wallet.' He bit back further nervous chatter. 'How does it concern you, Inspector?'

'Where did the paper come from?'

He shrugged. 'Probably from a block in her toy-box. I'll ask Jean.' They moved back to the kitchen. Sherry was now sitting happily at the table, her face smeared with jam. Mellor consulted his wife about the drawing-pad but she shook her head, frowning.

'No, she's only got a blackboard and chalks, unless it was paper from a school book that one of the boys gave her. Why? What's it got to do with a chief detective inspector?' She stood protectively between Browne and the child.

The door burst open and both boys shot through the kitchen and up the narrow staircase that divided the house. Mellor turned to his daughter. 'This gentleman likes Daddy's picture that you gave him to keep in his wallet.' Why, Browne wondered, did so many people speak of themselves in the third person when addressing small children? 'Can you remember who gave you the drawing-paper?' She regarded him solemnly, then took another bite of bread and jam.

He encouraged her further. 'If you get another piece, you could draw one for the gentleman. Who gave it to you?' She continued to chew in silence.

'The brother who carried her in,' Browne suggested. 'He seemed very good with her. Would she perhaps tell him?'

Jean Mellor sighed. 'Do we have to get them down again when they're quietly occupied for five minutes? When they're out the neighbours moan about them and when they're in, in a place this size, it's usually pandemonium.'

Mellor patted her shoulder. 'Don't worry. We'll soon get somewhere better. I've applied for some exam marking already and I could try to get some night-school classes.' He went out and they heard him going upstairs. They waited in silence, Dean doodling in his notebook, Browne gazing impassively through the window and Jean Mellor glaring defiantly at both of them.

When Mellor returned, his son came in with him, holding another piece of drawing-paper, adorned with his sister's scribbles. 'She did one for me as well.' He grinned at Browne, handed it over and sat at the table next to the child. 'Shall we draw some more pictures, Sherry? Where can we get the paper from?'

Sherry beamed. 'Kelly's,' she told him, succinctly.

'Oh, yes.' Jean had suddenly been reminded. 'Jackie Fielden looked after her for me when I had my last hospital appointment and she came home clutching a handful of pictures. By the way,' turning to her husband, 'talking of Jackie, we'd arranged to sit together last night and she never turned up. I felt really stupid on my own till Belinda Chance invited me to join her lot. Where was she?'

Browne bit back his annoyance at this self-absorption. 'I gather she was a bit under the weather. Nothing for you to worry about.'

Mellor felt the sarcasm. He escorted his visitors to the door. He could see that they were anxious to be gone but not as anxious as he was to be rid of them.

Dean climbed into the passenger seat and slammed the door. 'Are

190

we going to chase this piece of paper,' he asked Browne, 'through the house of every suspect?'

'We're going to chase it,' Browne told him, grimly, 'until we find out where it came from.'

The Fieldens were in their kitchen, washing up. Four of every kind of implement lay on the draining-board, but, having eaten, the girls were evidently not required to help clear away. Browne declined coffee and asked to speak to Kelly.

'What for?' Jackie Fielden had been looking quite relaxed after her emotional storm of the night before but the high-pitched voice revealed that the veneer of calm was thin.

Fielden, too, was unhappy. 'I'll help you in any way I can, Chief Inspector, but I can't have the girls hounded.'

Browne decided to be soothing. 'Of course you can't, Mr Fielden. We don't hound children. We just want to ask Kelly about the afternoon two or three weeks ago, when she helped Mrs Fielden to look after Mrs Mellor's little girl.'

Jackie relaxed. 'Oh, when she was at the hospital? That's all right, then.' She smiled at her husband. 'I'll just get her.'

Kelly came through looking important. She settled herself at the kitchen table and her parents stood behind her, glaring defiantly at the two officers as though they expected to be dismissed. Browne sat down opposite the girl and smiled at her. 'Most people go to hospital as outpatients on a weekday. Can you remember what day of the week Sheridan came?'

Kelly nodded. 'It was a Thursday, the same day they found the body of that girl, Denise.'

'I've told you, I won't have the children upset . . .'

But Kelly was manifestly not upset and Jackie Fielden hushed her husband and let Browne continue. 'How was it that you were not at school that day?'

'The weather was awful and I had a bit of a cold.'

And a maths test or a punishment to avoid, probably, Browne thought to himself. 'But you felt up to entertaining the little girl?' he asked, sweetly.

'I like little children,' Kelly told him, admitting more than she realised, 'though Sheridan's a very spoilt little thing. She tends to break things so I put most of my own things away. We played a

191

baby board-game that she'd brought with her for a while on the table in here. She didn't understand the rules properly and cheated but she loved shaking the dice and moving the counters. It kept her quiet for ages.'

'And then, Mrs Mellor tells me, you let her draw some pictures.'

'That's right.' Her face asked why he was asking questions to which he seemed to know the answers. 'I'd found some old wax crayons at the back of a drawer in my bedroom. I couldn't find my old drawing-pad at first. It was only when I looked in Dad's desk to – er – borrow some of his paper that I found it there. Sherry was no better at drawing than she was at Ludo . . . '

'You've told us what we wanted to know. Thank you for describing it so clearly.' She sensed that Browne was dismissing her and, accepting it reluctantly, left the room.

Browne and Dean stationed themselves one each side of John Fielden. Browne left Dean to issue the statutory warning, but added conversationally, 'Perhaps you'd come with us now, sir. It will save you the price of a stamp.'

Jackie Fielden stared at the three of them in turn. Suddenly, she began to scream.

Browne was not fond of Hunter's wife but even he forgave her much when he was drinking her excellent coffee. It offered now the physical soothing he needed whilst his mental faculties were coming to terms with his recent interview. Hunter was the only person he knew who could begin to understand what he felt about Fielden even if he could find all the right words to explain it.

Fielden had found them. He understood his own problems better than any psychiatrist would ever understand them on his behalf and was quite articulate enough to explain them clearly. It was just that he was too emotionally damaged to deal with them.

Browne knew that the interview, witnessed by Mitchell and carefully recorded according to PACE, had cured Fielden in the sense that he would never kill again even if they let him go. The system would grind on, of course, meting out its standard judgements. And, possibly, the incarceration it imposed on Fielden as his punishment would provide the only condition in which he could enjoy any kind of peace.

'I don't think,' Hunter said, slowly, pushing his cup aside, 'that Fielden would kill again, even if we let him go now. They'll have to bang him up, of course, after they've tossed a coin to decide whether or not he's sane, but what will have made the difference for him is having put into words to another human being the awful truth about what's been happening inside his mind.'

Browne had been expecting this degree of insight from Hunter, yet, at the same time, hearing it from him unprompted was astonishing. He didn't know where to begin his own account until helped by his sergeant's questions.

'What actually tipped him over, started him killing now?'

'It was going to a piano recital given by someone he was friendly with at university.' Browne saw Fielden's face in front of him again, glasses removed because he no longer wanted to hide behind them. He'd looked younger, less tense, more vulnerable, and his voice had been anxious, eager, now all was known, to explain.

' . . . I sat in the front row of the circle, watching Harry. His face was blank. He was staring into space, his mind lost in the theme of the music. His hands were moving quite automatically because he'd trained them so well. Then the concerto had an orchestral passage and he sat through that looking bewildered, as though he wondered what we were all doing there. And I knew that, if she hadn't ruined everything, it could have been me. I've had the music inside me for forty years, years that could have been spent learning and performing and listening so that the expression of what was inside my head could have been more skilful, more disciplined, more informed.

'It wouldn't have been more original, more melodic, more myself. Much as I've hated her, she's never managed to get inside my head and spoil what was going on there. But she's stolen my time from me, maimed my performer's hand as a cold-blooded punishment for a peccadillo. She pushed me into a nice, respectable, time-consuming job that paid quite well to give me everything I didn't want, everything that wasted more time and dried up my inspiration, television, theatres, a respectable house to entertain fools in. It was her fault I had to get up and dress up every morning to have inane discussions with people who didn't matter about things that didn't matter, instead of lying or sitting or walking alone, letting tunes float or whirl or fight inside my head until I had to let them out, play them, write them . . . '

'I can't put it as well as he did,' Browne said, lamely, not very sure in any case of how much his lips had conveyed of what he'd been remembering. Whatever he had managed to say, Hunter was obviously absorbed in Fielden's problems.

'Did you discover why those three girls were the unlucky ones?'

Browne nodded. 'It sounds so trivial. They just used common phrases that had been refrains through his childhood because his mother was always using them. They weren't trivial to him, I suppose. In her mouth they were bitter reproaches because her husband and son hadn't lived up to all her expectations of them. Denise was listening to an account of someone's winter break in the Caribbean and made some remark about some folk having all the luck. Old Mrs Fielden said that whenever anything pleasant happened to anyone she knew. Alison started it, saying something about his car. He'd offered her a lift to the station that night in November without any intention at all of harming her. He'd had delivery of a new car about a week before and that was the first time Alison had seen it. After she'd admired it she said, "It's all right for some folk!" – another of his mother's put-downs. He suddenly saw red.' Hunter was nodding, perfectly understanding. 'He didn't mention exactly what Jocelyn had said to trigger him off, but he did say that he hadn't been able to punish her for it straight away. He'd had to wait a few days for an opportunity to separate her from her companions, an opportunity which we'd been strenuously trying to deny him.'

He waved away the coffee-pot, replete. 'I've brought you a copy of the tape. Don't flash it around.'

'Thanks.' Hunter slipped it into his pocket. 'I think, if Fielden were really a genius, his drive to write and perform would have been more powerful than his fear of his mother.'

Browne considered. 'But a minor talent is possibly more precious to its possessor than a great gift. It will be interesting to see what he does with the opportunity to be alone that he's about to be given.' He took his leave, pleased to note that, after this session, Hunter still looked fit and alert.

194

Epilogue

Fielden found Christmas Day in the remand wing much like any other. He'd been there too short a time to know whether the food was meant to be anything special. There had been television in the day-room, closely supervised, with no choice of programmes. Depressing news had alternated with mindless jollity. Yet more trouble was brewing over the inspection of the Iraqi potential for nuclear weapons.

He was terrified of nuclear war – of any war that he might get involved in. He remembered watching the events building up to the Gulf War, praying that the Americans would not invade. Fear had squeezed his heart like a clammy hand and given a savage edge to his voice when Jackie had tried to talk to him about it.

He'd watched the war actually happening. It had come into his sitting-room, though it had confined itself to the flat, vertical plane of the screen in the corner. He hadn't, at that point, felt personally threatened, but his upbringing and education had given him at least a half-belief in Armageddon, a Middle East war involving God's people, the Jews, with sufferings unimagined before, and followed by the Second Coming to collect the Redeemed and to expose to all his acquaintants all his humiliating and sordid little sins that prevented his belonging to Them.

That frightened him more than the flames of Hell or the searing of a nuclear explosion. Perhaps they were the same thing. Whether or not, he half-believed he would have to live through them.

Sometimes he had a protection from it all, when he was playing or writing his music. Maybe here, in prison, he could escape, shake off the soft mesh of manipulative maternal concern that fell

195

softly and bound fast, and take control of his own life. This new self, or rather, the self he'd always been but hadn't known about, could face suffering with – not courage exactly, but with curiosity, a willingness to experience it. He'd been taught to take every precaution, to do nothing because that was the best way of not being hurt, not being blamed, not having to decide.

Now, he wanted all life had to offer him. He had something to offer in return. If life hurt him, he'd be sustained by this new and exciting realisation that he could bear it as well as the next man.

He wasn't sure now what country they were in – he'd stopped listening to the news-reader but the shells exploding on the screen filled him with a guilty excitement. They lit up the sky revealing silhouetted buildings of unfamiliar Eastern shape. He knew they were full of people, dark eyed, honey skinned, but having inside them red blood, plans for the future and fears about eternity all like his own.

He wondered if he'd ever get like other people completely. Would he ever learn to love? He'd married without it. If his emotions ever began to function normally, they might lead him to a person quite different from Jackie. He'd married her because he had to go through the motions with someone and she'd been there and willing. He wondered if she understood anything at all about his situation.

He'd thought when the girls were small that he might learn to love them. He'd felt fiercely protective towards them, anxious for their physical safety, but as they grew older he was indifferent to their adversities and their achievements. He'd felt responsible for them, but it wasn't love. Jackie, in spite of her problems, seemed to have all the right feelings for them – or was she pretending too? She was good at it if she was, but then, he was too.

She behaved as though she loved him, talked as though she did. He'd said all the right things too, of course, but how could her love feed on mere pretence? It occurred to him that he must believe that love existed, that it wasn't just an illusion or the pretence of it a useful convention, or he wouldn't be asking all these questions. Thank God, whom he half-believed in, for an excuse for opting out of the physical side.

He'd like to love the children. He'd like to have loved his

father, for whom he had at least felt a deep respect. He'd known instinctively, as his mother taught him and forced him to lie and deceive, that his father had no part in it. Knowledge of it, yes. As he grew older, especially since his father had died and he himself had been able to study the past more clearly because it was no longer changing, he'd realised that his father had lived in no fool's paradise. Maybe he'd been cowardly, or maybe wise, to grieve over but accept a situation he was powerless to change. Something had harmed his mother too much for a lifetime of his father's patient devotion to cure her.

He wondered if his father had expected him to bear his share of the mission to his mother, or whether he'd had no conception of the cage she'd raised him in. He wished he'd talked more with his father but he'd been afraid to. Not afraid of any physical abuse, nor of unjust punishment nor ill temper. He'd been afraid of his father's integrity. He dared not reveal to him the guilty resentment within himself. It was this inability to talk, this instilled necessity to pretend things were other than they were that was the root of his trouble.

If he could tell someone that he was completely indifferent to his wife and children, he might clear the ground, begin to feel something real. He willed the war on the screen to stay where it was and not spoil the bright new future. War would make everything expensive, make people value only what was necessary for survival and frenzied fun. The conditions would be all wrong for good music. No one would want to listen to his sonatas. He'd be set longing and left there as usual.

Again, now, the music was bubbling into his mind, where it hurt him until he let it out, got it on paper. When he'd managed it, he'd feel as though he were floating. However sordid his surroundings they would become transposed, would wrap him up in his euphoria. It didn't last, of course. It ebbed, leaked away slowly, but he'd be recharged when more music welled up inside his head, and the process could begin all over again. But, now, the world that should have encouraged him, rewarded him, appreciated him, was set on a course of self-destruction, drowning his notes with the screaming of jets and rockets.

Where did his tunes come from anyway? Certainly the genes

were not from his mother, who thought she knew what was best for him and who'd ruined his life. Not from his patient, honest, hard-working father who had dragged the church choir basses out of tune until the humiliation of his wife's constant and public criticism had crushed him and put an end to the Sunday roaring. He'd enjoyed his father's singing. It was fine for music to be enthusiastically out of tune in some contexts, so long as it wasn't mean, like his mother's unadventurous, piping little soprano that didn't know *piano* from *forte* but which relentlessly counted out the beats and stopped because it came to a double bar line rather than because the melody had drawn to a close. He took a grip on himself. He was letting her get to him again. His music must come from the God he half-believed in.

He'd been more glad of the short spells of the other prisoners' company he'd been granted than he'd thought he would be. It made him feel less different, less abnormal, to know that they too deserved to be here. He'd listened with some interest to the troubles of Danny in the next cell, though he didn't choose yet to say very much to him about himself. He still felt purged, cleansed, by his confession to Chief Inspector Browne. But he drew comfort from knowing that when the time came he would be able to speak.

Danny had stopped short of naming the crime that had brought him here. Fielden had wondered whether his own failure to inquire showed a lack of expected concern, but he didn't know the protocol here. *Better not ask*.

To Cully, Christmas had been an ordinary, boring Thursday, except that he'd eaten too much, surrounded by people he didn't specially like, and was now left with a mountain of dirty dishes. His visitors had offered, half-heartedly, to help with them but Cully preferred the work to more of their company. Outside, in the little courtyard, the trampled snow lay like a creased, chewed blanket, filling a giant bed for some enormous pet.

As he scraped and stacked, rinsed and left to drain, Cully was amusing himself by listening to recordings of all the smoochy carols he had refused to let the choir sing at the concert. The excellent soprano line of the Cambridge Singers was currently oohing and ahing yards of diaphanous sound that veiled the strong melody of a traditional carol, stoutly rendered by the equally excellent tenors and basses. How he did hate Rutter. It didn't sound, from this wishy-washy stuff, as though he could live up to his name!

He dried his hands and changed the tape. Jessye Norman sang to him and he was held in her spell as always. He thanked Providence for Christabel with her amiable common sense and a voice so similar and family commitments that kept her with Cloughton Choral.

He placed the last plate carefully on the rack and glanced round the room before turning up the fire. It hadn't seemed appropriate to decorate the house this year and only his cards marked the occasion, pride of place being given in the centre of the mantelpiece to the one Jack had pushed through his door last night. It announced the early but safe arrival of five-pound-two-ounce Oliver John.

He sang along quietly with the next carol, thankful to have evaded his relatives' attempts to drag him off to be sociable at their party. How could they accuse him of having no interests but music in his unnatural life when he'd just cooked them such an excellent and unusual meal? What they really wanted was to get him married. 'Single' was their definition of unnatural. He considered the girl they had brought along for him today. She was quite beautiful, and if they were to be believed talented, too – but there must be a catch if she'd nothing better to do with her Christmas Day than collude with friends in their matchmaking plans with a chap she'd never met before.

He got out a couple more bottles of wine. Young Simmons was coming in later on to discuss finding a new piano teacher. It was urgent that he found someone quickly since he'd made such a late start, but he had really summoned the lad tonight to give him a break from Christmas Day in his ghastly home. They'd have some real music and some St Emilion. He had not mentioned this commitment to his relatives. God knew what they would have made of that!

He might ring and invite Jake to join them if he wasn't legless already. If he could get the two of them to co-operate musically, it might be the making of both of them. He wondered, idly, why the glamorous Philippa had failed to charm him, then dismissed the question. *Better not ask!*

Mitchell's parents had arranged to spend Christmas Eve till Boxing Day with friends out of town, content that Benny would be spending most of that time with the chief inspector's family. His sister, a nurse, was safely on duty, and Mitchell had promised to be out, for her convenience, when she had her day off tomorrow.

The Brownes' Christmas dinner had been enormous and no one had found it strange that he and Virginia needed to walk off its effects. They had walked precisely three quarters of a mile to the Mitchells' back door. They had passed a group of Salvation Army musicians and Ginny had giggled because they were singing,

> 'O Holy Child of Bethlehem,
> Descend to us, we pray.
> Cast out our sin . . . '

Mitchell had rehearsed his request carefully, but in Virginia's presence he had been unable to utter the words. They had not been necessary. Their feet had led them, and, arms entwined, they had arrived here. Virginia seemed to know that he had arranged it all.

He'd carefully protected his parents' bed with an extra, unmatching sheet, hoping that she wouldn't comment, or, worse still, laugh. She hadn't, though she'd been uncomplimentary about their pink walls and flowered curtains. He hadn't taken her to see the bizarre decorations in his own room. The garish colours and weird posters there, that familiarity caused to go unnoticed now, had been chosen originally more as a challenge to his parents' authority than as a reflection of his own tastes.

What was he worrying about the interior decorations for, he asked himself, now that he'd finally succeeded in getting Virginia to bed? Soon, they'd get up and make coffee but, at present, he lay with her head in the crook of his elbow, with only the uncomfortable prickle in it caused by his impeded circulation

200

preventing his pleasure being more than he could bear. Mitchell considered himself sexually experienced but Virginia had seemed to know what to do all right. Ginny . . . have you ever . . . ? No! He'd tried that before. *Better not ask.*